I0667101

Earth Reborn

First Edition

Published by The Nazca Plains Corporation
Las Vegas, Nevada
2008

ISBN: 978-1-934625-76-7

Published by

The Nazca Plains Corporation ®
4640 Paradise Rd, Suite 141
Las Vegas NV 89109-8000

PUBLISHER'S NOTE

Earth Reborn is a work of fiction created wholly by *Shannon Rae's* imagination. All characters are fictional and any resemblance to any persons living or deceased is purely by accident. No portion of this book reflects any real person or events.

Cover Photo, MAXFX
Art Director, Blake Stephens

Dedication

My eternal thanks to the following:
    Hal (My significant other and better half)
    Dr. Grant (My Agent and wonderful editor)
    Jeana Fors (My BEST friend and JIF to those that know her)
    Chuck T.
    Chris Prescott

Earth Reborn

First Edition

Shannon Rae

Contents

Chapter 1 | 9
Love and Greed

Chapter 2 | 27
Loss and Life

Chapter 3 | 39
The Dawn

Chapter 4 | 57
Embracing the Dawn

Chapter 5 | 69
Trained Passion

Chapter 6 | 79
Bittersweet

Chapter 7 | 89
The Fold

Chapter 8 | 99
Mood Swing

Chapter 9 | 111
Revelations

Chapter 10 | 123
I Am

Chapter 11 | 131
The Trials

139 | **Chapter 12**
And Baby Made Four

147 | **Chapter 13**
Home Away From Home

157 | **Chapter 14**
Descent

165 | **Chapter 15**
Loss

175 | **Chapter 16**
Emergence

185 | **Chapter 17**
Earth Reborn

195 | **Chapter 18**
A New World

197 | **About the Author**
Shannon Rae

Chapter 1

Love and Greed

When I was only 800 years old… or 8th age, they still told the story of the Big Death in my village. After my nightly chores, we'd gather around the fire in the mountain caverns that hid us. The smell of burning wood filled the air as golden shadows danced along the stone walls as though they were alive.

We'd listen as the oldest of us told the tale. They spoke of the days of the Thorens' arrival to our planet. August 12, 2008, at approximately 12:03PM, those enormous brilliant spheres entered our atmosphere. They were so silver that it was beyond the reflection of a mirror, and more of liquid mercury just as they are today.

Looking to the sky all around the world, the Sphere Major, as we call them now, appeared. The sky filled, as far as the eye could see in every direction, with strange square patterns, like a silver dotted quilt had somehow been laid across the earth. Five over, five up, five across, five down, on and on and forever into the distance. As I gazed into the darkness I often wondered what it would look like to have only the moon and stars fill the sky.

The Big Death surged across our planet and all the women in the world died in a matter of days. It was a mere blink in history, and they were gone. Stories and paintings have been passed down over the centuries, but no one has ever seen a real female. They are little more than myth and legend.

The Thorens brought disease, death, and slavery into our already chaotic world. They justified their every action with the rationale that we were destroying ourselves and our world anyway. They were simply more efficient. They would control our infestation and let the world return to its natural state. There was no sense in letting a rodent problem ruin a perfectly good planet, I suppose.

Strangely, with all this, they also brought us life. The same virus that killed all females also caused the male population to age at a much slower rate. What would normally have been one year of bodily age now took 10 years to occur. A 200 year old man looked only 20 years old. We're also told that this was when we acquired our birth slots. Between our hips, all males now possess what can best be described as a pouch like a kangaroo. It is a small crease across the waist that only opens during birth but otherwise appears little more than a sealed, indented scar.

Sadly, I age only one year for every 100. My pouch father gave birth to me when he was 200 years old and named me Khore. After my rate of aging became apparent, I was labeled his 'Special' child. I am your average 1599 year old kid in appearance. What we now refer to as nearly 16th age. I am 5 foot 6 inches tall and shorter than most men my age with a lean, tan body more like what a 14 year old might possess. I do have muscle, but it's blended with that stubborn baby fat that seems to never fade away until one is in their 20th age. My mocha brown hair is wavy enough to lend a bit of movement across my shoulders, like a ripple in a pond. I've made a habit of keeping my bangs cut short, but long enough to cover my eyes if I tilt my head just right. My pointy thin but pert nose and average mouth make me nothing exceptional when it comes to beauty. What does make me unique however, are my eyes. They are the color of cold blue grey ice. Eyes that, when you see them, you'd swear they might glow in the darkness. It makes people uncomfortable to look at them, and I do my best to keep a downward gaze. I find it a good habit not to see too much. Their furtive glances only remind me that I'm different.

I never knew my other father and it was not something that I was allowed to mention. Briar, my Pouch Father, simply refused to speak on the topic. He was shorter than most men and I suspect it was from him that I got my height. In his prime he had hair much like my own. He had the same lazy curls of earthy brown, and a set of eyes to match. His body was strong with muscle as were most of the villagers. Our daily labor kept us in shape and ensured our survival.

In our society, most have a Father, and a Pouch Father. The Pouch Father is what we are told used to be called 'Mom' or 'Mother'. They are the ones that carry us to term and give birth to us. It is usually decided who will be the Pouch Father by simple chance. After a couple is together, any further children are birthed by the original Pouch Father as they are then more susceptible to carrying a child. I have heard there are some families where one man was Pouch Father to one child, and then the other was Pouch Father to a second, but I have never seen it.

When Briar died, at the age of 930, I was orphaned and became one of the many village boys without parents. Being 730 years old I should have been in my 73rd age but I still possessed the physical body of a seven year old. The constant threat of discovery by the Thorens kept our close knit community tight lipped, and my freakish aging was not a topic of idle conversation. I was an aberration in the eyes of my people, a fact they seldom let me forget.

As per custom in our village, orphans are taken in by the oldest family to aid them with farming and household chores. Until one is 160 or 16th age, they are not considered able to be self sufficient and a full member of the community. This is because a younger body simply cannot defend and perform the same tasks that require the strength of one in their 16th age or older.

It was never a simple life. Possessing the body of someone so young, and the mind of someone so much older, was a constant frustration. It wasn't accepted that I was likely the wisest of those in our village. Instead I was totally disregarded due to my physical appearance. I lived through two complete generations of our village and was finally nearing my 16th age.

Kalob was 16th age when my Pouch Father died. He was elected as leader of our village. Later, nearing his 106th age, and in failing health, Kalob's dying wish, of course, was to have his 18th age son assume the station as leader to maintain his family in a position of power over the others.

It was our custom to elect a new leader between the 16th and 20th age to replace the previous leader. The two oldest families then act as councilors to the new leader to ensure more balance within the community because, at any time, any given family could be the eldest and offer input into the workings of the community.

There were mixed emotions from the villagers regarding my coming of 16th Age. Some felt that I should be given the position as leader while others still feared what they didn't understand. There were also whispers that Rase, Kalob's bastard son, had every intention of taking over as leader and continuing his father's reign of terror. Now, however, he would not need his father's clout to protect him. He would be, by village law, untouchable. When I saw the look of complete, burning hatred in his eyes, as he glanced my way, I worried for my future there.

Rase was quite attractive if it were not for the constant sneer etched across his face. His furrowed brow and squinty eyes did little to hide his intentions. His arms and legs filled out to solid rope-like muscle that only comes to one in their 18th age. The long furrows of muscle that rippled across his chest and abdomen were hard not to admire underneath the bronze sheen we acquired from many hours of laboring in the gardens that fed our village. He had not yet developed the extra fat that fills a body in the mid 20th age. The same fat that seemed to collect as a more mature body fills in its own gaps and starts to save up for the more difficult seasons to come. His eyes and his silky shoulder length hair were nearly identical in the depth of their warm brown color. His locks framed his square jaw, weasel like eyes, and short pug nose. His round ass was of the sort that defied gravity by sheer force of muscle.

Jaron was the 5th in the line of families with whom I had lived over the years and was my current step father. It was strange to consider someone my junior by nearly 600 years to be my father, but I got used to it as the centuries passed. During a very heated 'discussion' between Councilman Tyler, my Councilman step father Jaron, and a very agitated Leader Kalob, I overheard my step father say that I should be village leader, and that I had every right to take over after Kalob's passing. I would be of age and eldest within the community, something that has never happened before.

My step father, Jaron, was a council member due to his advanced age of 1085 years. He was not nearly as ancient as I was, but remarkably old in comparison to the others. He was stately in appearance, though time had bent his shoulders. While he was quite old, remnants of his fleeting beauty could be seen beneath the wrinkles that etched his face. His full head of hair was cut short and white as snow which also contributed a dignity to him. He didn't get around as well as he used to, but was still quite mobile and lucid for a man of so many years.

I would be 1600 years old in thirteen days. On that very day, my love, my beautiful Vale and I, would announce our union, and move into the space I had made for us amongst the caverns in the mountainside.

Vale was a beauty to me that was difficult to describe. His powder green eyes and honey colored hair made my heart skip a beat every time I gazed upon his face. Having entered his 16th age four years ago, he still had that supple appearance to his muscle and skin that were absent in someone who is in their 18th age. From hunting and gardening, his muscles flexed and rippled as he moved, but not with the violence you might notice in someone older. His rear was chiseled but appeared delicate enough to pop like the bubbles in the froth of water on a surging river bank. He was remarkably tall being six feet three inches, and the perfect height to my five feet six to hold me in the warmest of embraces. I felt as though I could sink into him and disappear, centered and safe from the world. I loved the landscape of his body as I looked past his thin nose and pouting lips to see the love in his eyes beam back at me.

It wasn't always like that, however. Having seen so many grow old and die over the years I became a recluse. As I performed my chores I stayed to myself, not that I had many options for distraction. I suppose it wasn't very endearing to have a conversation with someone a fraction of your age in appearance, but ten-times your age mentally. Epiphanies that came with regular age to others I had already realized centuries prior.

About twenty years ago, Vale started following me around and making short but idle conversations. Not so much saying anything, but watching me with a look I had so often seen between others, but never directed toward me. I had had many come to me out of morbid curiosity, only to see the terrifying realization that I would one day have to watch them die, too. I would never age as they did, and could never fully join them through the natural cycle of life.

Vale was different. Foolish, I thought, but he wanted me, seemed infatuated with me, and I couldn't bear the notion of it. He was too handsome and new for me to conceive of the idea of being with him. He was subtle in his way, little more than a gnat that flies around your face. You barely see it, it doesn't really bother you much, but it's there... buzzing about, distracting you.

After ten years of pushing him away, we had a less than friendly confrontation. It was an unbridled yelling match that astonished everyone. For centuries I had barely lifted my eyes to another's face let alone to yell out in complete rage and frustration. I insisted he leave me be, and that it was completely inappropriate. It could never work. My being in my 15th age and he in his 16th age seemed fine, until one did the math and realized I was over 1500 years old to his 164!

I walked away meaning to end our battle of words, but Vale, through teary, bloodshot eyes, yelled, "What the hell good is it to live, if you don't love? You don't even exist as much as the trees on this mountain! At least they feel the wind!"

And he was right. His words stopped me. At that moment and in those words... my walls crumbled, and I did either the most foolish or the wisest thing of my entire life. I turned back, walked to him, pulled him down to me, and gave him the most passionate kiss I had ever shared with another man. It was a kiss where only he and I existed.

A dead silence rolled across our village. Vale's Father and Pouch Father were completely taken by surprise as was everyone. Vale's parents, being older and wiser, saw the future for what it was to become, but didn't have the heart to deny their son's love. I often wondered if it was out of pity for me that they barely hesitated in their blessing. As fate would have it, I would never truly know.

That was ten years ago. It was a mere blink in time, but such a blissful blink. In less than thirteen days Vale and I would be announcing our union, our unborn child, and our move into our own space within the caverns. Our son wouldn't be born for another 7 months, but Vale's pouch was already darkening and puffy like a mild scratch that doesn't break the skin but still causes raised red flesh. As I gazed past Vale into the surrounding forest, the old worries started to flood my mind.

'Will I watch my own son grow old and die as well... then his children, and his children's children? How much death will I have been witness to when my own finally comes around to greet me?'

"You're thinking again," I felt Vale's smooth arms brush my sides and wrap themselves around me from behind.

"Well, I can already tell what you're thinking." I felt his hardness press into the cleft of my ass.

"What are you up to lover boy?" I leaned into him, and turned my head to peer into his eyes.

Vale ground his cock into me and began to chew my neck. Through muffled lips he whispered, "I was thinking we could go to our spot."

"I don't know, I'm pretty tired" A grin stretched my lips and I couldn't hide my growing anticipation.

He slid his hand from my chest to my groin, with butterfly touches and found me more than ready. "Get moving old man!"

"Isn't it your bed time?" The true difference in our age became a joke long ago, but one we never tired of.

"That's what I'm trying to do!" He flashed me a mischievous grin.

"Well... chores are done. Let's slip out of here before we're missed!"

We clasped hands and rushed into the woods. We weaved and ducked through the trees and brush like some serpentine creature. It never took long to find our private hideaway. It was an area about five yards in diameter next to a cave entrance. In front was what we called god's table. In reality it was only a large flat-topped granite stone about knee high, nearly eight feet long and five to six feet wide that jutted out from the earth as if the makers themselves had decided to create a place to rest. We however... had other plans!

My chest heaved from our race to privacy, as I sat and rested. I caught my breath and pulled Vale's body toward me as I lay flat against the cool stone. We ground into one another and our tongues dueled hungrily. I shifted my weight and we rolled together, with me on top.

"Shhhh... don't move," I grinned as I pushed his arms above his head. We wore only the slightest bit of clothing as there truly was no need for it. The entire village was clad only in loincloths and, on occasion, short work pants depending on the chore. His young taut muscles writhed beneath his chest as he struggled.

As I straddled his abdomen, his pelvis lurched up to penetrate me but he was still confined beneath his loincloth and unable to reach his destination. I leaned further forward, out of his reach. With both of his hands held by my one, my chest brushed against his upturned lips as I started giving his wrist nips and bites. I slowed on occasion, to trace my tongue further down his arm and to his elbow.

Vale took the opportunity to run his tongue across my nipple and gave me a loving nip. I wouldn't be distracted, however. I dove into his sweet musky arm pit. The scent of an adult is different than an adolescent body, though each has their own savory aroma. I licked and chewed with fervor against his sensitive skin. Vale squirmed and struggled, but not enough to actually escape his torture. His body gave into the sensation and he whimpered. I pulled my hand from his wrists, and glanced briefly into his eyes to let him know he was to remain there. I had only begun my feast and he was to lie still.

Running my fingertips down his forearm and across his arm pit I tilted my head and placed feathery kisses down his side, stopping occasionally to draw the tip of my tongue across the ripples of bronze flesh that covered his ribs. He squirmed and whimpered again. I scooted further toward his waist, straddled his thighs, and he grinned as I undid the knot on the side of his loincloth. I gave a slight tug and he lifted to speed the process as I removed the rough fabric that barely covered his eight inch cock. It twitched and drooled as I gave it a whispered breath across the shiny tip.

Glancing along the line of his body and into his eyes, I gave him another squinty eyed look as a reminder to lie still. As further torment, I dove into the meaty flesh to the right of his engorged cock where the thigh and his hairless balls lay. I kissed and chewed as he squealed and squirmed in delight. From the corner of my eye I saw his hard cock leak even more fluid. A sticky wet itch told me I had a similar mess of my own.

Sliding forward I gazed at the muscled landscape of his abdomen and the red puffy line at his waist. It stretched almost like a smile from hip to hip. I blew across his pouch's entire length and Vale shuddered beneath me. It was something we hadn't experienced before and it seemed decadently erotic. His body began to writhe as though he was bursting through his own skin. His arms gripped the sides of the boulder, while his body twitched and twisted beneath my assault. I drew closer to his birth slot and fluttered my tongue against the swollen ridge.

Vale lost all restraint and it seemed like he was everywhere at once. He ripped the cloth from my waist and suddenly I was on my back and his hard cock was already entering me. He was so wet with desire he slid in completely. He began to fuck me, pounding his cock in and out of me with a fury. He gyrated his hips and touched the depths of me as only he could. I clutched the boulder, and hoped to keep what little control I still had. I dug my heels into his ass, pressing him into me as he throttled my most secret places. Moments later I cried out into the dark as my seed erupted between us. My twitching hole sent him over the edge and he grunted like a wild beast and howled into the darkening sky. His back arched and he buried himself within me one last time.

Moments passed as our minds floated back to reality. He leaned forward and then rolled us onto our sides. Still panting, we stared at each other, amazed. I felt my cheeks curl into an unbridled grin and leaned in to kiss his tender lips. It was a sweet embrace and my body molded into his, knowing those comforting arms would protect me from every evil in the world. Safe in my lover's powerful embrace, we drifted off to sleep.

I awoke in the darkness to the sounds of pain and sorrow in the distance. They weren't howls of idle pain. These were the morose shrieks of terror and anguished cries of a mortal wound. It is the sound made when something has ravaged their soul. Something was horribly wrong.

My eyes burst open and I realized that the cries I heard were, in fact, real. As the rest of my senses flared to life, I could smell smoke and recognized that the sounds of horror were coming from the direction of our home. I sprang upright at the exact same moment as Vale. We turned to face each other, and his eyes reflected the same horror that I was sure filled mine. We jumped up and, with fumbling fingers, retied our loincloths like some adulterous lovers trying to escape the wrath of a husband's return.

We ran breathlessly, hearts pounding, through the trees and brush, stumbling with reckless abandon to return to the caves and those we held dear. As we approached the clearing and entrance to our home in the caves of the mountain face, we saw strange figures. The area was bathed in a luminous, almost fluorescent, blue glow that cast broken shadows. Small fires belched smoke that seemed to stretch and bend as if it were alive.

I grabbed Vale's wrist and held him back. He tried to pull away and race toward the figures in the distance, but I pulled both of us to the ground.

The blue and black framed scene, just twenty yards before us, was almost too much to comprehend. What I assumed were Thorens, were 'herding' our entire village, single file, to a smaller version of the spheres that dotted the sky. It had somehow opened and used that piece of it itself to create a ramp with what looked like silver water.

Huddled, howling, and teary eyed families were pushed along by people much like our own village folk, but who were strangely dressed. They carried long metal sticks that urged the villagers along. As the tips were thrust against my people's skin, their flesh glowed with a bright blue flash like small bolts of lightning. Screams of pain and fear proved their function and I shivered at the sight of it.

Dread and a hollow emptiness filled my chest when I realized it was humans that were driving my people into the sphere. A familiar vibration in my skull threatened to steal my attention, but I fought against it. The strange sensation was becoming more frequent with each passing day, and now it was happening again. A hum, lodged in the base of my skull, was working its way forward. There was no time for distraction, and I tried to shake it away like a wet animal.

As I watched in horror, I realized I had never seen a Thoren before. There had been descriptions passed down through the generations, but I had always thought of them as giants that had come to crush the world. Through the smoke and flicker of fire light, however, it looked as though they were frail of body. There were two of them. One stood at the entrance to the sphere, and another at the base of the silvery ramp. They appeared to be supervising but not actually doing anything that required more than a simple hand gesture.

Next to each Thoren was a rather large, bulky human that was at least six feet tall and 350 pounds of pure muscle. Each was dressed in fabric I had never seen before. It reflected the light like water and appeared delicate in design. The cloth seemed to move of its own volition as it draped across their powerful chests and hung to their thighs. It was gathered and belted at their waists, but I suspected it was more for appearance than function. It was nothing like the work pants I owned, but reminded me of the robes the elders wore during our union ceremonies, except that they were much shorter and finer.

I was pulled from of my thoughts when I heard Vale's breath catch. Humans dragged his Pouch Father, Kenneth, from the cave entrance, and he was resisting. A flurry of flashes erupted, and he writhed with each touch of a different stick. Vale's other father Jerif burst from the surrounding wooded shadows brandishing a garden hoe screaming in a primal rage. He rushed the humans, making brutal contact with the first he met, upside the head. The man fell to the ground with a sickening thud. The hoe's blade was covered with something shiny and wet, and what I was sure, was blood. That moment of shock was enough for Jerif to advance and step between his lover Kenneth and three advancing humans.

The largest of the three yelled "Set to Kill!"

Vale jumped to his feet and ran screaming across the clearing. A blinding blue flash vibrated from the jumble of his parents and I saw my Vale stop. Kenneth and Jerif were reduced to a spray of ash. Vale charged the largest human with an anguished scream. The man turned, knelt, and brought the stick to Vale's chest with practiced skill. A flash of blue light reduced my love to grey powdery death.

"Ignorant Slag!!" The Thoren at the base of the ramp hissed and raised his arm. The man flew through the air into a tree. His head twisted in an odd angle by the impact and a sickening crunch joined the chaos.

My love, my child, and my world were ripped away from my soul. The hum in the base of my skull rose in pitch and climbed further forward to a point between my eyes as I stood. The alien creature turned in my direction and raised its hand. I felt a push brush against my body like a violent wind, but I advanced.

I walked, stumbling forward, in horror. I felt my soul pushing back through that thin line between my eyes until I was close enough to see clearly the creature responsible.

At that moment a figure emerged from behind the Thoren. It was Rase, the son of our ailing leader. Instead of a look of triumph on his face, there was only terror as he gazed back at me. I looked to the Thoren and lost myself in the glow of his eyes. They were too much like my own, ablaze and somehow more alive than they should be. The area between us began to brighten as though someone had lit and intense bon fire. As my rage and anguish reached an impossible level, the hum in my mind rose to a fevered pitch and a blast of white sent the Thoren, his bulky companion, Rase, and myself flying through the air in different directions. Wind swept across my body, and my vision faded to black.

Flashes of white and streams of sound blazed through my mind.

"Increase the intensity of the neural stabilizer by ten."

"How can this be?!"

"Kelay... report to Section E3 Level 10 immediately!"

"This is extraordinary! Where is Kelay!?"

"Kelay isn't aboard the ship, Sir. Sensor grids are scanning for him now."

"Ahhh... I see... DNA cross section comparison with Kelay and specimen 143977?"

"Positive Match."

"I knew you had ambitions Kelay... but I cannot believe you would go this far."

"Place the specimen in stasis on Secure Level and post a guard."

My world darkened again and I drifted until I felt a push. Not the same kind as when that Thoren had raised his hand to me, but something much more delicate. It was a subtle caress across my consciousness like when you feel your dreams begin, and your mind allows them to take hold. Then there was another more urgent push.

'You must wake up.'

As if tugged into reality, my eyes fluttered open and I felt a weight pulling at my limbs as though I had slept for days or, if possible, even longer. I began to focus on my surroundings and found a Thoren looking back at me. I jumped, or rather tried to. I couldn't move.

'Be calm, my son,' it said, not with audible sounds, but spoken loudly as though the words had been sent straight to my mind.

"Son?" I tried to ask, but still couldn't find the strength to speak.

'Think it, my son, and yes. I am your father, though I fear for not much longer. The stasis affects will diminish shortly enabling you to move, but there is something we must do. The device I carry won't hide me for much longer.'

'Are you Kelay?' I thought.

'Yes, Briar's lover and your father. I have hidden your location for the last sixteen centuries and now, due to a traitor in your midst, our love has almost been undone.' He knelt down beside the stasis pod and looked into my eyes.

My father... Briar never spoke more than his name, and always refused to discuss the past. Now I knew why. He had loved the enemy, and I was a result of that love. Looking at him now, with better focus, he really was quite beautiful. His body was that of a 14th age boy, but more like one that has been sick for far too long and is likely never to recover completely.

His eyes were my eyes. They were the color of gray-blue ice and seemed to glow like the first winter snow beneath a full moon. His eyes, like mine, also had the weariness of someone who had been witness for too long. His opalescent clothing reflected the light, like water flowing over his delicate pale skin. He couldn't have been more than five feet tall, with golden hair that framed his face in curls but barely brushed his shoulders. His pink lips and slightly upturned nose completed what I could only say was beauty. One might be more inclined to refer to his appearance as delicate rather than handsome. He was breathtaking, and still yet so frail.

'We must hurry my son. You must know what I know if you are going to save us all,' His every movement seemed deliberate and with purpose though his words sounded rushed and worried.

"Are you leaving me?" My voice was a harsh whisper, but it was a comfort that I had some control over my body again.

"No," he answered aloud for the first time and the amber timber of his voice made me smile. "I will blend with your mind. You will still be who you are right now, but with all of my knowledge and experience. You will know all the things I do at this very moment. It is what you must know to live. You will know me as only one other has and, through you, I will go on forever. After, this body will cease."

"What!" I couldn't contain my surprise as the words burst from my lips.

'Shhhhhh... My time is coming to an end, let me live within you,' Again he spoke to my mind. 'You must allow this; my time is finished no matter what you decide. I would have you live.' He stood, leaned over, and brushed his lips across my forehead.

'I love you.' He moved the hair from my eyes with his fingertips.

His touch became urgent and firm against my forehead, and my mind was awash with memories not my own. Images of traveling from world to world, loves, lost loves, sickness, and their dying race all came to me in wave after wave with nauseating speed. Kelay and my father, Briar, in the heat of passion, their joy and sorrow, my birth, and so much more, that it was deafening. When I thought I could take no more, thousands of more years of life and living were poured into me like so many raindrops into an already over-flowing river. After what seemed an eternity, the push weakened and Kelay began to fade.

"I love you, Father," I whispered, thought, and felt. The rush of life faded into nothingness and Kelay slumped to the floor as I sat upright in the stasis pod. His form faded, and his clothes drifted to the floor like clouds resting on the wind. His body merged into a singular concentrated sphere of silvery light that brightened, pulsed, and then burst out in every direction like a million stars at once. My father had moved beyond.

I climbed over the lip of my stasis pod. After changing into his somewhat tighter garments, I prepared for my escape. I knew what I had to do.

So many new thoughts entered my mind that it was difficult to absorb. I had memories of the cloth I wore, but that was the first time I actually felt the erotic sensation of the foreign fabric against my skin.

Memories of vast landscapes and exotic foods began to fill my mind, but I had to push them back. I would have to sort them out later. It was not the time, nor the place. I needed to get the hell out of there and meet with the human captain, Bransen, and current leader of the resistance. He was expecting me, and I could not miss the rendezvous. 'Strange... since when did I start referring to them as humans instead of people?'

I opened my mind and searched out into the hallway. No one was in the immediate area. Sending the mental command to the door, it opened, pouring away from view, as if absorbed into the door frame around it. What was left was an arch more than large enough for me to pass through. Stepping into the silvery azure-lit hallway, my body shuddered. I needed to calm myself and concentrate.

They would know I did not belong if I did not handle myself appropriately, and it is not like a Thoren to fidget or sweat in fear. Taking a deep breath, I suppressed my fears and calmed myself. It happened quite naturally. I was somewhat dismayed at how simply I was able to shut off my emotions, but then I remembered why. Kelay had had to do it for the past 2000 years or risk his own discovery and destruction. Thankfully because of our merging, I had the memory, skill, and horror of it at my disposal.

The hallways were endless and curved in a circular pattern, converging with bisecting hallways that led to the center of each floor. The layout of the Sphere Major was much like a 3-dimensional spider web. Each ring stood over another but linked to the center by crossways, except for levels 49 through 54, my next destination. I followed the brightly lit mirrored hallway to the lift.

Had it not been for the blue lighting framing each doorway and corner it would have been even more disorienting than it was. Fortunately, the liquid metal, or Cavrium alloy, was in a constant state of flux, so that one's reflection was never perfect. It made the contours of light much easier to discern in the orderly chaos.

It was a reflection more like what you see in the ripples of a pond as you lean over the bank and spy yourself looking back. It is imperfect, bent, and faded. As I mentally issued the command for the door to open, a Thoren and his Slag emerged from the curved hallway coming from the left. I entered the lift and maintained the command to keep the entrance way open. They entered, and I then commanded the metal to flow back into place at the opening.

Submitting my command for movement to level 50, the lift shifted and raced me toward my destination. The only way to realize movement was the pulse of blue that lined the corners of our compartment.

The lift stopped, and again the door merged into its frame and I stepped out onto the entry way of level 50.

The Thoren in the lift smiled and thought to me, 'Enjoy.'

'I most certainly will,' I replied in thought and rushed toward an unoccupied pod surrounding the arena. Luckily I found one about 15 yards from the lift. I entered and sealed the entrance arch behind me.

Level 50, or the 'leisure deck,' was far from leisurely. The area consisted of 5 levels set up much like a grand theatre. It was perfectly circular. Looking through my portal I could see a pit located at the base of the area that maintained an antigravity field where bodies writhed in ecstasy and floated throughout. The walls of the area were made of a smooth mirrored finish. Participants within the arena could only see their reflections, but those of us in pods could look on undetected.

The Leisure area had six entrances at its base, evenly distributed so that in any given direction one could make his way either into or out of the antigravity area. Bodies floated along, meshed together in groups of two to eight, jumbled, thrashing, and pumping. Occasionally ones flesh would brush against the smooth surface on the upper four levels seeing only their reflection. Part of the thrill was the knowledge that there were eyes behind the reflection that watched intently.

I was in one such portal hoping to locate Rase. A couple blocked my view as a Thoren savagely fucked one of the many Bucks in the arena. Bucks are the humans that were used for the sheer pleasure and entertainment of the Thorens. As the Buck clutched his heals into the Thoren's ass he moaned, convulsed, and arched backward. His cum shot out into the air and they floated away from my pod. I was given a broader view, and finally saw him. Rase was floating off to the left. His head was thrown back with a Thoren chewing his neck from behind. Two Thorens with legs entangled, and balls mashed together were pumping their combined meat into Rase's ass. A third was in a 69 position above him and they devoured each other's cock with abandon. Rase, through his betrayal, lost his father, his village, and his way of life, yet still appeared to enjoy his latest torment. A rage boiled within me that he might have any joy in his world after such treachery.

With my rage in check, I entered his mind, and created a mental barrier to keep my presence unknown. If I were discovered, Vale's death would be for nothing, and I could not allow Rase to alert the Thoren before I had my way with him. Seeking out his nerve endings and concentrating, I could feel both of the Thorens ravaging his ass as if I were the one in the clutches of flesh. The sensations around Rase's nine inch cock were expert, to say the least. I could feel his hunger as he devoured the Thoren's cock in his 69 position and his desperate yearning for release. Rase had been in the room for the past thirteen hours without rest or release. That was the crux of the 'Bucks'. They were there for the pleasure of the Thorens, not for their own. A Buck's lust was his torture during endless hours without release.

Poetic justice came to mind, and so did sweet revenge. I gave a subtle push to the nerves in his cock and ass, causing him to feel three times the pleasure. I heard him moan in his mind, as his muscles threatened to fail from the prolonged strain.

The two Thorens impaling his ass and the one sucking his cock sensed his new heightened level, and used their energy to push and maintain his decadent torture. He would not be allowed to cum. As the need in him grew, I increased his sensitivity. The cascading affect of the attached Thorens made him all the more insane with lust. His body was pure sex and his ass clutched the invading Thoren cocks in ways that I thought were nearly impossible. Rase was nose to nuts on the Thoren he serviced and showed no sign or inclination of coming up for air. He brutally clung to the Thorens ass with all his strength to drive him even deeper into his throat.

'Hello,' I whispered in his mind. He was too wild with sex to stop what was happening, but understood every word.

'You will be my diversion, my satisfaction, and my revenge,' My words were cold and distant in his mind as I revealed my own seven inch cock, and pulled my tunic to the side to grasp my member.

I leaned back and stroked my cock, enjoying every sensation, and began to increase Rase's sensation exponentially. His balls, cock, and ass were becoming liquid fire to his nervous system, and the Thorens, in the throws of passion, continued to subdue his ability to release. His mind howled strangled screams and I continued to push excruciating pleasure through his body. His threshold had been passed hours before, and, with or without the Thorens' control, was about to cum. I took a bit of his pleasure for myself, and flooded it into my already throbbing cock. After one final stroke, I shot across the room, splattering the viewing window.

My body shuddered with my orgasm as I worked out the last drops of cum.

'You will not cum this time, and you will not ever cum again,' I spoke within Rase's mind.

'In fact, you are going to die,' I thought to him as I increased his pleasure over and over and over again, until the Thorens fucking him lost all control and blasted into his mouth and ass.

That was all I needed. As they reached the height of their orgasm, they lost their ability to control his release, and release he did. In that instant his head exploded into a shower like so much crimson wet meat. Pink mush, brain, and bone burst from above his shoulders onto everyone around him.

Screams shattered their bliss and alarms sounded. I gave my wilting member a quick flick to shed its last dribbles of pleasure and stowed it safely away. I ran down the hall toward the lift, and sent the command to open. I dove through the arch and commanded it to close behind me.

"Level five," I thought the command, but there was no movement.

"Level five!" I thought again in a panic, but still no movement.

'Shit!'

"Level four?" I questioned as well as thought, and the lift started to descend. I forgot that vital ship levels were secured during emergencies.

"Fuck!"

The lift stopped and I reached out with my mind. There were Thorens, Slags, and Bucks, but in a complete state of mayhem. I hoped they would not notice.

I exited the lift through the arch but not before commanding its next destination to level 99. Then, turning back to the lift, I commanded the arch to open but, of course, the lift was not there. Clinging with my left hand to the arch and leaning out, I grasped the access ladder with my right hand and climbed on with unsteady feet. With a passing glance at those behind me, I saw a Slag pointing in my direction from down the hall.

Two Thorens standing on each side of the Slag instantly sent a burst of energy from their minds in my direction. I returned the blast. They were barely visible as if the air were liquid and they rippled toward each other. The first mental blast was stopped, but the second caught my left side and thrust me backward. My left hand lost its grip on the side of the arch way and my head slammed against the wall. The impact shook my body and the blow to my head stunned me. I commanded the arch closed and stumbled up the access ladder to level five. As I hung from the side on the access ladder, I sent the command to the arch.

The lift would not go to level 5, but the open command was still functional. As it opened, I leaned over and let loose a power blast of energy from my mind which rippled toward all those in the room. It threw them backward into the walls and equipment, and several Slags were tossed from the platform to their death.

Swinging onto the platform, I ran to its edge to board a small two man sphere. Another Thoren had emerged behind me and I was buffeted with a massive blast. My back burned in agony as I was thrown forward. At that rate I would go up and over the pods in front of me. I released another blast forward which slowed my arc, and I landed on the top of one of the pods.

'Enter,' I sent the command, and was enveloped by the sphere, as I sunk into its center. I landed in a liquid metal control chair which hovered in the center of the pod. I could see out in any direction while digital and tactical displays showed before me. From the exterior, one could only see a shiny reflective surface, but inside, I sat atop a floating chair within an obscure glass bubble.

'Emergency Eject!' I thought, and was catapulted from the sphere. When my pod emerged the sky was black as pitch, with only the moon, stars, and the occasional grid-points of Sphere Major dotting the skyline. I cloaked the pod with my mind and amplified the signal of the device I wore that protected my father Kelay from detection.

My body and mind had taken more damage than I had realized and it was becoming difficult to concentrate. I had to get to Bransen's location now! With that thought firmly in mind, the sphere increased to a blinding velocity and I soared across the sky like a flash of lightning. We were moving as fast as thought, and Cavrium liquid metal, however strong, was not made to handle this much strain within the atmosphere. We crossed an entire ocean and continent in a matter of moments and were heading to what was once called Mexico.

The pod slowed only momentarily and I was ejected in a downward spiral to the jungle below. The pod then regained momentum and raced toward preset coordinates deep within the Antarctic Circle. It was a crash heading and would hopefully lead them away from my true destination.

I was falling through the atmosphere and to a certain death, when my body began to slow. I hadn't noticed, but upon my exit from the pod, I was coated by the liquid metal. It acted, as much as anything, like a parachute. Weary, and in much pain, I finally descended to the ground like a lost and drifting feather. When I finally touched the earth, the metal poured away from my body, and evaporated into the air.

As I slumped to the ground, I took a moment to catch my breath. Blood was trickling down my face from a wound caused by the impact of the second blast in the lift shaft and my muscles were quaking from the exertion of the last twenty minutes. Resting on my hands and knees in the underbrush, I sensed them. Not only was I not alone, I was surrounded.

I struggled to my feet and commanded the weapons around me to come. Guns and knives emerged, flying through the air to a position in front of my outstretched arm.

"You will not harm me," I tried to sound menacing, but my voice was weak and betrayed me.

"It was never my intention." A familiar voice filled the night as Bransen stepped into view.

My vision blurred, and I felt the earth crush against my body.

Chapter 2

Loss and Life

I woke momentarily and saw Bransen sitting in the corner of the antiseptic, dimly lit room. The smell of bleach and other antibacterial agents wafted past my nose. Sleep pulled my eyes closed again. We would have to talk later, and I wondered if the look of fear on his face was for me or because of me.

My eyes fluttered open again. This time someone was taking my vitals and writing on a clipboard. I felt stronger and glanced about the room. Bransen sat in the corner, sullen and silent. I didn't know if he was still there or had come to visit again. There was a mixture of concern and distrust upon his face.

"Captain, I believe sleeping beauty has finally awakened." The medic turned to the corner to address Bransen.

"If you ever call me that again, I'm going to beat you until you quit moving! It's Bransen, not captain," he grumbled. "Now get the hell out of here!"

My caretaker glanced at a monitor above my head, made a nervous scribble, and rushed out of the room.

"Nice to meet you, cheerful!" I joked in a raspy voice.

"Cut the shit, freak. I don't have the time or patience for another smartass in my group," Bransen snapped back.

"Oh… so this freak is part of your group, huh?! I don't remember being asked or agreeing." I spat out the words while trying to pull myself up.

"In fact," I hacked, trying to catch my breath as my voice broke in and out of a rage, "they're probably still cleaning up the brains of the last asshole that crossed me!"

The truth was, though, had they not taken me in, I would probably have died or, at the very least, been dinner for one of the local critters that roamed the forest. The IV in my arm was becoming more tangled as I struggled to sit upright. The room began to spin and I slumped back.

"Hey, hey, calm down kid. I'm sorry." The tender amber tone of his voice filled the room as he walked toward me. He pressed the button on the side of the bed which made it rise.

"Kid?!" Bransen's eyes grew nearly twice their size in surprise.

A middle aged gentleman burst through the door and yelled, "What in the blue fuck is going on in here!? What the hell are you doing to my patient?!" Doc rushed through the room and stood between my bed and Bransen.

"Woah! Woah! Doc. It's just a misunderstanding," He backed away with his arms half raised.

"Get the fuck out of here you butcher." Doc spun and stared at me dazed. I was almost as surprised to have said it as he was to hear it.

"I'm sorry." Visions of the last few days of my life flashed through my mind and a hollow ache tightened my chest.

"Please... Just leave..." I begged them both as I clutched my hands to my face and sobbed.

Doc turned and left the room without another word. Glimpses of my unborn child, Vale's death, the slaughter of his fathers, and the entire ordeal of the merging flashed through my mind. My murder of Rase in my rage blazed across my thoughts as my body shook with an anguish I couldn't control. Who the hell was I? What the hell was I? What was going on? Hot wet tears spilled through my fingers and I barely noticed his arms pull me into an embrace.

"Hey guy, it's okay. It's okay now. You're safe. You're here with us." Bransen tried to comfort me as he hugged me even closer. He rocked me for what seemed like forever before I spoke again.

"They're all gone." An involuntary shudder rolled through my body and shook my words as I spoke.

He pulled away, lifted my chin and stared into my eyes. "You have a new family now."

Glancing past him and into the mirror across the room, I saw something that terrified me, my reflection. A set of blue-white eyes blazed back at me. They weren't the icy blue color I was used to, they literally glowed. Realizing what I was seeing, my breath caught in my throat.

"It's too much! I can't do this!" I wept and leaned forward again, hoping to hide away in the curve of Bransen's neck.

I had lost so much and my heart ached. There was no escaping the horror, and I didn't know how to react, so I let Bransen console me. I had lost everything, and I had maliciously killed a man. This wasn't me... was it?

Pulling away from Bransen one final time, I calmed myself and sniffled. He handed me a tissue and I wiped my eyes and nose. I had felt so much pain so quickly I was now almost immune. It takes time to gain the benefit of the numbness and acceptance of a true horror and I was thankful for the subdued pangs of emotion. It was done. I was there, and nothing I could do would change what happened. I would carry the scars of my actions as a part of me forever. As I have always told others, "It is what it is. Learn from it and move on."

"Kelay was supposed to be with you." Bransen picked at his fingernails as he spoke.

Staring into my lap, I whispered, "He is." I lifted my eyes to his. "All that he was and knew."

"Knew?" Bransen interrupted. "Knew? Where is he? What happened? What do you mean 'Knew'?" I could see the worry in his eyes.

"All the things he was and knew, I now know. All of his memories are now mine." I paused. "My father now lives within me, forever. He has moved beyond," Another torrent of tears crawled down my cheeks. The word 'father' seemed to surprise him.

I felt a burning anguish rush through Bransen's soul, which was then tucked away and hidden. "I understand," His voice was barely above a whisper and I wasn't sure if he actually spoke the words.

I looked into his eyes and knew. He loved Kelay, truly and desperately, but his love was a caged and bridled thing, never allowed to escape. Bransen had loved my father from afar for many years, but had kept his emotions safely in check. Kelay knew, but it was a fire that was never allowed to start. How sad. So much wasted time. What are we if not how we spend our time here?

"Are you sure?" There was a desperate pleading in his voice, but I crushed his hopes with a simple nod.

"We have merged and he has moved on. I know you as well as any, though you don't know me. Understand this though; I am all he was, and more. It is how he had planned it. He knew this day would come."

Another muted twinge of pain rolled through his chest, but never reached his face. I held out my hand to him, but he shrank away. I should have anticipated this. I had the memories, but I didn't know how to apply them.

"I need time alone, please." We both needed time to think on what had happened and now Bransen had his own pain to deal with.

A thought escaped him as he stood and turned away from me. 'You sound so much like him!'

"It was never my intention". It was what he had said to me when we met in the woods.

At hearing his own words, he paused and glanced back before finally leaving the room, and me, to sort out my new world.

Sleep overtook me. Coming to terms with everything would have to wait. I needed rest.

I woke, and once again found Bransen watching me from the corner.

"Hello again." I tried to smile.

"Hello Khore," he quietly replied.

"I will be ready for training in 1 day." I could hear the questions like a low rumble rolling through his mind as he studied me.

"One day?!" There was doubt in his voice as he eyed me suspiciously.

"Well, it's been long enough for my body to fully recover. Speak. I get the impression you have a question for me." I watched as he squirmed uncomfortably in his chair.

"Uhhh... how long do you think you have been out?" He eyed me as though he were ready to surprise me.

"I don't know. A couple of days?" I shrugged off the question.

"It's been two weeks." He spoke the words with cold abandon and seemed to want some amazed reaction.

"I see." I ignored the surprising news as though it were nothing. "Must be a result of your inferior medical practice."

"WHAT!?" He exclaimed, in denial more than anything.

"Got ya!" I chuckled. "You are sooooo easy."

I realized it was the first time a smile had stretched my lips since my last night with Vale. I remembered the joy of it as we lay on the cool stone, spent from loves exertions. The memory made me feel an instant guilt for even considering happiness.

"So, what happened?" Bransen glanced at me and then focused on something on the floor.

I recounted the events of my last hours of memory and he listened. Skimming over some of the more explicit behavior of my sexual escapades, I told him my story with the essential facts as I could best recall them.

He looked at me in disbelief. "So you were from one of the primitive groups then?"

I nodded my reply.

"Excuse me for saying so, but you seem to have adapted remarkably well." Branson's green eyes seem to search me for more.

"Do you think so?" I couldn't agree considering the rage of emotion that flooded my heart and mind. "I'm not obsessed with the future as the Thorens are. It is their failing, and will ultimately be their destruction if they don't change their ways. They have forgotten how to live for the day, and instead only worry about their own longevity. They are dying, and it terrifies them. One might think that the many millennia they have witnessed, would have taught them more than this, but vanity and fear are hard pressed guides in their lives."

"I have Kelay's memories, but not his wisdom." I looked deep into his perplexed emerald eyes and tried to explain.

"Knowing not to touch the cooking pot because it will burn you, is not the same as having made the mistake of burning your skin from its touch." Some understanding crept into his expression as I continued.

"We learn from experience and feeling of a thing. I believe it is for my own sanity that I have chosen not to allow Kelay's emotions to merge with my own. I don't know if I could keep my mind if I allowed that just yet." I paused, feeling a slight glimmer of hope move through him.

"Our emotion is what builds and maintains our soul. It is our pain, joy, fear, and triumph that molds us into who we are and who we will become." My life had not been an easy one, but it was simple, and the complexities of Kelay's memory made me glad for it.

"You speak like an old man." Embarrassment colored Bransen's cheeks a pale shade of pink.

"Today is my birthday." Feeling the growing pains increase within my body, another of Kelay's memories entered my mind. "I turn 1600 years old today, and need you to go so that I may change."

I could see questions forming in his mind, but interrupted him before he could speak.

"I need you to go now. Do not allow anyone to enter. They won't be able to, and I may unwittingly harm them. You will know when I have finished." My eyes started to shine with that familiar white blue which grew steadily in intensity.

I moaned in pain and writhed on the bed as my muscles and bones began to reform themselves. "Go now!" I said, louder than I had intended and Bransen jumped.

"Khore, are you okay?" Bransen's words were filled with concern but the rise in his voice seemed to hint more panic than worry.

Panting, with sweat forming on my brow and upper lip, I yelled out in pain, "GO!" and thrust him from the room with my mind. I centered an almost violent and immediate pressure on his chest, sending him stumbling backward, and out of the room. I slammed the heavy metal door with my mind and bent it into the doorframe. The extreme pressure curved it outward like a wind-caught ship's sail.

I had allowed him to stay too long and wasn't prepared. Focusing on the smallest of cells within my body, I was able to temper the pain. I knew from the shared memories that now was the time to merge, Kelay and myself, to become who I needed to be. I loosed Kelay's emotions from the prison I had created for them in my mind, and it began.

Wave upon wave of emotion rolled through my mind, finding their appropriate place with each memory. Pain, loss, sorrow, joy, lust, pride, shame, and more all took their place amongst the millennia's memories and experiences. The flashes of Kelay's thoughts merged with the images like watching someone's life on fast forward. The images were a constant blur at blistering speed, moving much to quickly to give more than a silhouette or impression of any one given thing. It was as though someone had painted a multicolored mosaic that was constantly remaking itself, shifting in complexity and hue.

As the emotions racked my mind, the growing pains that throbbed from my bones began to increase in intensity. I pinched my eyes shut, trying to chase away the agony. A blinding blue and white fire wrapped around my body. I was aging now, faster than anything my mind could imagine. My shoulders were broadening, and I could feel my hair and nails had grown considerably. I heard myself screaming, long and loud, between gasps and shudders of pain, though thankfully, I was more witness to the spectacle than active participant.

Time blurred as my body aged to that of a 21st age young man. Kelay had designed me this way. Knowing it was true, and that he had tinkered with the building blocks of life did little to ease the transition. In hours my body had aged what would normally have taken 5000 years. Well, what would have been normal for me anyway. The fury of light and emotion that coursed through my mind and body finally began to fade. Only my eyes glowed, and the pain was barely a dull ache, accompanied by an occasional cramp or muscle spasm that stole my attention. Exhausted, I dozed off, leaving the final changes to complete themselves while I lay in the ignorant bliss of sleep.

I awoke with matted eyes. Rubbing them with balled up fists, I massaged away the sleep and sat up. The weight of my hair stressed the muscles in my neck as I struggled to sit upright and I nearly scratched my face with my incredibly long finger nails. Commanding the lights to rise, I began to look at my hands and arms in the dimly lit room. As I stretched, new thicker muscle played across my arms and chest. A trail of hair traveled down the center of my taut abdomen like a small stream, growing in strength and color at my naval, and then lower and to more private places.

Pulling myself to the side of the bed, I stood and grabbed large handfuls of hair. Long chocolate brown ripples and ringlets cascaded passed my shoulders and to the floor. Even though I hefted it in my arms, my hair still trailed behind me as I stumbled to the bathroom.

Sitting down on the toilet, I cut my fingernails so that I would be better able to manage and reach the more important things without accidentally castrating myself. Looking at myself in the mirror, clad only in pajama bottoms and bare-chested, I stared. My hair now framed a more squared face, but the changes in my appearance weren't dramatic. My nose had grown to accommodate my face and my lips seemed somewhat larger, but not exactly plump. The muscles in my neck seemed more defined. My chest and abdomen lost the baby fat that used to hide the farm-built muscle beneath. I had to admire the new look of it, as my chest and abdomen narrowed at my waist.

Grabbing an armband used during the taking of blood samples, I gathered my hair at waist level and tied it into a mammoth pony tail. I found a pair of scissors on the counter and hacked away until it felt at least 7 or 8 pounds lighter.

I started the shower, kicked off my pajama bottoms and stepped in. The water felt like silk sliding down my new body. Running my hands across my skin with massaging grace, I glanced down the length of my body and to a somewhat larger cock. It rested atop powerful thighs and strong calves, and started to plump from the sudden attention. Limp, at five inches, it showed a lot of potential, but I didn't really have time to discover more. I would become better acquainted with my new body later.

I stepped further into the stream of water, letting it flow through my hair, and down the rest of my body in tiny rivers. Turning with my back to the spray, I let it beat against my skin to help relax the muscles of my neck and shoulders. The hiss of water was so soothing; I could have stood there in a bliss filled daze for hours without a second thought. I ran my fingers through my hair hoping to straighten the more stubborn tangles before turning one last time to rinse myself.

After toweling off and stepping back into the room. Cool air chilled my skin and an involuntary shiver traveled down my body raising goose bumps in its wake. On the arm of the chair where Bransen sat before, was a set of clothes. I pulled on a pair of brown pants. They were made of better cloth than I was used to and felt silky and seductive against my skin. I laced them up the front, much like one would a pair of shoes or boots. They were extremely form-fitting so I reached inside and adjusted myself so they were not quite as revealing though I was beginning to wonder if that was possible. The shirt was sheer and nearly transparent. The fabric was tinted a weak sky blue and rippled like a sail with every movement. Next to the chair was a pair of slip-on shoes made of tawny brown leather. It almost tickled as I pulled them on. In my old life I would never have dreamed anything so delicate existed.

It was the best I had felt since all of this began.

"I suppose I should get this over with. There is so much that must be done." I mumbled to myself and turned toward the door.

"Thank the gods that was only the door and not Bransen." I stretched toward the ceiling like a cat and breathed a sigh of relief.

Focusing on the door, I bound my mind to each molecule, increasing the speed of the protons and electrons as though I had built them myself. It was little more than that. It was a simple direction of energy to manipulate the environment around me, completely scientific and as natural as a drop of sweat. Or at least now it was. Before my encounter with the Thorens I would never have dreamed I was capable of such things.

As I directed more energy from my mind to the door, the metal began to warm and became more malleable. With a thought, I brought the metal back toward me and it groaned with a loud metallic yawn in complaint to its contortion.

The door swung open as I leaned against the end of the bed and waited for Bransen to enter. The noise from my manipulation of the metal must have alerted the medical personnel that I was awake, because Bransen immediately walked in.

"Happy birthday to me." I grinned and watched his eyes dance from my face to the rest of my body. His gaze lingered a little longer at my crotch than he should have allowed himself and I wondered if he was the one that picked out my clothes.

"I guess so!" He smirked and shut the door behind him.

"Could you take care of the cameras like before?" He glanced at the corners of the room and then back to me.

"Take care of what cameras? Ahhh, of course there are cameras. What kind of show would I be if I weren't caught on video?" I felt somewhat exposed and violated as blood flushed my cheeks.

"Well, don't feel too badly. They never worked much beyond the point when you kicked me out of the room." He seemed almost disappointed by the fact but grinned.

"They were on while you were getting dressed though. I hear it was quite a show." He chuckled and glanced back to my crotch. "I'm almost sorry I missed it."

It was the second time I had seen him blush and it was precious. It reminded me of how Vale used to blush when we were intimate and traveled into new and undiscovered areas of sex.

"I'm sure they have it recorded." I grinned mischievously. "As the captain I'm sure you have access to all video records."

"Ohhhh you do like to push don't you." He laughed. "Just call me Bransen, alright?"

"Yes Cap.. err Bransen," I goaded.

"So, the cameras please?" He glanced to a corner of the room and then back to me again.

The energy I released during my transformation had interfered with the video feed. I reached out, sensing each and every camera and recording device in the room, and then drew energy into myself, causing my eyes to glow. I let the power radiate outward and knew that it would be enough to interfere with their function.

"They will not work again until you request otherwise." I blinked at him and knew the strobe like light coming from my eyes unnerved him.

"You're different." His eyes traveled their familiar path along the length of my body. "Your face, everything about you... is older."

"Yes, and this is the appearance and form I will possess until the end of time." I focused on a nondescript section of floor and tried to hide my horror.

"I thought that only the Thorens lived forever." Bransen was picking at his fingernails again and I knew there was something on his mind that he didn't want to admit.

"No... the Thorens are dying, but unless I am horribly wounded or incinerated, I will recover and continue on. I am my father's life's work made real through love, and the Thorens' ultimate goal. He kept it a secret from them, but now that secret, me, is out. They'll be searching for me. They would have already been here if they knew my location, so I think we're safe for the moment. My diversion must have been successful or this place would surely have fallen by now." The prospect of living forever was something that plagued me and I was glad for the distraction.

I watched his eyes widen as the gravity of the situation gripped him. With my admission of this information, he knew he had my complete trust, as he did Kelay's. I could feel his terror for it, and also something else. His heart moved. He was confused with his past feelings, and that part of me that is now Kelay. I will never be more in awe of anything, than the ability of the human mind to shift gears so completely, regardless of the momentum to its destination.

Bransen stood speechless, staring at me. A moment passed and I began to smile awkwardly at him.

"Perhaps we should go see the others. They're still waiting." I nodded hoping to bring him back from his thoughts.

'I wish you wouldn't do that. It takes so much fun out of the conversation.' Bransen thought the words.

"I'm sorry," I answered before he could speak what was on his mind.

"Quit that!" He chuckled and shook his head.

"I'm sorry, it's just that you keep so much hidden away. When a thought does cross your mind unbridled, it's like a scream that echoes about the room." I paused. "I will make a conscious effort to make sure that it doesn't happen again. I don't want you to fear for your own personal thoughts and privacy."

His mind seemed to shift from one thing to another and then settle. "Thank you. I appreciate that."

"Okay then, let's go meet the crew. Go easy on them, okay Khore?" Bransen grinned as I approached.

"Yeah, yeah. No death by sex. I swear!" I made a crossing motion over my heart and we both burst into laughter.

"Oh! And ratchet down those eyes. Let's not freak out everyone on our first day out, okay?"

Gods it felt good to laugh again. Who ever said that 'Laughter is the best medicine' was more brilliant than the world will ever know. Bransen made my heart smile and it frightened me. It didn't seem I should let myself feel even the slightest joy after the Vale's death, but my life was racing forward and out of control, and every simple happiness seemed to ease me along the way.

I followed him out the door and all eyes focused on me as we walked to the lift.

"Thank you for your most excellent care." I paused for a moment and looked at Doc. "My apologies for my behavior."

It's strange how a few words can affect a person. It seemed as though Doc's whole body relaxed. The man was tense; way too tense. He needed some hard core sex, and soon. It's not safe to linger too long when you're on the edge. I gave him a wink. Yeah, I'm a bitch. I never said I was perfect, and who's to say I wouldn't cure him of his 'dry streak.' He wasn't unattractive by any means. His short, cropped, sunny blond hair, with a perfect part, tired slate blue eyes, pale skin and medium frame was kind of sexy in fact.

He had the body of someone who exercised because they cared. He seemed like someone who strained in and out of life. There was never enough time to put his soul's effort fully into anything. Hot, but just too damned busy to care more about himself than others. I mentally decided, 'Definitely doable'.

A bell sounded and the lift doors opened. We stepped in and Bransen hit a button that would take us to the tenth level. We were on our way to the recreation and exercise area. Even though I was new here, I had Kelay's memories and knew each member of the crew by face, name, and the skills they possessed. I also knew enough that they weren't going to accept me instantly. This was a hard group of people where trust was earned, and never given. We didn't have the luxury of time, and I needed their cooperation *now*. Each would get the proof they needed and learn who I am. There didn't seem a way do it all at once, until a less than kind thought crossed my mind.

The bell rang again as we reached level ten. The doors opened and we stepped out. Bransen led the way to the large sparring area. It was a simple open space with nothing but 50 square feet of mats on the floor. We passed the dining area and I felt the press of eyes as we strolled through the room.

I had Kelay's memories and knew each of them. Not on the level that Bransen did I am sure, but we had had several meetings in the past and each had proven themselves. It was strange to have them look at me with suspicious eyes, but then again, they hadn't ever seen me before.

Sweed and Neek were sparring, exchanging combinations of kicks and punches as we approached.

"So this is the new bad ass, huh? Kind of puny, don't you think?" Neek glanced at Sweed and puffed out his chest.

I calmed myself and settled into a defensive stance.

Bransen stepped back, "Don't hurt them, Khore. They don't know you."

Neek took the comment as a personal insult and ran toward me. As he was preparing to land his first combo, I stepped to the side, letting him pass me, and kicked him square in the ass and sent him sailing out of the training area.

Sweed watched and studied me. He was a mass of a man in size and stature. Nordic would be the best way I could explain it. He was tall, thick, and a short blond mop of hair topped his head. He had a square jaw, and fists that more resembled flesh covered clubs. He was a sight to behold. He moved more gracefully than he should considering his mammoth size. With a deceptive grace he advanced into a fighting pattern that telegraphed his every move. I read his thoughts, and found he was going to sweep my legs and then execute a change-over to mid rift kick.

I took a step back as he attacked, grasped his ankle, shifted my weight, and used his own momentum to send him flying into the wall five yards away. The massive power of his own assault was completely turned against him and made me appear stronger than I was.

This seemed to get the attention of Raven, Rift, and Twist. They all charged me at once. Raven sent a flying kick toward my face as Twist initiated a sweep and Rift went for a kidney shot from the side.

Throwing my hips, I went into a cartwheel kick, moving below Raven's attack, but above Twist's foot sweep. I made contact with Rift's knee, blocking his kidney shot, and dropped him to the floor. Raven and Twist then bore down on me in a two man free-for-all. I leapt into the air and planted the balls of my feet into each of their chests, sending them backwards. At that moment, Neek and Sweed attacked me from behind.

I turned, facing them. My eyes went ablaze, and the surprised expression on their faces made me smile. Stretching one arm in their direction, I used the energy around me to grip them and raise them off the floor. Clutching their throats, I cut off their flow of air. Before Rift, Twist and Raven could react, I raised my other hand, lifting them as well. I brought them together in front of me, and let them dangle in the air.

"Hello Gentlemen. My name is Khore. It's a pleasure to meet you." A white blue fire exploded out and around my body, and I released the pressure on their necks, so that they could breathe again.

"You freak son of a bitch! Who the hell do you think you are?" Raven spat out the words as he glared at me.

I turned and stared into Raven's piercing black eyes and smiled. I drew in more and more energy, glowing so brightly they had to squint their eyes against the blaze.

"Khore, that's enough. You promised." Bransen didn't hide his worry and spoke the words quickly.

I increased the energy another level and a pure icy blue light surged so brightly from me one could not discern what was at the center.

"I promised I would not kill them." Pulling and concentrating the energy into myself I formed it into a small ball of rolling power.

"I do not appreciate the name calling. I can make you feel pleasure." I released the ball of energy, letting it explode outward, enhancing the nerves and giving all whom it touched one of the most intense orgasms of their lives. There would not be a dry pair of shorts in the room. It rippled like the waves created from a pebble thrown into a pond, but with extreme speed. There were moans and gasps to be heard for several moments.

When everyone seemed to come back down from their orgasm I was still staring at Raven who was now sweating and panting, looking somewhat pleased with the recent developments.

"Or... I can cause you pain. Personally... I'm not into pain." With a flick of my wrist I sent the five of them flying across the training area into the padded walls behind them with a staccato of thuds.

Bransen had recovered from the surge of sex, but still looked at me with a dopey expression etched across his face.

"I promised not to kill anyone with sex. See... everyone lived," I chuckled.

"Bransen, report to the infirmary immediately. Bring Khore with you." The intercom belched Doc's words. It seemed as though he was 'trying' to sound angry, but failed.

Twist's eyes lit up and he laughed, "Well that has got to be a record. What's it been, twenty five minutes out of your room before you got into trouble?"

"Seriously... uhh... when you get a free moment I'd like a repeat of that thing you did before you tossed us across the room." Twist blushed and diverted his eyes to the floor.

We all laughed and Bransen elbowed me in the side. "Let's go see Doc. I think your little 'trick' went a bit further than this room."

Chapter 3

The Dawn

We walked over to the far end of the room toward the lift. As Bransen hit the call button I turned and saw the team staring. It was like mass whiplash. I had never seen so many heads snap away from my direction in my entire life, and that has been a very long time. Sure there was the time when a bit of gas escaped from me with a thundering rumble during a union ceremony, but that was when I was only eight hundred years old. Even then that caused everyone to glare *at* me. Seeing them shy their eyes away from me was something quite new.

There was a little sadistic satisfaction in it for me though. It was the feeling you get when you think to yourself, "Yeah, fear me!" Then you have to slap yourself because there is 'ALWAYS' someone else out there who's bigger and tougher. I had never had anyone truly fear physical harm from me. It was like I had a sign posted on my chest that said, "DON'T TOUCH" and, of course, everyone's first reaction was going to be… "poke".

The doors opened and Bransen and I entered the lift. He pressed the '20' button, and we descended further into the complex. We were heading back to the infirmary faster than I wanted. I'd kind of had my fill of people poking and prodding me. There was too much to do, and I didn't have time for this. I suppose it would be wiser to hear what Doc had to say, or scream about, but I truly wasn't up to the task.

The lift stopped its descent and the doors opened. We exited and, upon first glance at a staff member, I could see that Bransen was right. The nurse had a bit of a stain still on the front of his scrub pants which he was desperately trying to hide while searching for a replacement pair. By the shine of his skin and the smell of cum riding the air, there had been sex, and lots of it. I was in trouble. I tried to strangle a giggle that threatened to burst from my chest. If I started laughing now, I wouldn't be able to stop, and while I'm sure it was an excellent orgasm, I wager it wasn't exactly timely.

Looking around at the rest of the staff, it was obvious that everyone on this floor had been affected and surely all those between level ten and twenty had also juiced their shorts.

It was then I realized something wasn't quite right, but I didn't have time to think about it because the door we had been wandering toward was now right in front of us and opening. Doc sat behind his desk with that same sheen of sweat on his skin as I discovered on the others.

"Come in," Doc's breath caught, as he looked in my direction.

We stepped into the office and the door shut behind us. Yes, the smell of sex was still in the air and I was sure Doc sat in a mess of his own.

"Have a seat, please," He seemed a bit flustered and fought to regain his composure.

He was building up to admonish my ill thought behavior. Well, I didn't really have time for it. Bransen had seated himself while I remained standing.

"Excuse me, Doc, but I have much to do," I said, raising my hand as a signal for him to please let me continue.

"I see my energy blast reached further than I had intended. It was a mistake I will endeavor not to repeat. There are some anomalies that Kelay had not anticipated in our merging and my creation. I will be more cautious in the future," I stated matter-of-factly.

"So, did the energy wave radiate upward as well as downward when I release it, and how far in each direction were the affects felt?" I asked clinically.

"Please have a seat," Doc asked again, the wind now somewhat knocked from his sails. This seemed to give Bransen a good deal of amusement as he pursed his lips to hide his smile.

I sat down and took a deep breath. I was a little tired after the release of mental energy, and I really could use one good nights rest before everything spun out of control again. The Doc leaned forward, rested his forearm against his desk, and looked directly at me, only occasionally glancing in Bransen's direction.

"The 'wave' of energy you released was felt on our lowest level, but fortunately," he emphasized, "none above level ten were affected."

Doc continued, "I do not need to tell you that you would have compromised the entire facility and everyone in it had the wave gone through the upper levels. The entire populace..."

"You're right." I spat out the words as I interrupted. "You don't need to tell me."

This seemed to ignite a small spark of anger in the Doc, and the room became uncomfortably quiet. I leaned forward, now only inches from Doc's face. I looked deep into his tired slate blue eyes. "So, was it good for you?"

Doc eyes stretched wide, and Bransen erupted into laughter. He flipped over backwards and rolled out of his chair onto the floor. Doc and I couldn't help but to laugh with him. The golden tones of Bransen's laughter were infectious. After all, luckily no harm had been done. A few moments later Bransen stumbled back onto his feet and righted his chair long enough to slump back into it. He panted from his lack of breath, and wiped the tears from his eyes. We calmed ourselves and smiled at each other while snickers escaped from Bransen in uncontrolled bursts.

"Well, Khore," Bransen said, looking in my direction, "I guess you shot the hell out of 'not freaking out everyone' on your first day."

"Yes... that is definitely regrettable, and something we need to deal with, but there's something else we need to attend to first." I straitened my back and composed myself as best I could before I continued.

"There was a device with the clothing I wore when I first arrived. We need to install it in the structural integrity field generator on level 51. It is a Molecular Fusion Mirror, or MFM. By specifying the area of affect and incorporating it into your structural integrity generator, it will completely cloak the complex from even the most thorough scans the Thorens possess. Basically, it folds and mirrors the external environment to the surface of its opposite side.

Doc squinted his eyes and then turned to face Bransen.

"Would you care to explain exactly how Khore knows the layout and location of key systems in this complex?" There was a little more edge to his baritone voice and the smirk on Bransen's face was not helping.

"I'm sorry to interrupt again, but can you explain this to Doc, while I get to work? Where are the clothes I was wearing when you brought me here?" I turned to Bransen and ignored the Doc. He was going to throw a fit, but it would have to wait.

Doc looked questioningly at Bransen and he nodded in reply.

"The nurse at the monitoring station has your personal affects. Someone had better fill me in on what's going on here," Doc snarled.

"Thanks, Doc," I said with a grin, "for everything."

I turned and exited the office and walked to the monitoring station to collect my things. He, I would later learn his name was Chris, already had my things on the counter as I approached. Apparently he was eaves dropping, but I was glad I didn't have to battle for my things.

"Could you hang onto the rest of my stuff here until I'm assigned quarters please? I only need this at the moment." I asked, placing the MFM in my front pocket.

"That should be no problem." The blond nurse blushed.

With a quick thank you I was in the lift and on my way to the bowels of the complex.

Level 51 was the absolute basement of the facility. The generators, oxygen filtration, water purification, as well as all other essential systems were located in the jumbles of shadow and twisted metal. Filth lay everywhere. There were more layers of dust than what could be remembered or written. I found the access panel that housed the SIG, removed it, and began the arduous integration. The components weren't exactly compatible, but this would provide us with more time while we decided what to do next. Almost two hours passed when I sensed someone approaching from behind.

"Stop!" I commanded his muscles to freeze.

Turning to see my would-be assailant I eyed him from head to toe. By his filthy grey uniform, I knew he must be a maintenance man. Terror filled his eyes and he screamed within his mind as I approached.

"Relax, I am not going to harm you or anyone in this complex. I am performing an enhancement to the structural integrity system on Bransen's authority. I am going to release you so that you may use your COM to contact him personally. Tell him that you have someone here with you calling himself Khore. I won't let you harm me, so please don't make any foolish or sudden moves." I returned control of his body to him.

He was somewhat shaken, and immediately called for Bransen over his wrist COM. After a few moments, and some grumbling, he finished his conversation.

"Well, someone could have let me know a new face was going to be down here. I nearly shit myself!" He wrung his hands as he spoke and glared at the COM as though it might shrink from his gaze.

"Well, then, I suppose you'd have two messes to clean up after your shift." I grinned, letting my eyes fall down to the dried stain in his crotch.

Puffing out an exasperated breath, he took a moment to think it over as he peered at the work I had been doing.

"What modifications are you making, if you don't mind my asking? I'm the one that gets stuck fixing this skeletal bitch when the shit hits the fan, you know," His words were defensive but curious.

"I'm Khore. Pleased to meet you. I'd be happy to explain the modifications, if you don't have other pressing duties." I reached out my hand while again letting my eyes drift down his body.

He hesitated before a small smile crept across his face, and shook my hand. "My name's Jason, but most folks call me Dusty. You can guess why."

I suppose the circumstances of our meeting must have stopped me from noticing before, but Jason was absolutely breathtaking. The dirt seemed to cling more to his clothing than his skin. His 6'2" frame was clad in coveralls open from shoulder to midriff, exposing his thick neck, broad shoulders, and powerful chest. His abdomen was taut and chiseled to perfection and a trail of hair led down with the promise of more tantalizing things below.

He looked to be close to his 30th age and had all the muscle and appearance of a Greek god. He simply exuded power without the faintest attempt. His skin had the color of someone who had fixed so many things for so long in filth, that his flesh had somehow absorbed the grime around him. It possessed a deep dulled brown hue of something else not quite natural.

His disheveled hair promised the color of a medium blond should it ever come into contact with enough soap and hot water. His lips were strangely flatter than most, not the least bit pouty, but prominent beneath his once broken nose that now bent slightly to the left. His eyes, though, were hazel and flashed little flecks of green. It was difficult to tell, with the odd lighting of the area.

A bulk of muscle strained against the fabric of his rolled up sleeves, and I was thankful I had sensed his presence. Otherwise, I would probably have a two and a half foot long coil burner as a permanent addition to my skull. Now the coil burner only swayed in his downward stretched arm.

Crouching back to the access panel, I waved Jason over to join me and review the modifications I had made so far. He literally devoured everything I told him. His full comprehension of what I had been doing, and my ultimate goal for the incorporation of the MFM, was impressive. In fact, he proved helpful enough, that we were able to complete the modifications at least an hour earlier than I had expected. Gorgeous and a brain; it was a rare a combination indeed.

As we stood and admired our work, I reached out to shake Jason's hand once more. He didn't hesitate this time, as his large palm engulfed mine.

"I've been meaning to ask you something." If he was nervous, he hid it well. "Exactly what was that earlier?"

"My apologies. I made an error in energy strength and accidentally caused everyone from levels ten and below to have a sexual 'episode'." I diverted my eyes to the floor and felt my cheeks flush.

"Oh... uhh well thanks for that, too," he stammered, "but, actually I was referring to how you stopped me from moving."

My face burned and I chuckled. "Ohh that. Well... same concept... different application."

I left the explanation there, knowing that within days, if not hours, the entire complex would know more about me than anyone ever had. I'm sure that the whispers had started soon after Bransen and I entered the training area on level ten earlier today. I was a new face and, coupled with the orgasm wave, there weren't going to be many that didn't know who I was.

'Well, at least I started out with a bang.' I thought to myself.

"Thanks for your help with this. I appreciate it, and the conversation was a pleasant change. I hope that we can meet again under different circumstances. If you ever have a moment of free time, I'd love to hear from you," I told him, still wondering about what his grey coveralls hid from view.

My eyes fell south again, and I could swear the bulge in front had somehow started sliding down his pant leg. It was then I realized I hadn't let loose of his hand, and he showed no signs of letting go either. I glanced upward to his face and I could see I had been caught gawking.

I wanted to let go of his hand. What the hell is going on? It wasn't supposed to be this strong! I tried to release his hand as flashing white and blue flames of energy licked my skin and danced up the flesh of his arm. It was slowly climbing up to his shoulder. I could see the blue white light of my eyes, in the reflection of his and he pulled me into his arms.

Our tongues swam together as we ground our bodies together, trying to get as much contact our hard pressed arms could give.

"Oh shit!" was the last lucid thought I had before pulling back from his lips and diving into the muscled curve of his neck. I licked and chewed my way to just behind his ear and back again.

The fire had spread from me to Jason, engulfing us completely and we both lit the walkway like two writhing fireflies in the night. Taking my hard pressed hands from his ass I pulled his coveralls down on each side, only losing contact with his body enough to let them drop and gather around his ankles.

There was no controlling my desire as I ate my way down his flesh with vicious starved nibbles. My tongue delved into the cleft of his muscled chest. He tasted of musk and sweat as I ate my way from one nipple to the other. His gasps and moans fueled my desire as I hungrily devoured every inch of fevered flesh I could find. He groaned and ground into me as I drifted down to his belly button leaving a slick wet trail across his hardened abs.

Brushing the underside of my chin was his long and meaty cock. It, like him, was a thing of beauty and a good eight inches long. His pendulous balls swung below and swelled with the anticipation of release. I would dine on those egg sized jewels soon.

Licking and teasing I continued to torture his naval and pushed him backward onto the equipment table. He shifted his weight and scooted back just enough for his ass to be supported by the top of the table. I continued my assault as I brought my fingertips up to his knees and slowly pressed them apart. When they were as far as his body would allow, I dove into the musky crevice to the left of his hairless ball sack. I licked and chewed him into a frenzy of whimpers and strangled breaths.

Slowing... I brought my hands from between his legs to behind his knees and lifted them higher for access to that precious skin between his ass and balls. Flicking my tongue across his perineum, I watched his body spasm to the dance of my tongue. Some time later, working him into a false sense of calm I lowered his legs enough to flutter my fingers across his massive thighs and dove into the right cleft of his leg between his thigh and balls. I feasted again chewing more than licking with tender urgency.

Glancing up from my meal I gazed across the landscape of his body. I saw the upturned curve of his taut abdomen and arched spine while his head hung back swinging from side to side in ecstasy. His powerful arms bent at the elbow supporting his weight and I yearned for their embrace. At the center of this most savory view was a throbbing, and twitching cock that drooled its thick prize. With feathery touches I glanced across his smooth balls switching from one to the other before taking each into my mouth and massaging it with my tongue giving a gentle tug every now and then. Letting it pop from my mouth I gave his juicy sack a weak breath across its slick surface watching it draw closer to him for warmth.

Letting his sack fall from my mouth with an audible pop I dabbed my tongue into the river of cum that was making its way down his engorged pole. Almost painfully my mouth strained to cover his swollen helmet getting as much of his sweet nectar along the way as I could manage.

Giving his shaft one last pass with the tip of my tongue from top to bottom and then back again, I took his beautiful cock into my mouth. As he moaned loudly and thrashed about, I struggled down the mammoth girth until I felt his bush tickling my nose. He was mine now.

My left hand kneaded his thigh as I tickled and massaged his heavy balls with the other. I increased my motions on his cock and gave up any notions of regular breath. We were racing to his release and the blue white fire traveling across our skin was now brighter with intermittent bursts of white erupting from us like shooting stars.

I released him from my mouth, threw off my shirt and untied my pants nearly ripping the laces apart. My imprisoned cock was covered in its own juice. I gripped him again behind the knees, and pushed into his tight ass not stopping until I was completely inside him. I commanded his arms outward on either side so that he could not tend to the aching need of his own twitching member.

Working my seven inches of thick meat in and out of his ass sent sensations to my groin that traveled up my spine and sparked within my mind. The blue white fire about us intensified to an almost silver hue as my mind switched over giving each of us the others feelings of pleasure to combine with our own. I could feel his warm pulsing ass around my cock as well as the fullness of being entered as if it were my own. Moans nearly on the verge of screams escaped out throats as I increased the pace of my thrusts, hammering his prostate. The feeling intensified and we both came.

His cock leapt and shot heavy ropes of cum over his head onto the wall behind him and I unloaded in convulsed rhythm into his clenching depths.

A blinding white explosion flashed. A super nova moved outward in all directions in a growing ball through the complex, shaking equipment and sagging wires in its wake.

A heavenly forever passed as we drifted in our bliss. I rested my head on his sweaty chest, panting and spent as his breath threatened to rock me to sleep.

Pulling myself from him, I stood and fumbled with my pants and knotted them back into place. Grabbing my shirt I fluffed it a couple of times in the air and tugged it over my head, situating it as I went.

Jason still lay flat against the table, his legs dangling over its edge. His chest was busy with labored breath. His eyes were glazed, giving the appearance he was still lost in his orgasm while his body twitched like a sleeping newborn puppy.

Grabbing his coveralls from the floor, I gave them a few good snaps. I shook so much dirt and dust from the cloth I nearly choked. The buffeted smack of the fabric seemed to bring Jason back around. He sat up relying too much on his tired arms.

"While that was surely the most incredible sex I have ever had, "he rasped, "a simple thank you would have sufficed." A strange grin crossed his face. He was still gone.

"Thank you for being here for me." My sanity returned and a feeling of shame and betrayal filled my chest. It was too soon, Vale hadn't been gone even a month.

"It was never supposed to be that intense. All of the models showed... well never mind," I tried to explain.

"Khore. Report to my office immediately!" I jumped at a very pissed off yell from the COM on Jason's wrist.

"Okay Stud, I think you'd better come with. Let's get you decent before I go face the executioner. The view is fabulous, but I think I'm pretty much fucked on this one." I pulled the coveralls back up his legs and made Dusty as presentable as possible.

With little help, I was finally able to get him dressed. He slumped his weight against me as we stumbled toward the lift. Hitting the call button, I shifted his weight a little to relieve the stress in my shoulder. He was heavy and I was more than exhausted.

"Khore. Report Immediately! That means now!" I jumped again as Doc's angry words erupted from Jason's COM.

'Fuck!' I thought as the doors of the lift opened.

"Well, what's done is done. Accept it, learn from it, and move on," I said matter-of-factly, and dragged Jason into the lift.

Hitting the '20' button, I felt our assent whisk us to my most assured ass-reaming bitch-fit of epoch proportions. Yeeee Haaaaaaww! I guess I could always just dump Jason here and bolt. Nahh, that wouldn't work. Jason needs medical attention. Come to think of it, I'm not feeling quite right either. I hear me, but I don't sound like me at all! What the fuck?

I punched the button a few more times, knowing that it was only my stress I was relieving and not that it would make the lift move any faster. It was a futile gesture I would never have indulged before. Something definitely wasn't right.

The doors opened and we passed a very satisfied, blue eyed, sweaty Nurse at the monitoring station on the way to Doc's office.

The door opened as soon as we passed the nurse. Inside the office sat an extremely pissed off and sweaty Doc.

"Get your ass in here right now!" he hissed. I dragged Jason with me, his arm swung over my shoulder stumbling toward the door.

"Wait. wait!" Doc stood and came around the desk toward us. "Chris, prep a bed for Dusty STAT."

Squinty eyed, he glanced in my direction and spat the words, "You! Wait in my office."

With that I shuffled Jason off of me and onto Doc and trudged into his office. Damn I was tired. I flopped into one of his recliners a bit harder and heavier than I meant to. My world swam with a bounce and everything went black.

I found myself lying in the same hospital bed that I had been in thirteen days ago. The smell of antiseptics assaulted my nose yet again. I knew this place.

"Morning Bransen," I said with sleep slurred speech.

"Morning Khore," he answered, looking very well rested but concerned.

"Sleep well?" I asked as I tried to sit up.

"Sleep well, did you ask?" Doc snarled, barging into the room, slamming the door behind him. "Did you ask him if he slept well?"

"That's all anyone could do after your orgy induced escapades from last night! It was by sheer dumb luck that it was so late when you spiraled that energy through the complex. Most couples were already in their beds, but I can tell you this much, the maintenance people are not impressed with the mess that was made in the Rec room!!" Doc paced back and forth like a caged animal.

A giggle escaped me at the thought of it. "How's Jason, err, Dusty doing?" I smiled, in my dopey expression.

"What the hell's wrong with you!?" Doc said, defeated, as he crossed the room to check my vitals and reflexes. "He's doing very well in spite of the workout you put him through," He finally added.

"If I didn't know better I'd swear you were piss drunk," Doc muttered.

"You are going to stay here under observation until I find out exactly what is going on with you."

"You've got 'til noon, Doc," I blurted, flopping my head to the side to look at Bransen. At least he wasn't yelling at me. "Noon, Doc. By then Bransen should have my quarters assigned and I will be moving there. Have Jason install a smaller version of the MFM device in the room so that if this should happen there, no one will be affected," There seemed to be a burst of clarity, but it was short lived as my mind clouded over again. Nope, too hard to think right now. Not going to bother.

"Take some more blood, run some tests, show that naked video of me dressing," I chuckled. "Have a field day!"

For the first time since Doc's entrance, Bransen finally spoke up. "It might be for the best, Doc. We can have Dusty install another MFM and keep him away from others, at least for the moment."

"Yep, yep," I quipped, "nap time!" I mumbled as Doc turned and glared at me. The sounds blended around me like distant echoes and I drifted into one of many forgettable dreams.

My eyes opened to the sound of steady breathing. A quiet snore escaped at regular intervals, like some machine that was in desperate need of maintenance. Looking around, I knew this room. It was the same quarters usually reserved for Kelay. The grey metal walls were darkly lit, with only the stray picture hung here and there to break the monotony. The room was ten foot across by ten foot deep. A desk, with work table connected, filled the right wall from corner to corner. Adjacent from the bed sat a chair tucked between the table's legs barely allowing enough room for passage. In the left corner of the room, on the front wall, was the entry door to the quarters. Next to it, on the left wall, was the door leading to the bathroom that contained a very small sink, toilet, and standing shower. A shower sounded like a wonderful idea, but not just yet.

My bed was a small twin that would fit two persons should the need arise, and I didn't see any reason it shouldn't be used for that right now.

"Bransen," I whispered....

"Bransen," I whispered, louder this time, taking him from his dreams, or more possibly his nightmares.

"Huh...?" he grunted as his eyes opened to slits. He stretched while pulling himself up into the chair.

"Come here. There is no reason you should sleep in such an uncomfortable place. You know how you get when you don't sleep well." I scooted over beneath the woolen blanket to make room for him to join me.

He stood and stumbled, and climbed over the end of the bed to the pillow I now shoved over for him. With as much flair as a bull in an outhouse, he climbed under the covers behind me, rolling onto his right side as I was. Not knowing what to do or, possibly unconsciously, he flopped his left arm over me for lack of anywhere else to put it. These beds were made for functionality, not convenience, and there simply wasn't enough room to avoid the contact. Besides, I didn't mind the comfort of a warm body.

His breath tickled the back of my neck and made me smile. I pulled his arm tighter around me and enjoyed the warmth of him against my back. I felt safe.

I awoke some time later, feeling the best I had in days. Bransen's arm was still in tow as a shield, holding me close in his slumber. Lifting his arm, I felt him resist and pull me in closer, grinding his obviously aroused body into mine. I lay still as he adjusted in his sleep. After a few moments passed, I lifted his arm from me and slid out from his embrace and the tangle of covers, trying not to disturb him. Finally free from the bed, I looked back at him. He looked so peaceful. Shifting, he grabbed the pillow in my stead and gave it a tight squeeze.

He was gorgeous. His blond hair spilled around his face onto the pillow in a tangle of golden chaos. His body was muscular and many battles had left their shiny scarred mementoes here and there across his skin. His eyes were closed, but I remembered them being the deepest green I had ever seen.

I crept to the dresser on his side of the bed, opened the wardrobe and pulled out a pair of black loose pants, and a billowy cotton blue shirt with sleeves that reached almost half way down the arms. This would do perfectly. Finally in the bathroom, clothes in my arms, I closed the door behind me. Putting the clothes on the sink, I lifted the toilet lid and released. The shower was small, but served its purpose as I did my best to scrub myself clean from the last few days of fighting and sex.

I didn't want to leave the near scalding cascade of water, but I was beginning to wrinkle and as always there was much to do. The towel felt like feathers against my skin as I dabbed myself dry and tried to wring the last of the water from my hair. Damp curls left their marks on my collar and shoulders. I had had bangs before, but after the transformation and my hack job on my mane of hair, I simply combed it straight back. I let it fall where ever it might, occasionally brushing a wet ringlet of hair back from my eyes.

I felt absolutely refreshed. It was the first time in days. I gathered my dirty clothes and the wet towel and tossed them into the tiny hamper that was wedged between the sink and wall. I got a fresh towel from the cabinet beneath the sink knowing that Bransen would want a shower as well and hung it up on the hook by the shower door.

I opened the bathroom door and peaked out and found Bransen sitting up in bed staring back at me. I was trying to be quiet. Well, no sense in it now. I walked out casually and made my way to the chair he had occupied earlier. Bransen looked somewhat perplexed and I knew instantly what was on his mind.

Looking at his quickly wakening expression, "No, we only slept," I answered his question. "You looked so uncomfortable, and the bed had room for two, and well… I needed the comfort of someone I could trust," A heated blush burned my cheeks as I thought of things we might have done if I wasn't already exhausted the night before.

"I need to shower." There was a hint of disappointment in his voice, and I wondered if it was me or Kelay he longed to lay with.

"There is a fresh towel on the hook. We'll talk when you are finished. Please help yourself to the clothing in the wardrobe. There should be something in there that will fit you. I know it is policy to keep a stock of different sizes just in case." I gave him a mischievous smile and nodded toward the wardrobe.

With that he hopped out of bed and passed me. It was a tight fit and I got a nice view of his muscled ass as he twisted to get by. He picked out a black pair of denim pants and teal short sleeve shirt. The shirt, we both knew would be too small, but would accent his powerful chest and arms and make his eyes stand out like stars in the night. He disappeared into the cramped bathroom and I listened to the hiss of water. I made the bed, and took a chaste moment to stop and bring his pillow to my nose. It smelled of him, fresh with the aroma of sleep and his natural cologne. I settled back into the chair and waited for him to finish.

When Bransen emerged from the bathroom, I had to stifle my surprise. Damn he was exquisite. He had selected a pair of pants that accented how very small his waist really was. The fabric now barely contained what I felt the night before in my sleepy daze. His chest was broad and strong and tapered to his waist and then burst out again as his muscled thighs filled the legs of his pants. The shirt, as I suspected, was like a second skin and clung to every inch of his strong chest, rising and falling with his every breath and muscular twitch.

"Wow!" The word seemed to escape my mouth without control. "You look very nice," I said awkwardly, trying to cover my interest.

It wasn't appropriate, and he already had issues he needed to sort out with his previous infatuation with Kelay. I didn't need to fuel his confused desire, but the urge to rip his clothes off and run my tongue across his body was almost too much to control. There was no time, and we had business to attend to.

Strapping on his wrist COM, he tapped it and raised it to his mouth. 'He has such pretty pink lips.' The random thought entered my mind.

"Doc, if you have a few moments, Khore and I would like to meet you in conference room 3 on level 5," He lifted his eyes to me from across the room as he spoke.

"Well, it's about damn time!" Doc's words raged out of the COM.

"Lose the attitude, okay? There are more important things. Check yourself or don't bother," Bransen hissed into the COM.

"Shall we?" He smiled and waited for any indication that I might be ready for another encounter with Doc.

"Sure... what the hell." I rose from the chair to join him.

To be honest, I felt like a new person. I had gone through so many changes, but this was the first time I felt like I was really me. A new me, none the less. I didn't know quite how to explain it. Clinically, I knew what had happened, and feared Doc's confirmation, but we were still on course, and I would have to explain to him what had gone on in the last 48 hours.

"Call the team, please. I'd like them to get this first hand. We owe them that much." The reality of the situation stole my joy and I could feel my brow furrow with darker thoughts.

"All alpha team members report immediately to Level 5, conference room 3." Bransen made the command and looked back at me expectantly.

"Okay then," I gazed into his eyes and tried to hide my sadness with a smile. "Let's do this."

We took the lift to level 5 and waited while Doc, Sweed, Twist, Rift, Neek, and Raven entered the room and found places at the table. Doc, Bransen and I stood at the front of the table.

"Please call Jason, too. He needs to hear this." I spoke more to Bransen than anyone else.

He made the call and ten minutes later Jason, whom everyone knows as Dusty, emerged through the door in his coveralls, looking at me and then Bransen with worried eyes.

"Have a seat, please," I smiled at him, hoping to ease his mind.

Dusty made his way to an empty chair beside Raven.

We were all here and I had some explaining to do. This was not going to be fun. As I looked across the table from face to face I remembered their abilities with memories that had been given to me from Kelay.

To my left was Dusty, though I know him as Jason. When you have sex like that, it's hard to use nicknames, though from now on I would refer to him as Dusty. I did not want to cloud the situation anymore than I already had. He sat, resolute with expectation, as his eyes stole furtive glances at my body. A bit of pink rose to his cheeks as he diverted his hazel eyes to the surface of the conference table.

Beside him sat Raven. He was an ominous looking man who appeared to be in his 27th age. Dark black hair matched his upturned midnight colored eyes. There seem to be only pupil, and when he looked at you it was as though he could read the deepest fears of your soul. His mop of poker straight black hair brushed the tops of his ears and collar with bangs nearly as long in front that cascaded down to his chin on both sides of his face. He was cold and quiet, with ample pink lips and a small nose. We were nearly the same height, 5'8", but he bore tight compact muscle across his body, letting you know he could make the killing move. The sadness behind his eyes, however, told me he had done just that too many times in the past, leaving a bruised look about him. He is what most would simply describe as dangerous and, rightfully so, his area of expertise was hand to hand combat.

Beside him sat Sweed. The Nordic mass of a man was more power than he was skill. That adept ability was not something to scoff at when it came to a fight, however. He was more cunning than his Neanderthal appearance portrayed. It was a deception that had worked to his advantage on many missions. The contrast of him and Raven side by side was stunning. It was as though someone had made a negative of Raven and enlarged it. His blond hair, blue eyes, and strong square jaw gave him the look of the Vikings long since lost in history.

While very strong in spirit, Sweed gave furtive glances at Raven. It was the look of a dog afraid you'd yell at him but with the anticipation of some kind gesture. It was a strange thing to see someone of such strength to be cowered so easily by emotion. They were lovers but, as it had always been, Raven treated that love as something to be flicked off after passion had run its course. I could sense the love Raven felt in his heart for Sweed, but it was caged and hidden from the light. He had seen too much pain and been hurt one to many times. My heart went out to Sweed. He was traveling a difficult path.

Across the table from Sweed sat Neek, the name having been whittled down from Sneak. He was a small, frail looking thing that seldom if ever let daylight touch his skin. In his 18th age he bore the body of someone of 14th age, being small boned and almost weasel-like in appearance. His bland, brown shoulder-length hair was pulled into a pony tail, making him look younger still. His wide set brown eyes sat atop a nose that seemed to escape from his face. While he could hold his own in a fight, his skills were in communications and electronics. He acted as sentry to the group, twisting and contorting along the way as only his small five foot frame could, leaving no trace behind.

Neek fidgeted like a nervous animal, preparing for slaughter as though too much energy had been packed into too small a package. He, much like Doc, was our worrier, and when Neek worried, there was usually a damned good reason. Neek was a loner and we all knew why. His lover, Chance, had been killed on a mission not long enough ago for him to forget or forgive. I could feel it burn in him, as he looked up at me. He sat in a silent anguished rage and it was my fault, though I didn't know why.

In front of him sat Twist. Twist was a holy terror, to say the least, and known for making brash decisions in the heat of the moment, barely cheating death by the skin of his ass. He was also our comic relief. If there was ever a smart ass comment to be made at any opportunity, it was made by him. He was the team's weapons specialist. He was forever coming up with new gadgets and items that would kill all the quicker, but he never seemed to dwell in the death of it. He seemed to thrive on the discovery and mechanical science and I wondered if that was distraction enough to ignore the end result of his work.

He was taller than most and stood a little over six feet in height. He had the upper body muscle of someone that always carried too much but never moved great distances, though we all knew his stamina to be on a par with the rest. He was, to say the least, pretty. His sharp features, murky brown eyes, and short cut spiked hair seemed to reflect his personality; sharp and painful to the touch.

Rift sat in front of Twist. Explosives were his forte and I suspected that in his youth, he was the child you had to hide the matches from. Guns and bombs seemed to go together as well in topic as in bedfellows. Rift and Twist were lovers, by more than just practice. They loved each other deeply and it could be seen in their eyes as they gazed at each other. Rift had blown shit up for as far back as anyone could remember. He didn't just blow shit up though, he made it an art in only destroying what need be, to get the team further to its objective. He mirrored Twist nearly enough that they could have been brothers, except for his wavy auburn hair. While his jaw was more pointed and his shoulder-length loose hair was a contrast, I could not help but to look on in admiration at a pair better matched. Being the quieter of the two, when Rift did speak, it was always best to listen.

The room seemed to languish in silence and Twist broke the awkward silence. "So, what's up Doc?" The ancient reference garnered a weak snicker.

Glancing over to the Doc, I interrupted before he could begin. "Tell them everything, Doc. We don't have time to sugar-coat this."

"Well.." he fidgeted nervously with the test results and many print outs he'd gathered in the last few hours. "You are all now part of Khore. Khore is also now part of you."

He raised his hand to stop any questions before they began.

"From the blood tests, Khore has somehow infused himself into you and, by proxy, also has taken parts of you into himself. He now has a DNA make up of proportions I cannot begin to understand. The computers can't split it out like a normal genome. There is simply too much data, too much complex genetic code. And now, from the scans I have taken, you are all part of it." Doc sighed and his eyes threatened to close at any moment.

"What the hell is that supposed to mean!?" Twist blurted out.

I placed my hand on Doc's shoulder. "Let me explain." My voice held an authoritarian tone I didn't know I possessed.

"Surely you felt it when you awoke this morning." I paused. "The feeling that you are now more than what you were before. I sense it in you as easily as you can in those next to you."

"I should start from the beginning. I am from a primitive village. Until three weeks ago, I knew little of this world or how it worked." If they weren't listening before, I definitely had their attention now.

"My fathers were Briar and Kelay." The statement seemed to stop a heartbeat or two. I watched as the realization gripped their minds and continued.

"It was through their love that I was born. I am now 1600 years old though in appearance 21st age." A sharp intake of breath could be heard from Doc.

"This was never meant to happen, at least on the schedule we've all now fallen into." Looking into their confused faces, I took a deep breath, and continued.

"You are now as you will always be, and what I mean by that is this. You will not age. Not from this point forward. I did not know that this would happen so quickly. It was not meant to occur for another 30 years," I explained.

"Everyone in this complex will no longer age. It was the only way Kelay could ensure our survival. The Thorens are dying. You will find yourself stronger and less susceptible to influence by Thoren tricks of the mind. I have given to you as much as you have given to me. I had planned a better time but something has gone terribly wrong. This was never meant to happen so immediately, and I cannot explain why." I focused on the surface of the table to avoid their stares.

"I can." Bransen spoke barely above a whisper.

He glanced at me, and let loose a pent up breath. "I was there during your conception".

Suddenly my eyes blazed with their familiar white-blue light. "What?!" Rage swelled within my chest that was more Kelay's than my own.

"I'm sorry, Khore. I'm so, so sorry," Bransen continued, somberly. "I had no idea that this would happen. Kelay was acting strange, and flew a sphere minor to god's table to make love, I suspected, with Briar. They had been going each night and I was jealous. I would listen to words spoken by them, wishing I was the one hearing them first hand, but it just wasn't so."

He called it god's table. I saw it in his mind, and it was the same place I had gone so many times with Vale. Pain reverberated through my soul, poking tender places of sorrow that I wanted to forget.

"Over 1600 years ago I followed them to the table. They made passionate love, but this time, something happened. I was pulled in from my hidden place behind the rock-face. No, I did not participate, but something devoured my being just the same. They took my soul, and from that day on I did not age."

I could feel my anger boiling over. The white blue fire had erupted along my skin. "What have you done!!!!" I nearly screamed, lifting him into the air by force of mind. The rest looked on in horror.

"We knew. We knew something was different that night." It was Kelay's memory and words that burst from my lips.

Glancing at him as tears threatened to spill from my eyes he continued to speak through me. "An extra... had joined us in energy and we thought by chance it had been..."

I grew cold and looked at his suspended form in the air. "You had NO RIGHT!" I yelled, more out of rage remembered than my own. A gash slid across his abdomen through his clothing in a quick upward slash.

"GODS!" I screamed. "What have you done!"

The others jumped up from their seats.

'SIT!' I forced them back into position at the table. Laying my hand along the slash I had just created, I sealed Bransen's wound. Hanging my head, I released Bransen, letting him fall to the floor. I ran through the door to the lift. I had to get the hell out of there and away from the truth that burned my ears and reality.

With tears rolling down my cheeks, I continued to pound the level one button. I needed air, fresh air. I needed an open sky and a quiet place. Finally the doors opened and I bullied my way through the guards, freezing their muscles as I made my way into the night.

I was atop a mountain. It looked like the top of the world as I gazed out at the landscape of shadow and haunting moonlit night. Climbing my way to the peak of the mountain, away from the access shaft, I finally found a plateau on which to rest. I hung my head and ignored the tears winding down my cheeks.

I hadn't expected this. We, I or Kelay or whoever the fuck it was, had never expected this. Three souls had brought me into being. I laid there feeling the cool stone against my tired body hoping my thoughts might make some sense of what happened so long ago. The brisk air seemed to soothe me as the wind rustled the fabric of my shirt. It was peaceful and my most favorite place, or at least Kelay's once upon a time. I had never been here before, but it was a stolen memory of Kelay's experience. The air smelled like wet earth as it brushed past my face, and I lost myself in the diamond dusted night sky. This was always a good place. Closing my eyes, I prayed the sun would incinerate me in my sleep. Just let me drift in dreams through the sunrise and die inexplicably. It would have been so much easier.

Time passed and I was pulled from my thoughts when I heard his voice.

"Khore. Please forgive me." Bransen begged.

Regardless of the merge, and everything else, I was normally not a

creature of vengeance, and refused to become one now.
    I reached my hand out to touch his lips and quiet them.
    "What's done, is done," and I slept.

Chapter 4

Embracing the Dawn

When I opened my eyes I could see that only an hour or so had passed. The stars had barely moved in the sky. It wasn't Bransen's fault. It wasn't Briar's fault, nor was it Kelay's. I suppose I should be grateful for his intrusion that night. Had Bransen not been so infatuated with Kelay I might never have been born. Kelay should have noticed that Bransen hadn't aged in all that time. When you're life is surrounded by those who never die, I suppose, it doesn't seem out of the ordinary when someone else doesn't as well. I searched back in my mind and to Kelay's memories. There had always been that suspicion. Kelay had locked it away, and dismissed it.

It scared me to think of the carnage Bransen had witnessed over the past 1600 years. I guess when so many die around you so quickly, few notice you're the one that lives. Bransen became a permanent fixture as much as the building had; watching people step in and out of his life. The only constant had been Kelay. Now he was gone and here within me at the same time.

I stared at the starlit sky, lost in thought. Emotions take so much out of a body and I had been on a whirlwind tour these last few days. I was acting like some ignorant child, and felt ashamed of myself. Bransen lay beside me lost in his own worries.

"So, what do we do now?" I asked, pulling him from his thoughts.

"We fight." His baritone voice was resolute and determined.

"No, I mean what do 'we' do. I know you care for me, though I can't say for sure if it is the part of me that is Kelay, or if it is me alone. It confuses me. I know I have his memories, but I certainly haven't been acting like myself or him these last few days. It seems so wrong for me to have feelings for someone else so soon after Vale's death, but I am no longer who I was. I feel like I've lost myself. It's becoming harder to sort out which memories are mine and which are Kelay's," I couldn't hide my frustration and the sound of my own voice aggravated me.

Sitting up, I turned to face Bransen and continued, "I don't want to walk back into that complex not knowing who I am. We don't need any more chaos than what we already have. Everyone will be going through a lot of changes, and they are going to be looking to you for leadership."

Bransen lifted himself from the cool stone and turned to face me. "Who are you?" he asked, staring into my eyes.

"I'm Khore!" I said quickly, and paused, "and Kelay, and I guess partly you." I was quickly falling back into the chaos of my mind.

"You aren't me," Bransen said, a bit too fast. "I'm here in front of you. Who are you?" he asked me again.

"I'm Khore... I think... I don't know anymore."

"You told me, just a couple of days ago, that our emotion is what builds and maintains our soul. That it is our pain, joy, fear, and triumph that molds us into who we are and who we will become. How has that changed in only a few days?" Bransen asked me.

I pondered his question before answering. "A few days ago, when I spoke those words, I had only the memories and none of the emotions or feelings behind them. Kelay knew."

"No, you knew," Bransen interrupted. "I think that is part of the problem. You keep trying to separate his memories and experiences from your own. You need to reconcile your mind."

"Now who is speaking like an old man?" I couldn't help but smile at him.

He was right though. I had been trying to separate the memories ever since the transformation and I was losing the struggle. The realization moved through me. I am Khore. All of the memories, all of the feelings. It's who I am now. I am Khore. Kelay is a part of me, not separate from me, and not something to keep locked away like some file on a computer, to be accessed at my leisure. We merged and I let him enter my mind, but I hadn't accepted it. I had subconsciously rejected it like some splinter in my finger too deep to dig out.

The epiphany was coming to me in waves now. "I am Khore," I thought to myself. These memories are mine now. They are me. All of the good and the bad.

"Hey! Don't be going all supernova on me now. The MFM doesn't work out here," he said, seeing my eyes begin to glow.

"Oh, sorry... let's go inside." I stood and waited for him to follow.

He rose and we began to walk toward the entrance to the complex. Bransen opened what looked like a rock that exposed an access panel. Placing his hand on the imager, a weak light moved from his fingertips toward his wrist and the door opened.

"You know, I really hate you some times," I said. His eyes widened in surprise. "But, I think I love you too." We smiled at each other and entered the complex.

The imitation rock that camouflaged the entrance slid back into place, and we continued past the guards I had frozen earlier.

I released their bodies. They were less than pleased at having been so easily subdued.

"It won't happen again. I'm sorry," I tilted my head to the floor but still watched them incase they might be holding a grudge.

They gave us a wide birth because I was with Bransen. Had he not been there, I think they would have shot me without a second thought.

"We should probably go back to the conference room," Bransen suggested.

"Ahh shit, I forgot. They're all still sitting there, aren't they?" I cringed, already knowing the answer.

We hurried to the lift and back to conference room three on level five. Doc was sitting there, tapping a nervous foot on the floor. I hadn't frozen him but he was not happy. I had unknowingly left him to tend to six statues resting in their seats.

"My apologies," I said, as I released them all, sounding as timid as I could manage.

"Ohh, oh, ohh!!! I gotta pee!" Sweed jumped up knocking his chair backwards to the floor and raced out of the room.

There was a deafening silence as they stared at me. Some faces were filled with rage, some with confusion, and some with sympathy. I hung my head and waited for Sweed to return.

Sweed bounded back in like the giant graceful lummox he is, righted his chair, and took his place again at the table. You could see he had reservations about sitting there again after his torment, but he sat anyway. 'Who the hell goes to a meeting having to piss??'

"Please accept my apology," I broke the silence. "Now, does anyone else have any other surprises they'd like to share with the group before we continue?" I prayed no one would speak.

Twist spoke up almost immediately. "Rift has an ass hair problem, Sweed likes to play with dolls, and Raven has a third nipple!"

"They're action figures!" Sweed protested!

"I do not have an ass hair problem!" Rift growled defiantly.

"It's a fucking mole, damnit!" yelled Raven.

The room paused only a moment before everyone burst into fits of laughter. "Damn you Twist, and thank you at the same time," I thought.

"Ohhh please!" Twist continued, "it looks like two raccoons fighting to escape your pants when you walk. I love my little raccoons though," Twist retorted looking lovingly at Rift as we laughed.

"Well then," Bransen started, as the laughter faded, "Now that we have all of that out of the way, let's get some rest. Tomorrow will be a long day."

"Neek, I'd like you to stay for a moment please," I glanced in his direction. Nothing but rage glared back at me.

"Would you mind waiting for me outside?" Bransen answered with a nod, and he and the rest of the crew exited the conference room.

Once we were alone, I looked at Neek. "I did not kill Chance, and I'm sorry for your loss," My voice was cold and without emotion.

"Yes you did," he hissed. "You may not have pulled the trigger, but you killed him just the same. It is because of you we were on that mission, and it is because of you that he is gone."

"Don't lay that bullshit on me," I spat back. "He chose to go on that mission. You didn't protect him and he died. It would be as much your fault as anyone's." I saw him blanch from the words as much as if I had slapped him across the face.

I could see the anger in his face as his jaw clenched, threatening to shatter his teeth.

"Go ahead," I goaded him. "Take the knife from your ankle sheath and kill me. Ram it in my chest until your muscles cramp. It won't bring him back, and you'll still be alone. Or," I paused, calming a little, "you could aim your anger where it belongs. The Thorens killed Chance. Not me, not you, or anyone in this complex. You need to move on, Neek. You waste your time and energy," I turned and walked to the door.

"What the hell do you know about loss, you freak!" he screamed across the room.

Spinning around, I sent him sailing out of his chair and slammed his body against the wall, dangling him there several inches from the floor. My mind sent the table against the wall on the right, and it burst into a thousand splinters as I walked toward him.

"Loss?" I yelled. "Because of the Thorens I lost my love, my unborn child, and my entire village. Don't think because you hurt, that you are the only one who has ever felt pain, or that no one has felt it as sharply!"

I advanced, sending chairs and anything else in my way crushing into either wall.

"They're gone now," My voice wavered as I fought to hold back my tears. "I can't change that and neither can you." I turned and released him.

I walked back towards the door. I could sense him reaching for his knife and felt it leave his hand. He threw it in his despair. I grunted with the impact, and stumbled forward. I felt the blade grinding against bone as it plunged into my right shoulder blade. I turned my head to see the horror on Neek's face.

"Khore!" he started toward me and stopped. "I didn't mean to," he said through his tears. "I'm sorry!"

"So am I." I reached back and pulled the blade out from my shoulder and tossed it to the floor. My body had already started repairing itself and sealed the wound before I made it to the door. It hurt like hell, but it wasn't fatal, and soon it would be just another memory.

"Dusty has feelings for you, Neek. You shouldn't waste so much energy on hate. Get some rest, we've got training in the morning." I opened the door and found Bransen waiting for me.

Eyeing the destruction in the room he seemed somewhat relieved to see we were both alive, until he noticed the blood that had stained the back of my shoulder. Glancing at the knife on the floor he knew what had happened and rushed over to check my injury.

"What the hell!" He spun me around to check my wound. There was none, just my torn shirt, the blood soaked fabric where the knife had entered, and an inch long line of newly grown pink flesh.

"Everything is fine, Bransen. We just had a little talk." I waved it away and walked to the lift.

"You coming?" I asked, looking back at him.

Bransen stood there looking at me and then back to Neek. I turned and continued to the lift, hearing Bransen's steps approach from behind.

"What the hell was that all about?" he asked me as I pressed the call button.

"You don't know?" I asked as the doors opened and we entered the lift.

"Neek wanted to kill me. He blamed me for Chance's death." I stared into his eyes but there was no hint of surprise.

"But you weren't even there!" Bransen argued in my defense.

"No, but you were there because of me. Grief seldom accompanies reason. I think he's okay now. A little shaken, but he should be fine."

"You're alright with this, aren't you? That he tried to kill you?" Bransen's voice rose in volume in his frustration.

"If he had wanted to kill me, he would have aimed better. He just wanted me to hurt. And it did hurt, like a bitch!" I smiled back at him.

"I don't get you, Khore. Tomorrow I'm going to bust his ass. He won't see the light of day for a decade!" Bransen muttered as he crossed his arms.

"Let him be, Bransen. He's already punished himself enough."

We stood in silence until the doors opened. We exited and started down the hallway toward our quarters.

"Could I ask you a favor?"

"Sure, anything!" Bransen replied, looking back at me.

"Uhh... would you mind keeping me company tonight? I don't want to sleep alone," I muttered, embarrassed.

A smile crept across his lips as he nodded.

"Sleep. I said sleep! We'll discuss other things later." I could feel the heat rise off my face as we arrived at my door.

It opened as I pressed my hand against the scanner and we entered. The door closed behind us with a barely audible whisper. I stripped off my shirt, pulling it up over my head. Finally escaping the tangle of cloth, I saw him doing the same. Blushing, I turned away after catching him looking at me as much as I was him.

I practically ran into the bathroom to relieve myself and hide my expression. Either I was moving extremely fast, or he was deliberately tormenting me, because when I came back out he was still shirtless, showing off his muscled chest and abs. He sauntered toward the bathroom as I moved to the right side of the bed. The small walkway forced us to brush against each other, chest to chest. I was getting ready to remove my pants when I realized I hadn't any undergarments on. I never wore them. Instead, I untied the knot at the top and loosened the laces. I climbed into bed, and rolled onto my right side. Damn he was beautiful. I was now more than glad that I was facing away from him and that the covers hid my predicament.

After returning from the bathroom, Bransen finished undressing and I was too afraid to look to see just exactly 'how much'. I strongly suspected, by the amount of clothing I heard drop to the floor, that he had taken off more than just his shirt.

Suddenly, I heard a giggle and glanced over just as he dove into the bed, practically knocking me out the other side. He had nothing on! He quickly climbed over the top of the blankets and gathered them around himself as he rolled away from me onto his left side.

"What are you doing?" I asked as he reached to shut off the lights.

"Turning off the lights. Aren't you ready to sleep?" He asked.

"Not that, you goof. What are you doing facing that way? Turn around here." I demanded. There was a long moment of silence before he spoke.

"Uhh... I probably shouldn't," he mumbled.

"Having some control issues, are we?" I jabbed my elbow into his back.

He bounded onto his other side, reached around me and grabbed hold of my cock. A wrestling match began.

"It seems to me you're having a problem of your own," he said as he gave my cock a rough squeeze.

"Hey!" I squealed.

He scrambled, climbing on top of me and now had my arms pinned by his knees under the blankets, tickling me mercilessly. His impressive cock was aimed straight at my face. I looked, but couldn't control myself as I was in spasms from the relentless barrage of pokes and prods.

Between breaths and shrieks I managed to get out, "Two can play that game," and he instantly stopped attacking my sides and moaned. I heightened the sensations in his cock and raced him toward orgasm with my mind. Struggling, I got an arm loose and pushed him over onto his back as he exploded into the air, shooting all over his chest and face, grunting a deep satisfaction.

"You cheated!" His chest heaved as he protested and grinned. "I think I like it when you cheat."

"Okay, go clean up and get to sleep." I chuckled, fully aware of the mess I had in my own pants.

He climbed out of bed and went to the bathroom. As he was cleaning up, I removed my pants and used them to swab up the cum that matted my pubic hair. After pitching my pants into the corner, I covered back up with the blanket. Bransen came out of the bathroom, and thankfully, this time he didn't launch into bed. Instead, he was giving me a nice view of himself. His powerful thighs were separated by a very impressive cock and balls and I had to fight to keep from staring. 'Time to sleep, damnit!'

As he climbed into the bed, I flipped off the light. He scooted in close to me and I could hear the intake of his breath as he realized I too was naked. Pulling his arm over me, I snuggled back into him, partially for the comfort of it and partially to torment him.

"Thanks, Bransen," I smiled in the darkness. "If I wake up pregnant, I'm gonna kick your ass."

I enjoyed the feel of his chest, as it expanded and contracted against my back. The delicate tickle of his breath against the back of my neck made me want to squirm and have a longer more extended encounter, but the necessity of sleep helped me decide otherwise.

I awoke the next morning to the sound of water running in the bathroom. Bransen had risen before me and was taking a shower. I lay there for a few minutes and waited for the haze of sleep to leave my mind. As I sat up the blankets fell to my lap, hiding my morning excitement. With any luck I would be under control by the time he finished. I leaned against the wall, and the cool surface made me shiver.

The door opened and out stepped Bransen... naked. He made no effort to cover himself, and what little control I had a second before, was now gone. He flexed and stretched his muscles lewdly in front of me.

He was getting the best of me and I had to turn the tables.

"Thank the gods! I've got to pee!" I threw off my covers, and revealed my hard cock. I slid off the mattress and faced Bransen. His eyes widened and I think he stopped breathing. Stretching my arms toward the ceiling, I arched my back, pointing even more in his direction, and grunted. Bransen's gaze was locked on my groin.

"Don't mind that." I swayed my hips a little before walking toward him. "I'll get it under control soon enough," I couldn't hide my grin as he finally broke eye contact with my cock and looked me in the eyes.

As I approached I gave him a little tug to bring him closer and gave him a sweeping kiss on the lips.

"Morning," I flashed my most decadent smile and stepped into the bathroom, shutting the door behind me.

'Point for me.' I thought as I turned on the water and grabbed a fresh towel. I would have released my tensions there in the shower, but thought better of it. After I finished rinsing off I stepped out of the shower, dried myself, and then exited the bathroom.

Bransen was sitting on the end of the bed, stealing glances at my now limp meat.

"Serves you right, you know," I said, seeing him jump from the unexpected words.

"Huh? What do you mean?" His eyes scanned me from head to toe as he asked.

"It serves you right for coming out of the shower, looking that damn good, knowing what kind of affect it was going to have on me," I giggled.

He blushed and smiled as he watched me dress. "Well, I like to tease," he grinned.

Opening the wardrobe, I leaned forward, doubling almost in half to get my shoes giving him a very intimate few of my ass. "Oh?" I paused, "I wouldn't know what you're talking about," I laughed as I started digging through the clothes to find something to wear.

"Okay! Okay!" he said resting his hands in his lap. "I get your point!" he grinned at me.

"No, but maybe someday if we're both lucky," I said over my shoulder.

I found a nice pair of deep blue lace up pants and green half sleeve shirt. Finally dressed I sat down on the end of the bed beside him.

Leaning into him, I asked, "So, ready for breakfast? I'm starving!!"

"Now that you mention it, so am I. Let's go," he said hopping up off the bed.

We took the lift to level 11. The cafeteria was more of an assembly line of unhappy servers and semi conscious patrons. We trudged our way through the make shift buffet. I chose a cheese omelet, egg whites only, and wheat toast, while Bransen had what looked like half of a dead cow teetering on his plate.

"How can you possibly eat that much so early in the morning?" I gaped at his tray as we made our way to an empty table.

The mound of food he had stacked on his tray was almost frightening. "How do you eat that much and stay thin?" I was completely at a loss.

"You said it yourself. We are now as we will always be," he replied with a grin, as he gripped his fork and violently stabbed at the slab of meat.

As we ate I felt the occasional stare. I guess I had made quite a spectacle of myself in the last few days. It was going to take a while for everyone to adjust, and most of them hadn't heard the half of it yet, though I could feel their curiosity surging through them. They felt different, better, but didn't know why, and now wasn't exactly the time to tell them. They would all be notified by their instructors as they trained in their classes today.

Sweed, Rift, Raven, Twist, and Neek entered the cafeteria, looking as tired as I felt when I first opened my eyes. I watched them amble through the serving line and waved them over as they searched for a place to sit.

"What are you doing?" Bransen whispered in a panic.

"I'm inviting them over here, what the hell does it look like I'm doing?" I looked at him, wondering if he had suddenly gone insane.

"We don't usually eat together," he whispered loudly to me.

"Why not?!" I asked.

My wave had gotten their attention, but they all stood frozen, like field mice seeing an owl swooping for the kill.

"HEY!" I yelled. "OVER HERE!" I waved again.

I almost laughed. It looked like both Bransen and they were ready to shit themselves.

"I command these men," he said quickly before they got too close.

"These are friends. Someone who keeps your ass alive is more than welcome at my table," I nudged him with my knee as they approached.

"So, have a seat. Damn, what's wrong with all of you this morning? Not had your coffee yet?" I chirped.

They took their places, pulling a chair from an adjacent table to accommodate us all. Everyone sat quietly, staring into their trays, not saying a word. "What in the hell?!" I thought.

"So, are you all looking forward to training today?" I tried to start the conversation.

I got four shrugs, a grunt and a very unsteady, "Sure," from Sweed. Still, no one had picked up their forks to eat.

I sat back in my chair and looked at the lot of them. I had never seen such a close knit unit so unbelievably awkward, eating at the same table. Nope, this simply wouldn't do. Almost instantly... inspiration struck.

I mentally lifted the hash browns from Sweed's plate, and sent them sailing across the table. They splattered against Neek's face. A good size chunk clung to his cheek as the rest fell to his food tray with a plop. Everyone in the cafeteria froze, looking to see Neek's reaction. You could have heard a popcorn fart it was so quiet.

Suddenly, a wet splatter flew from an adjacent table, where Dusty sat, coating Sweed's face. It was a splatter of egg cooked over easy and the yellow residue dripped down his nose onto his plate.

Complete and total chaos erupted as breakfast flew from every direction, making contact more often than not. A rain of eggs, potatoes, and meat of various origins began. Food flew everywhere, and I slid below the table, waiting for the chaos to run its course. I couldn't help but to laugh as speckles of oatmeal dotted my hair from the fall out.

Having spied my escape route, Bransen joined me.

"You're bad, you know that?" he asked, as much as stated, with a grin.

Flinching as someone's grits blasted my cheek, I smiled in reply. "Everyone needs a hobby."

I pulled him into a kiss. Our tongues dueled as we lay in the midst of battle. I leaned back and brushed his butter caked hair from his face while gazing into his eyes.

"I do love you," I said, amongst the insanity, touching his brow with my finger tips.

"I love you, too."

My heart swelled with his words and I pulled him into another kiss, feeling the impact of food as it blurred across my peripheral vision and onto me and Bransen.

"What the hell is going on in here?!" we heard Doc yell.

Everyone paused, food in hand, completely caught off guard. The room grew silent as a lone wad of hash brown traveled through the air, landing on his head like a snow cone capped with more ice.

"Bury him!" I yelled, sending with my mind what debris I could find from the floor and trays around us in his direction.

Moments later, Doc stood at the entrance to the cafeteria, tray still in hand, and laughed in spite of himself. What else is there to do when you have breakfast creeping down the crack of your ass, because you like 'loose fit' clothing.

I leaned into Bransen again, and we kissed as I ran my fingers through his food soaked hair.

"Thanks for breakfast." I gave his cheek a lick.

We crawled our way to the door and away from the carnage. We were stopped by Doc, and rose to our feet. Before us stood a breakfast-covered man knowing too much for his own good.

"Somehow," he said smiling, "I know this is your doing, Khore."

"You can thank me later, Doc. We have to get out of here and go train. As it is, it's going to be delayed a while," I grinned and nudged Bransen in the side.

"Let the others know, would you? Training is rescheduled for noon." Looking at Bransen, I changed my mind again.

"Okay, make it 2pm. We'll see you then. Please be sure that Dusty and Chris are there." I gave Doc a peck on the cheek as we walked toward the lift.

Chapter 5

Trained Passion

"How about I shower real quick, and you do the same. I'll meet you in your quarters in 20 minutes. Then we can decide on a place for training," I grinned as I turned to Bransen.

"Oh, uh, okay," he said, crestfallen.

I chuckled and sent sensations to his cock and balls with my mind. I intensified the feeling slowly, bringing him quickly to the edge.

"There are many forms of training you know," I said, waiting a few more moments. I halted the sensations just as he was reaching the point of no return and a wicked grin crept across my face.

"This is going to be the best training session ever!" His breath was stilted and beads of sweat were forming on his forehead.

"Well, it won't be like any you've ever had before... I hope," I reached out and tweaked his nipple.

"Good luck hiding that monster on the way back to your room," I chuckled and glanced at his crotch as the door opened to my room.

Looking over my shoulder as I entered, I waved and the door closed between us. His cheeks glowed from embarrassment and I couldn't help but laugh.

It took longer to get breakfast cleaned from my hair than I expected, but I finally managed. It never seemed to fail. When I rushed, it seemed to make everything I did take twice as long.

"Now... what to wear... what to wear..." I thought to my self.

I picked through the clothes, scrambling to find just the right thing, and then I realized what would be perfect; the clothing I had arrived in. I only hoped that they had been cleaned. They were still at the medical station on level 20.

I pulled on a shirt three sizes too big for me and slipped on a pair of clean shoes. Everything essential was covered as I raced to ward the lift, but still I hoped I wouldn't have to explain my appearance to anyone.

Besides, I didn't want to keep my Bransen waiting. With the state I had left him in, there was no telling what he might do to alleviate his frustration. I needed him 'intact' so to speak.

The lift doors finally opened and I pressed the '20' button eight or nine times, trying to rush the heap along its way. The lift's ascent finally slowed, the doors opened and I jogged over to the nurse's monitoring station.

Chris was yet another specimen of beauty. He was nearly six feet tall with light brown hair that dusted the tops of his ears and neck. His sparkling blue eyes reflected the love he felt each time he glanced in the direction of Doc's office. It was obviously more than just infatuation. His jaw was more square than most, and sported a cleft in his chin. He didn't have the muscle many of the others did, however. His body was lean, but without the bulk that results from too much manual labor.

"Hey, do you have the clothes that I was wearing when I first arrived?" My voice was hushed and I was nearly panting, though it was excitement and not effort that stole my breath.

"Certainly. They are right here," he answered as he pulled a box labeled 'Khore' from beneath the counter.

"I don't suppose you had them cleaned did you?" I asked, afraid to hear his answer.

"Not at first, no. It's policy to leave them as they are, in case we need to investigate possible contamination from any DNA and debris we encounter in the field." My heart started to sink.

"But," he continued, "you were found perfectly fit so I had them cleaned."

'Thank the gods!' I thought to myself. "Thank you so much, you're a life saver!"

With that, I pulled the clothes from the box and inspected them. They were clean and ready for wear. Pulling my over-sized shirt over my head, I got lost in the tangles and couldn't manage to get the damn thing off! I heard a gasp come from Chris's direction. The fabric was bound up under one arm. In my fit to get the shirt off I had managed to tie it around my neck and was nearly strangling myself. I was stuck there with my shirt hiked up and my left elbow was wedged and suspended at head level, while my lower body was completely exposed.

"Hey, do you think you could give me a hand?" I asked, fighting against the fabric.

A moment passed and he began tugging on a portion of the shirt and I was finally able to break it loose from my body.

"Thanks a lot," I said, grinning at him. I watched his eyes as they glanced from my face to my crotch and back again.

"You did see the video didn't you?" I pulled on the silken tunic and fastened it at the waist.

"Yeah," he answered, in a daze, still staring at me. "But it's not the same as seeing it in person," he continued, obviously referring to my cock.

I chuckled and he seemed to snap out of his trance, blushing. "Sorry," he said, focusing on the pile of paperwork atop his desk.

"Don't be," I paused. "It's flattering to know that others find me attractive, or at least parts of me," I laughed.

"Could I ask you a big favor?" I pleaded. "Could you keep these until tomorrow?" I offered him the clothing I had worn during my jog there. "I have to meet someone and I'm running late."

"For you, I'd keep them for an eternity," he said, with a wicked grin as his blue eyes sparkled at me.

"Great, thanks!" I turned and raced back to the lift. "You're a life saver," I belted out as the door to the lift opened.

I slipped inside, immediately pushing the '30' button over and over again. The lift doors seemed to close slower than normal, taunting me. Maybe these aggravating delays were life's way of saying 'relax.' I didn't want to relax though. There was a hot body attached to the man I loved, waiting for me.

Checking myself in the reflection of the door, I straitened my clothes. It was a tunic of sorts comprised of a large opalescent shirt, open at the chest that tapered and belted at the waist with just enough fabric to conceal your 'interest,' hanging only as low as mid thigh level. Straitening myself, the doors opened and I walked quickly to Bransen's quarters. His room was just down the hall from my own. The temptation to run down the hall nearly consumed me, but I fought the urge and walked as fast as my legs would take me. After one last primp I pressed his call button and placed my hand on the entrance scanner to identify myself.

The doors opened immediately and I found Bransen standing behind them waiting for me.

"I wondered if you... You're beautiful!" he said, eyeing me from head to toe.

Scanning him from top to bottom I was more than impressed. He had chosen a two piece workout set of black silk that draped obscenely across his muscles. The top seemed to caress his skin with each movement and I was almost jealous of the fabric. It was open at the shoulders, much like my own, and tapered into a V and belted at the waist. A pair of black shiny silk pants covered him from hip to ankle barely able to contain his muscular thighs.

Returning my eyes to his face I lifted my hands to his temples and ran the tips of my fingers through his thick blond shoulder length hair. It curled just enough to wrap around my fingers as I explored.

His emerald green eyes and high cheekbones tilted as I brushed his sweet plump pink lips with my own. He had a moderately muscled body, that was not too big or too small, but beautiful by simple but powerful lines that tapered to his hips. His thighs were massive, separated by a very ample concealed cock I had committed to memory. He was perfect and I craved him.

"So, do I get to come in? Or are you going to make me stand out here?" I asked, with a grin.

"Come in, come in," he repeated, as he stepped back to allow me access.

"I was thinking we could train in Hydroponics on Level four. What do you think?" I asked, as I pressed against him, letting my fingertips trail across the flesh of his neck.

"I think that sounds like an excellent idea." His words were a heated whisper as he pulled me against his hard body.

Sliding my hands down his strong arms, I stood on my toes to reach his lips with my own and gave him a sweeping kiss as I ran both hands through his mane of hair.

"Well then, we better get going," I whispered.

Nearly ripping my arm from its socket, Bransen activated the exit and we left his quarters, him yanking me quickly in tow to the lift.

"Hey!" I giggled, "be gentle."

His grasp on my wrist loosened as he continued to drag me toward the lift.

As we entered and he slapped the '4' button in passing and pressed me against the wall, grinding into me before the doors had even begun to close.

I wanted him desperately, but pushed him back, grinning. "Lesson One. Control," I said, panting.

We separated as the lift slowed to a stop. He led me to our destination. Even the way his hand engulfed mine was sensual as we let our loose fingers dance across each others palm.

It was a good thing we didn't meet up with anyone in the hall. It was not by coincidence that I had picked this level. No one came here because of the environmental controls. It was hot, sticky, and wet, the kind of humidity that makes you sweat just from sitting idle. Luckily the breeze from the ventilation fan made it less than stifling. This was the perfect place for our first training session.

Bransen led the way out into the depths of the hydroponics bay, moving along man-made paths through the palms and underbrush. Traveling for nearly ten minutes, he veered from the path, and he pulled me through thicker growth to a small clearing. We stopped at a lagoon-like area, surrounded by palms and near a deep pool that was fed by an overhead waterfall. Around it was a white sand beach that sloped downward and disappeared beneath the water.

We listened to the rush of water beside us and felt the spray collecting on our bodies and clothes.

"Remove your clothes please." I said as I loosened my belt and pulled the tunic over my head. I lay it on a low branch only a few steps away and turned to watch him disrobe.

Bransen removed his clothes and laid them next to mine on the odd shaped branch.

Fully nude, I sat on the sand and motioned Bransen to do the same, directly in front of me. With knees touching, we sat with our legs crossed. We were both already hard with anticipation, which made concentrating that much more difficult as precum dribbled from our cocks.

"Okay, relax your mind." I touched his temple gently with the fingertips of my right hand. "This is going to be a little intense. Try to let it roll through you. Don't resist," I said, and paused a moment before flooding his mind with memories. Our backs arched and trickles of sweat traveled down our bodies to the sand. Finally finishing the transfer, I released his mind.

"Whoa!" he said as the knowledge was absorbed. "Is that what it was like when Kelay merged with you?" he asked in a whisper.

"No," I took a breath. "When I merged with Kelay, it was about 182,000 years worth of memories," I explained. "What I've given you just now was about 5,000 years worth of information."

"How, how did you handle it?" he asked, amazed.

"Not well, from what I gather, but you helped me sort it out," I said, smiling back at him.

"182,000 years," Bransen whispered, shaking his head.

"Anyway," I interrupted, "what have you learned?"

"We'll play a game similar to one I played a very long time ago, but we'll make it fun." I grinned.

"I will give you a sensation, and then you return it," I said as I activated the nerves in the head of his softening cock.

"Ohhh!" he said, his breath changing. "Just out of curiosity, how much can you increase that?" he asked as he squirmed from the feeling.

"There is no limit," I said, remembering my escape from the Sphere Major.

Bransen was quiet for a moment as his mind wrapped around it and then asked, "That was the method you used to kill Rase wasn't it? I saw it in your memory but it was only a flash."

"Yes," I said flatly, not really wanting to think about it. "We'll get to that later. Now, concentrate."

"Return the feelings I have given you. Think of the nerve cells, and of the electrical impulses that pass between them. Enhance the signals and maintain them. Weave them like a tapestry within your mind." I said to him.

His face became resolute and I could literally see him strain.

"What are you doing? You cannot force this. Envision it in your mind, know what your goal is and let it happen. Guide it," I urged.

I felt a pulse in my cock which quickly faded. "Yes, that's it!" I told him as he lost his focus.

"Listen. Close your eyes. Let it happen. Give it a little nudge and do it."

Bransen took a deep breath again and relaxed. I felt his mind clear and he released control. The sensation hit me almost immediately and my breath caught.

"Yes, that's it. Damn, that feels good," I said, grinding into the sand where I sat. "Now, back off a bit. Let's not kill it with kindness." I urged him.

The sensation diminished but didn't stop. He was doing very well.

"Now, I want you to increase the feeling to match this." I said in a whisper as I increased the sensations coursing through him ten-fold.

He groaned and his concentration wavered. "Let it happen, but be gentle," I whispered, as I felt his mind shift.

"MMMMmmmm yes," I groaned. "Just like that." It was like being touched in every perfect place all at once.

"Now match this," I panted and sent additional sensations to his ass and balls.

"Uh, uh, uh," he grunted. His body shifted and his eyes squeezed shut as more sweat beaded up on his skin. We were both speeding to our climax.

After a moment to regain his composure, he was able to send my ass and balls to the same level of pleasure as my cock. It wouldn't be much longer for either of us.

"Now, maintain this level," I said as I leaned forward. This would definitely test his concentration. I took his leaking cock completely in my mouth until I felt his neatly trimmed blond hairs tickle my nose. Arching back, he thrust his cock forward and began shooting instantly into my mouth as I worked the length of him with my tongue, watching his muscled abdomen expand and contract. He had slipped in concentration and had tripled my own feelings of pleasure and I shot out across my chest and legs as I drank in his copious load, and groaned around his cock.

Giving his now shrinking member a last tug with my lips and tongue, I let it fall from my mouth with a slight pop and rested my head on his thigh as we recovered. We lay there for several minutes, just enjoying the roar of the waterfall and the touch of each other as I ran my fingertips along his abdomen. I traced along his length of his wilting cock and it sprang back to life.

"Oh, you are a horny devil aren't you," I grinned wickedly as I began to massage his balls with my tongue. In a matter seconds I raised the sensations through his cock at lightning speed, causing him to yell out and shoot a somewhat smaller load across his chest.

"No more! No more!" he begged, as I crawled up the length of his body. We wrapped our gritty hands around each other and kissed passionately.

"Let's get some of this sand off of us," I gave him one final soft peck on the lips and stood.

We walked to the lagoon and down the slope of sand, hand in hand, stopping as the water covered our feet. It felt cool to the touch, but not uncomfortably so. It was the ideal temperature to refresh. We waded further into the water, clutching each other as we made our way carefully to the side wall of the man made lagoon.

On the far side was a waist high ledge beneath the water. It kept us emerged to our shoulders but was high enough to lean against without having to worry about sinking below the water. I was sure this was by design and not just coincidence. We leaned back, completely relaxed and rested our heads in the sand. The water's current caused our legs to brush against each other like two dandelion seeds floating in the breeze.

Leaning my head to the left against his shoulder, I used my hand to pull his head toward me for a few swift, but gentle kisses.

"Are you ready for the next lesson?" I asked him, staring into his emerald eyes.

"I don't know if I can take another lesson like the last one," he answered, giggling.

"Good," I said, smiling to him, "because this one isn't quite the same." I reluctantly wiggled from our partial embrace and searched the rock face around us.

Finding a black stone about the size of a marble, I placed it on the ridge behind us and scooted away from him.

"Pick it up," I said.

He moved to pick up the small stone with his hand. I pressed the molecules closer together with my mind, maintaining a constant pressure upon it, making it equal to something approximating 250 pounds.

"What the hell? You're holding it there?" he asked, looking somewhat confused at me.

"No, it's just heavier now. Try harder, push on it. At least try to scoot it a little." I couldn't help licking my lips as I watched his muscles flex and strain to move the pebble.

Pressing with a great deal of muscle and effort, he was able to budge the stone a foot or so.

"Okay," I said, picking the stone up with my finger tips and dropping it back to where it had started.

"Now blow on it," He looked at me as though I were crazy.

"Okay," he sighed heavily, causing the pebble to waft off into the air like a leaf circling on the currents of air.

He just stared watching it drift its way back before finally settling again onto the sand.

"How'd you do that?" He said, a little too loudly.

"Much like the way we quickened and amplified the sensations in each other. You compress the atoms and molecules closely together to increase the density and weight, and then the opposite to decrease it. I don't expect you to get this right off, but I want you to practice this every chance you get. It is an important skill, and may save your life some day," I explained to him.

"Okay, moving on, lesson three. You know the barrier or seam of matter. The rock stands separate from the sand. There is a barrier there. The atomic particles cling to each other to maintain the thing that they are not wanting to merge with the other. I want you to see the barrier around the rock and lift it from the ground," I explained again. "Don't force it up. Just simply lift the barrier upward around it. There is no real effort involved."

Staring at the pebble, I could feel Bransen's mind clear. Concentrating deeply, I interrupted, "Only upward," I reminded him.

Moments later the rock shifted its position, kind of tumbling in place, and then rose about five inches from the ground.

"I did it!" he practically yelled, as the rock dropped with a dull thud back into the sand.

"Yes, you're a fast learner and should be proud of your accomplishments today. If I do say so myself, some of them were quite enjoyable, too," I grinned.

"I need you to practice this every day as well. You must move and direct these small objects. Once you have this mastered, I want you to practice with larger objects. The size never matters, but being able to concentrate and see the barrier in your mind is key. There is no limit to this skill other than your ability to concentrate and see." My voice took on a more serious tone and I hoped he understood the gravity of this lesson. "Every rock, every pebble, and every blade of grass can be your weapons if you master this ability." I then moved the pebble with my mind to the front pocket of his black silk pants where they hung on the tree branch.

"You keep saying there is no limit. How can there not be some kind of limit to this?" He looked at me and his brow furrowed the way it always did when he was thinking too much.

"Well, I don't know how to explain it other than to say that your limits are set by your own mind. If you can conceive it in your mind, then it is possible. If you do not believe it is possible, then it will not be." Bransen squinted his eyes and looked at me skeptically.

"Okay, I will show you," I said, wading out to the center of the lagoon.

Clearing my mind, I gathered energy and sent out a small sensing pulse. Every molecule, its position and purpose, drew their myriad function and position in my mind. Opening my eyes, I let them blaze with the blue white light and, focusing my mind on everything around me with all my senses, I let the blue fire erupt across my skin. Lifting myself completely from the center of the lagoon, I floated a few inches above its surface.

"Watch," I said to his mind, by thought only, as I bound every barrier to stop its movement. A moment later everything stopped, as though time itself had come to a grinding and abrupt halt. It looked like a quick snapshot of a thing moving too fast. The waterfall and each drop of its stray mist, the leaves of the trees, and every insect and dust particle froze in place. There was complete silence. Raising a 6-foot boulder that dotted the exterior of the man made beach, I told him, "Pick a drop of the mist."

He watched me, amazed, and moved through the air as the suspended droplets clung to his skin. He pointed out a single droplet of water.

"Okay," I nodded, and compressed the water to a linear blade only perceivable in two dimensions. I molded it into something so thin that, unless you were above or below it, you would not see it at all. The artificial light of the bay danced on the watery surface. Increasing its density, I sent it through the boulder, slicing it in half. The lower portion fell to the ground with an enormous crash. Then, to get the point across, I brought up thousands of water droplets to writhe around me like a living tornado of diamonds.

"Each of these is a killing thing if used properly," I said to his mind, letting the drops of water flow around me. "It can just as easily be done with grains of sand, blades of grass, or even the air around you."   I let the tornado of water gradually lower back onto the surface of the lagoon. I released my hold on everything and then lowered myself back into the water, letting our surroundings stutter back to life again.

Bransen looked at me in horror and it broke my heart. I turned to hide the tears as they fell from my eyes. I walked out of the lagoon, and to where my clothing hung on the tree branch.

"Yes, I know I'm a monster, a freak even by Thoren standards." My chest tightened and I was filled with a mix of anger and sorrow.

This 1600 year old wound was still fresh. Even though I was blessed with loving parents and foster parents as a child, this one truth remained. I was always an oddity and shunned by those around me. My life had never been easy, and of all people, I had hoped Bransen might understand.

"Wait! I'm sorry!" Bransen bounded in my direction through the water. He hugged his wet body to mine, and rocked me back and forth as he placed light kisses on my neck.

"I'm sorry! It just surprised me is all." He whispered in my ear as he tried to explain.

We stayed like that for some time before he released me and turned me by the shoulders to face him. I diverted my eyes to the ground to avoid his gaze.

"One thing I don't understand..." Bransen furrowed his eyebrows as though he were trying to wrap his mind around something.

"Is why I don't use these abilities to kill them all, right?" I interrupted him and a new horror shook my chest.

"Could you?" I asked, looking up into his eyes? "Could you live with that? Could you kill an entire race of people who were already speeding to their own destruction? Which is worse? The monster you think I am, or the monster you're asking me to be?"

Chapter 6

Bittersweet

I stared into Bransen's eyes, waiting for an answer. He seemed lost in thought, trying to grasp the enormity of the question I had asked him.

"I suppose not," he said, letting out a deep breath.

"Why?" I asked him.

He paused in thought again before speaking. "Some of them are innocent," he finally replied.

"Certainly most are guilty of one thing or another, only a few innocents would be lost. 'Collateral Damage' they call it. Why not kill them all and put them out of their misery?" I asked coldly.

My devil's advocate line of questioning seemed to confuse him. He was fighting with what was right and what was easy. Surely it would be as simple to just yell 'collateral damage' and have done with it. I was hoping he would find it more difficult to become a cold blooded killer.

"It's just wrong," he said, sounding agitated.

"Why? After all they've put us through, wouldn't we be justified?" I squinted my eyes and waited.

"Because if we kill even one innocent person, then we are as bad as they are! Kelay was an innocent. He did everything he could to protect us and you. He gave his life! How can you ask me this?" His voice rose as the anger built inside him.

"Now you have the answer to your question," I said with a sigh. "Now you understand. The Thorens are as much my family as you are to me now. They are far from perfect, but I do not wish their death. I will tell you this though, if I had to choose, I would pick you."

"I'm sorry." Bransen stepped forward and wrapped his muscular arms around me. "I didn't realize what I was asking."

"Don't apologize. Had you answered differently, you would have broken my heart and I doubt I could have survived it. Thank you for being the person I know you to be," I pressed my lips against his and stole a quick kiss.

"You have the ability to fight the Thorens hand to hand now. Soon you will be able to protect yourself from their mental efforts, and block their intrusion into your mind. You know this from the memories I've given you," I pulled away from him and continued.

"We need to disperse this information amongst the team, and give them the memories of this day as well. It might be a little embarrassing, but it is something they will benefit from. You must share the memories with them as I did you. Then, they must select 10 people to train, who will then train another 10, until the information is passed to everyone in this facility. The process should take approximately two days to complete," I diverted my eyes to the ground and stared at the sandy beach beneath my feet.

"They will also know that I am not one to be fucked with." A bitter tone tinged my voice and it made me chuckle.

"What's wrong?" he asked, hearing the sadness in my voice.

"When the training is complete, we are going to have to get to work and people are going to die," I said, trying to avoid the thought of coming battles.

We left the humid jungle of hydroponics bay four. It felt like we were racing down a path, out of control as the lift descended. As soon as everyone was trained, we would be making plans to extract humans from the Sphere Major.

The lift doors opened and we entered the recreation and training area. The team members sat waiting on mats that dotted the room. I gave Bransen a squeeze around the waist and we parted. We walked past the game tables, dining section, and into the training area.

As I had asked, Doc made sure that Dusty and Chris were here as well. Doc stood waiting, with the usual look of worry etched across his face. As we reached the floor mats all eyes were upon us.

"Khore and I have spoken, and we would like to invite you to join the team. Dusty, from what Khore tells me, you are adept in your understanding of this alien technology. Chris, you are well skilled in medicine, and would also be extremely valuable in the field." Bransen indicated each with a nod as he spoke.

Dusty paused for a moment and answered. "I would be honored and I'll do my best, but don't be expecting me to perform miracles with this place. This old bitch is moody and I've got a lot of work to do."

"If you thought you were busy before, then you're in for a lot of surprises," I said, knowing he was more than able to keep this place running.

"It's settled then," said Bransen. "You'll be partnered with Neek."

You could see Dusty's face brighten at the thought. Neek glanced at Dusty and gave a curt nod.

"You will train together. Whether or not you room together, will be entirely up to you," Bransen grinned as blood flushed Dusty's cheeks.

"Chris?" Bransen asked, looking now in his direction.

"Of course!" he blurted out too quickly, earning a few chuckles as he tried to divert his eyes. You could see he was anxious to spend more time with Doc.

"Good then." Bransen smiled.

"You will be partnered with Doc, and from what I hear you two don't need much more than the infirmary to get your workouts." We laughed.

"Neek, Dusty, Rift, and Twist, come with me. Doc, Chris, Raven, and Sweed, you are with Khore," Bransen ordered, as we scattered to separate sections of mats about 20 feet apart before finally sitting in circles facing each other.

"Everyone join hands," Bransen instructed us from where he now sat.

"This is not a time for play," he said, after a few giggles escaped the groups. "Khore, please explain to them what is about to happen."

"I'm going to kill you," I stated matter-of-factly and watched everyone's eyes widen.

"Khore! That's not funny!" Bransen did his damnedest to hide his grin but I could still sense the chuckle he fought to hide in his chest.

"Sorry. Bransen and I will be sharing approximately 5000 years worth of knowledge with you. Skills, mental abilities, physical combat techniques, and much more will be transferred to you in a matter of moments. Do not resist it. It will only make it painful for you. At first, it may seem overwhelming, but if you relax, it could be quite pleasant," I grinned and glanced at Bransen.

"You will be expected to do the same with ten people, and they with another ten until everyone has this knowledge. In two days the entire complex should share these abilities and information. You will not be perfect in ability however, and will have to practice." I had everyone's full attention and continued.

"There are methods of practice you will learn that will aid you in your development. In one month, I will test you all. If you do not meet standards, it will be very unpleasant."

"But I thought we had all the time in the world now?" Twist wined and furrowed his brow as he looked in my direction.

"We may be able to live forever, but as the Thorens draw nearer to their own death, they will become more ruthless in their tactics to capture Khore." It was the first thing I heard Rift say since I arrived, and I couldn't help but admire his grasp of the situation.

"Why would they want to take you away?" Bransen asked me.

"Keelon, as you know, is the leader of the Thoren people. He is a terrible and ruthless creature who has let his obsession with eternal life corrupt his mind. When we discovered we were dying, some four thousand years ago, he abandoned the path to advance himself in mind and spirit. He now clutches desperately to his one and only purpose. To live."

"After many years of searching the galaxy, we finally found this planet. After a decade of study I was the one who recommended you as a species. You were our best chance at finding the solution in the time that we had left. Your species is strong, and your genetic code showed enough similarities that we saw fantastic possibilities. Even though your culture was still violent and destructive, you showed great potential. We thought both our species could benefit greatly. We wanted an exchange of technology, for our admittance to your world. My hopes were that we'd blend our cultures, species, and knowledge."

"Keelon used everyone's fear of oblivion to guide us in our search for a solution. Many of us wanted to find a compatible species that we could mate with who would possess the solution to our problem." I paused.

"There was great debate on the course of action, once we found a compatible species. The arts and science communities felt we should merge cultures. The military faction had a much more abrupt notion. Keelon, as leader, and an original member of the military community, embraced the idea that we should simply take what we needed from an inferior race."

"We thought we had convinced Keelon that a more peaceful solution would benefit everyone. Another hundred years passed as we collected ourselves outside this solar system. We called together all those that remained of our race with promises of great advancement in the solution to our problem. Our scientists were able to extend the life span of those who had been fast approaching their time of passing, but it wasn't enough."

"When the last of our kind had finally gathered, we made our way to this planet, encircling it completely. Once in place, and after having caused a great deal of havoc and chaos on a global scale, a transmission was finally sent. Keelon broadcast a message containing just four words. "You Will Serve Us."

"We watched in horror as a virus was released into your atmosphere." I paused as shame and sadness spread through my body.

"Keelon believed our solution was an inferior one to his own. He, with the backing and aid of the military community, had secretly developed a viral agent that would simultaneously remove the female populace, forcing your culture to simulate our own, while at the same time adapting your genetic code to better accommodate ours. It was a contemptible atrocity, but we were unable to do anything to stop it. We had become frail over the millennia. We needed stronger bodies that could contain our minds as well as a reflection of Keelon's deviant perception of his own perfection," I finally lifted my eyes from the floor and blanched from the look of horror that raged back at me.

"Keelon made it clear that we were not to interfere with his plans and announced that anyone found to be acting in contradiction to his goals would be executed. This is a threat that hadn't been made in hundreds of thousands of years of our people's history. The mere thought of it was completely deplored, and had been long since forgotten in our culture. In one fell swoop, he had resurrected it, and it was then I knew he truly was insane." A shiver crept up my spine as I felt their realization brim in their minds.

"Over the next several hundred years, Kelay secretly changed his own genetic code in hopes of cross breeding with one of the humans. At the conclusion of this process, he met my Pouch Father Briar, alone and hunting in the woods not far from the caverns. They came to meet there regularly, and fell in love at God's Table, and eventually I was conceived," I explained.

The room felt somewhat colder now or maybe it was the relived horrors that sent the chill down my spine. "While Keelon is not as strong in ability of mind as I am, he is most surely a frightfully powerful being. He is ruthless and cunning and above all, a resolute opponent, set out to complete his task. You must remember, he is fighting for his life. In addition to this, he commands armies of Thorens that would decimate us should we be discovered before we can better prepare ourselves and increase our numbers."

"They have no intention of killing me. They need me to charge the remaining humans to ensure their eternal life, much like what I have done with all of you here. Then they intend to transfer their conscience to you and the rest of the humans, essentially stealing your body and evicting your souls. The technology is not yet perfected, but they are getting closer every day. We are running out of time." I finally finished the horrid tale.

"You heard the man, let's do this." Bransen's voice was stern and I knew it was the tone he used to command his team.

Bransen and I, in our respective circles, joined hands with those on either side of us and released the memories like water flowing down the steps of a ladder. First filling one, then overflowing to the next, and then again until everyone was full.

When the merge was complete, all eyes went to Bransen, making him blush furiously, and then to me with a different look. They were afraid of what test I would be administering at the end of this month. Especially now, after having seen with their minds, what I had done in the hydroponics bay.

"Some of you will absorb certain aspects of what you have learned today, faster than others. While you all possess the same memories, you have been given two different perceptions. Half of you have my view of the events. Those with Bransen possess his. You will extend yourselves beyond what you are now, learning fastest in your particular area of expertise, because it is that part of you that makes you who you were, and who you will become."

"Train with each other, with those you teach, and alone, at every opportunity," I said firmly.

"Doc and Chris, I have something extra for you in private," I said, and looked over to Bransen. 'I'll explain later' I thought to him.

"Come with me please," I said to Doc, as I rose from the floor, extending my hand in his direction. Grabbing it, I helped him up and waited for Chris to stand. I led them to a side room off the Rec area meant for staff meetings.

"I need your help," I said quietly, looking at his slate blue tired eyes.

"Of course," Doc said, before turning to look to Chris.

"I don't think you understand. I need to give you knowledge, and yet another one of my many mistakes," I dropped my gaze to the floor.

"Anything, Khore. I can't deny I'm envious of what you know," Doc said, too eagerly.

"Whatever we can do," replied Chris.

"I'm sorry," I said, and touched their temples. "Know," I whispered, and sent all I knew medically about what I had done. A millennia of memories flooded their minds. Long moments passed in silence as I fed them the last of the medical knowledge I possessed.

"I need you to fix this for me. I don't have the time to do both." I couldn't hide the sadness in my voice.

Chris and Doc slumped into chairs around the table. They were dizzy from receiving so much information. Sharing of knowledge and memory can be extremely disorienting and they had just received more than anyone here save for myself.

Doc nodded after the rush finally settled in his mind. "We'll do all we can," he said finally.

"Thank you. Your discretion is appreciated," I said, looking from Doc to Chris.

Some nights later, as I lay in bed with Bransen after making love, I thought back to my conversation with Doc. He had begun his work on a solution to one of our many problems, but we were missing some of the necessary equipment to progress further. This ancient facility and its culture simply did not possess the needed technology. We were going to have to takes steps to procure the necessary components and equipment if we were going to win this battle.

Noticing the change in my mood as my mind wandered, I felt Bransen give me a squeeze and roll over to face me, propping himself up on his side.

"What's on your mind?" he asked me in a whisper.

"Our future," I said, looking over to meet his eyes.

"Doc is working on a solution for the children to come. As it is, those born now will age so terribly slow that it would take an eternity to outnumber the Thorens. A seven hundred year old child will have a difficult life. It's a prison of my making and it's my hope that Doc's work might release them from it," My voice sounded emptier than I expected.

"The problem also remains, that if we multiply too quickly we will overrun this planet like an out of control plague."

"I see," Bransen nuzzled his pillow and trailed his fingers through my hair.

"So that is what you spoke to Doc and Chris about the other day. I know you have come to terms with your merge with Kelay, but I do hope you don't let the weight of responsibility for his actions become your own."

"How can I not?" I asked, a bit too quickly. "I'm responsible, and this is just one of so many mistakes I've made in the past." I felt as though the fate of the world and our kind were upon my shoulders and I couldn't stop the worry from bleeding into my voice.

"Kelay made those mistakes, not you," he whispered to me.

"I know, but the problems are now ours, regardless of who caused them. I have the memories of Kelay's actions as if they were my own, and I also bear the guilt."

"We need equipment from one of the spheres so that Doc can continue his work. That is going to have to be our first priority after training is complete. We must have a future to look forward to, or we will not have reason to fight, but I do have an idea," I said, as my mood began to brighten.

Kissing Bransen and giving him a quick embrace, I rolled over on my right side, pulling his strong arm over me like a blanket.

"Can we talk about this tomorrow? I'm exhausted. You are insatiable." I giggled, as he pulled me in tight to him.

"Of course, and thanks for sharing that with me. I love you." Bransen kissed the back of my neck.

"I love you too," I whispered, and drifted off to sleep.

Waking the next morning, we showered together and then dressed. Finally in the cafeteria on level 11, we shoveled in our breakfast, and made small talk at the table as we prepared for another arduous day of training with our new team.

"So how is your training going, Neek?" We had sorted out our personal issues with each other, but the tension between us still lingered in the air. I was making a special effort to heal our past.

"Actually, pretty good!" He grinned his weasel-like smile as he flipped hash browns from Twist's plate against Dusty's cheek.

"Hey! I was going to eat that!" yelled Twist.

"Don't even think about it!" Doc snapped, startling us while taking his place next to Chris at the table.

I had to laugh at the memory of our first meal together. We were becoming a family and it gave me hope. I loved them all. I feared for their future as well as my own, but just couldn't ignore the good feeling in the air.

"How are the individual MFM's coming, Dusty?" I asked, looking into his familiar hazel eyes.

"They should be finished in a couple more days," he replied as he pushed another strip of bacon into his mouth.

The proximity alarm suddenly sounded and we all froze. When the announcement didn't come that an animal had set it off we all sat staring at each other.

Lifting his wrist COM to his mouth, Bransen tapped the communications button. "Status Report".

"There appears to be a human some 100 meters outside the complex. His life signs are weak and he seems to be unconscious," the metallic voice informed us.

"Chris, Khore, Neek, Raven, come with me. The rest of you gear up and guard the entrance," Bransen ordered, and we rose from our chairs.

On level 1 we entered the weapons room. Clipping portable MFM's to ourselves, we then pulled our weapons of choice from the racks that surrounded us.

Twist had been busy. Guns, knives, and equipment I wasn't familiar with lined the walls. We strapped on sheaths and holsters to accommodate our weapons.

Chris pulled on a vest that covered his chest and abdomen and would protect him from projectile weapons. He had also grabbed a medical kit and draped it across his neck.

Neek clipped his MFM to the underside of a much lighter vest, which I suspected was designed for his ease of movement. He strapped two black leather sheaths to his thighs that contained sharp and deadly knives. On his waist hung a belt that sagged to one side and held a short blade for use in close combat.

Raven and I grabbed similar protective vests and MFMs and attached them to a flap of fabric underneath that seemed to be designed for just such a purpose.

Bransen holstered two large handguns with triple barrels that glimmered as he buried them into their dark brown leather confines. He clipped his MFM to his belt which caused the waistline to sag against his narrow hips.

Bransen Leaned into me, we kissed and then separated.

"Okay then, let's go see who's knocking on our door." Bransen grinned and waved for us to follow as he left the room.

Chapter 7

The Fold

"You know this is a trap," I finally said aloud what we'd all been thinking, as we gathered in the hallway.

Bransen nodded and glanced over at me with unsure eyes.

"So we're going to walk out there with only the MFM's to cover our asses and hope for the best?" I asked him.

"No," Bransen answered, somewhat agitated. I suppose he wasn't used to anyone asking questions before he spoke his plan.

"Team One will be Twist, Rift, Doc, Raven and myself. Team two will be Khore, Neek, Dusty, Sweed, Raven and Chris," he paused. "Our mission here is two-fold. First, to see if the human out there is a lure and two, to gather medical equipment from any Thorens that come to kill us," he said, with a stern stressed voice I hadn't heard him use before.

I didn't have to voice my disapproval of being separated from Bransen. He saw it in my eyes as I glared back at him. It was going to be a difficult argument we would have in the near future, but now wasn't exactly the time.

"Khore, your team will take access tunnel 34 that leads out behind the target and advance to the human's coordinates. We will move from the main entrance here. We should converge on the target. Khore I want you to keep your team back a bit in case it should get hairy," he explained.

"When we find the target, we'll place an MFM on him and then try to get him back safely to the complex," he continued.

"Doc, do not let him become conscious," I added. He knew what Thorens could do to a mind and body.

"Chances are when the target becomes cloaked we will be surrounded, so we are going to have to be fast. They will most likely be monitoring his position and when he suddenly disappears they will descend to our location almost immediately," Bransen continued.

It reassured me to know he had a good grasp of the situation and circumstances, but I still worried that he would be left in the open and captured. They'd rape his mind and subject him to horrible tests. I couldn't bear the thought of it. The fear rose in me like never before as a cold sweat climbed across my skin.

"You are taking a terrible risk," I thought to Bransen. "At the first movement of the human, they will come from the sky faster than we can escape."

"It's what I'm counting on," he thought back to me as he turned and smiled.

"After you're in position, there is to be no verbal communication. We cannot risk them triangulating the signal. Radio before you exit the access shaft behind the target," he said to us.

I nodded my understanding to Bransen and we went off through the darkened hallways that led further down the mountain. Finally in position, Raven raised his wrist COM. "Team 2 is a go."

"All communication from this point will be telepathic," I heard his voice come across our wrist COM's as we exited into the jungle.

It was mid summer and the heat was stifling. The air was thick and the smell of damp earth choked the air. As we made our way to our position through the thick underbrush, I reached out with my mind and saw Bransen setting explosives in the perceived landing zone of the Sphere Minor. He planned to blow them up and use the chaos to escape with the target in tow.

Something was rolling around in my mind but I couldn't remember, a reason why this wouldn't work, and the fear of it made me sweat all the more.

"Please be careful," I thought to him.

"We are in position," I thought, as we hid in the brush circling the position of the unconscious human.

I felt, as much as watched, Neek move through the foliage as he made his way to the unconscious body. Finally arriving undetected, I watched in horror as he clipped the MFM to the body and activated it.

"WAIT!" I sent out the thought, but it was too late.

Almost instantly, eight Sphere Minors blurred into view and surrounded Bransen's team position. The explosives were activated, destroying six of the spheres. One of the remaining spheres, however, directed a beam of light that pierced Neek's chest, burning through his heart. After the flash of light released him, his body slumped across the unconscious human.

We were in deep shit, and my body exploded into blue white flames. More spheres appeared, taking positions where the others had been destroyed, surrounding Bransen's team. They found cover in a ravine behind a giant tree, but it was barely enough to avoid the deadly pulses of light erupting from the spheres.

An exhilarating light burst from me with a blinding flash. It was so bright that even the rising sun behind me was paled in comparison. I walked slowly from the trees behind our target almost in a trance. The chaos paused only momentarily, as more sphere minors appeared, surrounding the team and me, broadening their circle as I made my way toward Neek's body and the human he had tried to save.

"Go back and prepare," I thought to Chris and the team. They scuttled back looking at each other unsure of the command.

I walked into the clearing and I could sense the feeling of triumph that prickled along the Thorens' skin. They began to buffet me with a multitude of mental attacks. It was a constant onslaught, and even though I knew each attack weakened me somewhat I felt them little more than a feather's touch. I reached out with my mind.

"STOP!" I commanded as every particle and body, Thoren and human alike, froze around me into stillness. Bringing the earth from beneath me, I surrounded myself as I rose into the air. A maddening tempest of debris swarmed around me. Building the energy, I noticed a few of the Thorens were breaking free of my hold.

Glancing upward I sent a beam of energy from my soul to the Sphere Major that filled the sky above us, causing it to explode.

Turning my attention to the Sphere Minors, I sent barrage after barrage of compressed soil blades that tore into them, making them burst into flashes of white fire.

I folded space, landing the much needed equipment to the infirmary, from the last sphere minor before finally destroying it. Using the same technique, I bent space around each of our party members, moving them to safe points within the complex, leaving only Bransen behind. He wanted to stay and I didn't have the energy to fight him. Looking out at the recent devastation, I felt the wet of my tears travel down my cheeks as I proceeded to kill them all.

I gathered up the earth beneath me into a greater tempest and sent it outward with blinding speed. The energy built into a super nova, and I incinerated the remaining Thoren where they stood. Slumping forward, I drifted back to the ground where Neek's body lay across the human that had been used as bait. The other Sphere Major would be sending forces in moments and we had to go.

Folding space, I moved the human, Bransen, Neek and myself to the infirmary, where I had sent the rest of the team. Appearing in odd flashes of bending white light, we arrived. I had already used so much energy, I marveled at the way I could see through my own arms. I was becoming transparent. I was more a lightly colored silhouette of light than anything else.

Looking into Bransen's eyes, I felt more tears fall as I placed both hands onto Neek's chest. I filled him with my remaining, but quickly drained, energy as his body glowed a deep white-blue on the floor before us. I could feel my energy waning and noticed that my arms and body had all but disappeared, except for a faint outline. I was on the verge of oblivion.

Fixing the damage created by the disrupter that had pierced Neek, I poured my life into him. I had given too much, and darkness filled my world.

I woke some time later, feeling Bransen's head against my chest. Looking down, I watched it rise and fall with my breath. I was alive and I was complete. I pushed out the words "I love you" in a whisper, before falling back into the darkness.

I awoke again to the feeling of Bransen's head on my chest as his arm reached across, pulling me closer to him for comfort. I lay there for a while, running my fingers through his hair. He looked so innocent in his sleep. He resembled a god-like cherub. The lines of stress and worry were gone from his face and he seem so contented, I didn't have the heart to wake him.

I was enjoying the sight of Bransen as he awoke and gazed up into my eyes. I smiled back and he seemed to spring to life.

He jumped up and kissed me, reaching his arms around me, between the press of my body and the mattress, pulling me into a hug. His breath betrayed his happy sobs, and I reached around him, pulling him tighter into our embrace.

Releasing me, he finally shifted so I could see the beautiful emerald green of his eyes looking down at me.

"You know, I end up in this bed far too often," I whispered, and we both chuckled.

"I thought I lost you," Bransen said with glassy eyes gazing into my own. The memories of what I had done surged through my mind. I peered back at him and ran my fingertips along the line of his face.

"I knew I would pick you, given half the chance," I said, as a quiet sob shook my chest. "I didn't know I would be so ruthless, though," I sighed, pulling him closer to me trying to chase away the memory. I had killed them all.

Pulling Bransen into the bed with me, I wrapped my legs around him trying to get him as close to me as I could. He felt so good within my arms as the weight of his body pressed against mine.

I folded space again. A white light opened and then seemed to swallow us with a small pop as we now lay on the bed in my quarters.

Stretching out my mind, I saw Doc as he drilled Chris's ass in a fury, and I sent the message, "We are okay," and left him to his work.

After we finished making love, Bransen folded me into his arms. Feeling him relax against me, I pulled him in closer for comfort as I drifted back to sleep.

Morning came with a start, as my eyes slammed open, searching the darkness. Nothing moved and the only sound I could hear was Bransen's heavy breath. My eyes focused on different objects in the room, as my mind tried to grasp and recall what each was, and if something extra was here that shouldn't be. I don't know what woke me, but it felt like I had been awoken by a loud noise, but didn't really remember hearing it. Reaching out with my mind, I sensed the area around me and in the hallway outside my door. Nothing. It must have been a dream.

I turned my head to see the display on the digital clock that sat on the work table across from my side of the bed. It was 5:30am. I woke up a half hour early. I was tempted to close my eyes, but knew now there was no hope of getting another 30 minutes of true sleep. By the time I would be drifting off, the alarm would sound, and I'd feel twice as tired as I did right now.

I slowly lifted Bransen's arm from around me. He responded with a grunt and I draped it behind me, so that I might be able to slide out of the bed without disturbing his sleep too much. I sat up, moving my legs out in front of me to the floor, and climbed out of bed. I was still nude from last night's love making, and walked into the bathroom, closing the door quietly behind me.

Flipping on the light, I was blinded and shielded my eyes as the glow seemed to burn the back of my skull. Damn, why don't they make bathroom lights with lower wattage!? I blindly fumbled with the shower door, reached in and turned the knob, and listened to the splash of water against the wall.

My eyes finally adjusted to the light. A flash of white in the corner of my eye caught my attention, as I stepped toward the shower. I backed up and looked into the mirror. A white stripe of hair, slightly left of center about an inch wide, stood out against the deep brown. The white shock of hair cascaded down from the roots of my bangs to their end at my waist. The snow white color was such a contrast it looked like it had been painted on.

Moments passed as I stood there, staring at my reflection. I had been closer to death than I realized. I could only hope that it was worth it. The Thorens would now come searching for us in full force, or they might use a bit more caution, and a slower pace, having seen their own kind killed. I was hoping for the latter.

Taking a deep breath, I stepped into the shower and leaned against the wall, facing into the jet of steamy comfort. I reveled in the warmth of hot rivers as they slid over the back of my head and down my body. My mind calmed and I rested for endless moment thinking about nothing at all.

Hearing the bathroom door open, I didn't turn my head. I could feel it was Bransen. He stepped into the shower with me and wrapped his arms around me.

"Good morning, beautiful," he whispered.

"Good morning, beautiful," I said, as I leaned my head back against his shoulder. Finally opening my eyes, I gazed down at my hair as it clung to my skin.

"I was kind of hoping this was going to wash out," I said as I lifted a long strand of white.

"I think it looks sexy!" rasped Bransen as he gave my neck a nibble.

"Yeah, well, if I manage to get another one, it'll probably kill me," I said, quieter than I had intended.

"How is Neek doing? Did he make it?" I was almost afraid to ask.

"He got out of the infirmary a couple of days ago. It's as though he were never dead," Bransen replied with a little too much enthusiasm.

"He'll probably be a little put out when he goes to see you this morning and you're not there." Bransen chuckled.

"He's been coming to visit?" I was awestruck.

"Yes. Actually, he visits twice a day, once before and once after his training." Bransen informed me.

"Hmmm, well, either he's pissed because I didn't let him die, or he's glad," I said with a small chuckle.

"According to the sounds reported to be coming from his room... I think both he and Dusty are happy that he made it." Bransen chuckled and the baritone tenor of his chest vibrated against my skin.

'Well good for him,' I thought. Neek deserves happiness as much as anyone and, to be honest, I didn't relish the idea of having another knife sticking out of my body."

"We can't do that again, you know," I said as well as asked.

"How do you mean?" Bransen searched my eyes trying to understand the question.

"We can't go unprepared like that into a certain ambush, and expect to come out of it alive. We weren't ready, and almost got ourselves killed. I'd be dead already if they didn't want me alive. We were lucky," I said, feeling a little angry with myself. It was a foolish and irresponsible thing to do and we both knew it.

"If they would have captured one of us, they would have torn through our minds until they discovered the location of the complex, and then it would have been the end for everyone." I scolded myself mentally for being so foolish.

"Doc has all the equipment now to work on our future." Bransen whispered the good news in my ear hoping to lift my spirits.

It made me smile. Our efforts weren't for nothing.

"How is the human doing?"

"He didn't make it. From what Doc says, he was probably dead before we got there. The Thorens did their work well." Bransen's breathe tickled the back of my neck as he spoke.

The cascade of water began to cool as we stood there, and my skin was threatening to wrinkle. "We'd better get out of here before we shrivel up to nothing," I said and turned enough to graze Bransen's lips with my own.

After rinsing off, we dried and picked out our clothes for the day. I wanted desperately to go back to bed and hide under the covers, but there was much to do.

"So... how many days?" I asked, breaking the silence.

"Huh?" Bransen paused to look at me as he laced his pants.

"How many days was I out this time? You said that Neek had recovered two days ago. How long was I out, total?" I repeated.

"Ohh, you were unconscious for five days. You didn't become solid until the second day. Once that happened, Doc said that you were out of danger, and we just had to wait for you to regain your strength. It was on that second day, when you became solid, that we noticed the white streak in your hair." Bransen trailed his fingers along one of the bleached strands as he explained.

"Yes, the latest in skunk wear. Just what I didn't need. I suppose it could have been worse though. It felt right to wake up with you by my side," I said, smiling at him.

"Hey, help me with something?" I asked.

"Sure, anything!" Bransen replied.

"I want to cut off some of this hair. It's too damn long, and it's getting in my way. Could you cut it off for me at mid back level?" I begged.

"Are you sure you want to do that?" he looked at me with doubt.

"Yes, it'll still be long enough to tickle you when we're having fun, and it'll be more manageable when we're in the field. Scissors are in the top drawer in the bathroom, if you wouldn't mind," I said, smiling at him.

A few minutes later he had lopped off a good 8 inches of hair and I felt better almost instantly. The unnecessary length had been removed and it looked much fuller now that it was not being pulled taut by its own weight. I shook my head and pulled my bangs back and to the side. The white streak was definitely going to take some getting used to. I still hadn't made up my mind if I liked it or not.

After cleaning up the hair from the floor, I took another look into the mirror, but stared at Bransen in the reflection. Even though we were both in the mirror, the only real thing I could see was him.

"Breakfast then?" he asked, raising his eyebrows a little.

"Sounds good to me. Let's go. I'm hungrier than I thought, now that you mention it. Hell, I might even have a whole egg omelet for a change," I grinned at him.

We arrived at the cafeteria about fifteen minutes earlier than we normally would have. Hefting our trays of food before us, we settled at our regular table and ate. It wasn't long before the rest of the group appeared. They walked through the door, looking exactly like the morning zombies I had come to know. I gave them a wave from our table, and they all seemed to push through the line in record speed, waking up faster than I had ever seen.

The first to reach us was Twist and, of course, the first thing out of his mouth had to be a smart ass comment.

"Heya, skunk boy!" I instantly responded by moving his chair from behind him and he fell backwards, flipping his tray full of food onto himself.

"Heya, graceful," I grinned back as we laughed.

"Where's Neek," I asked, looking around.

"My guess is he is running through the corridor between the lift and here." Dusty no sooner finished speaking, when I saw Neek dash into the doorway. Having spied me, he composed himself as though these last weeks had never happened.

He gradually moved through the line as he selected his breakfast, and moseyed over to the table. Walking up to me he gave my chair a weak kick and a quiet "Thanks" escaped his lips.

Neek paused a moment to glance over at Twist, as he sat on the floor picking food from his shirt. "Get off the floor you twit... your embarrassing me."

"I'm glad to see you're doing well," I said, smiling at him. "I hear that you and Dusty are getting along, too."

"No, I hear them, and they're doing much more than just getting along!" blurted Twist from the floor. We all laughed as Neek's cheeks blazed a bright crimson.

"Well, it's good to see everyone has fully recovered and is in good spirits. You have two weeks until I test you. I hope you've been training," I announced with a deadly tone in my voice. The entire room seemed to stop as if trapped in time.

"I will be harder on you than I was the Thorens. That goes for ALL of you!" I stood and yelled angrily across the cafeteria, and listened to my voice echo back from the walls.

"You had all better be ready." I paused and let my eyes glow with power as I looked around the room.

There was complete silence as my eyes drifted over the room only pausing here and there for affect. I let a few more stress filled moments pass before I sent each and every one of their trays splattering into their chests, and ran toward the cafeteria exit.

Only feet from escape, the door slammed shut in front of me and a hail of food followed. 'Sneaky little bastards!' Twenty minutes later, tired and caked with food, I gazed at the mess around us.

"Training opportunity?" I questioned in thought to Bransen. A smile crept across his face which was followed by a curt nod.

"I want this mess picked up completely. You are not to use your hands, broom, dustpan or any other device other than your mind," I said and found grateful smiles beam from the kitchen.

The cooks had to clean up the last mess I started here, so it was only right they shouldn't have to clean up this one.

"Lester!" I called to the cook in the kitchen area. "I want a count of broken dishes when they're done and who broke them."

'I want you to keep any broken dishes. Separate them by person in bags.' I thought to him.

"Ahhhh man!!!" exclaimed Twist. "This is going to take forever! You made half the mess!" he whined.

"Is that how you all feel?" I asked, and watched furtive nods roll across the room.

"Okay then... fine," I said. Raising my palms upward, I drew in the energy around me and sent it out to the right hand side of the room.

I sensed each barrier and form of every particle and piece of debris within my mind. Focusing I set about to right everything. I moved the tables and chairs into place. With a thought I sent food sailing through the air into the trash cans that stood at the end of each table. It was like watching a cup of water filling up, but in reverse, as fewer and fewer pieces of food remained, until there were none, and one half of the room was immaculate.

Finally stacking the dishes and utensils into the cupboards, shelves, and drawers, one half of the room appeared as though no one had even set foot in it.

Letting the glow leave my eyes, I lowered my arms, and allowed the energy to flow back outward to its normal balance. "Okay then, I'm done. You now have until noon to finish. Half the job, half the time." I said, looking directly at Twist.

"Fair now?" I asked, hearing several mumbles from the crowd. I could tell he wanted to say something but decided against it.

Bransen's smile was so wide had he been any happier I think he would have burst out laughing.

"Before any of you get the bright idea that broken dishes don't need washing, please keep in mind that Bransen will be the one to put those plates back together." I watched the smile fall from his adorable face.

"Hey!" he said, louder than we both expected.

"You did say it would be a good training opportunity, didn't you?" I interrupted him. "And I'm sure no one here would want toilet duty for the rest of eternity for upsetting their Captain."

"Ohhhh you are sooo in trouble! You know I hate being called that!" Bransen hissed the words in my mind.

I made my way to the exit, turned, and spoke with a deadly serious tone. "By the way, I wasn't kidding about the testing. You've got two weeks." I folded myself to my room, and vanished before their eyes in a flash of light.

After stripping down and taking a quick shower, I crawled back into my bed, which is where I wanted to be ever since I first opened my eyes. My little display to put the fear of, well, 'me' into them, had taken more out of me than I wanted to admit. I still hadn't quite recovered from my run-in with the Thorens. Showing weakness right now was not going to motivate them to train. Fear... fear however, would work quite nicely.

Chapter 8

Mood Swing

I awoke angry. It was just one of those things that happens once in a while, like when my mind has been busy with something in my sleep, that it can't figure out. I woke up frustrated and pissed off at the world.

I dreamt a memory from long ago. It was a perfectly horrible day. I could remember the dew on each leaf, and the mist that hung in the air as it collected against my skin.

I awoke earlier than the rest, as I often did, and made my way out of the caverns. The chill in the air crept into my bones, and the smell of green and life wafted past my nose. It was one of those cool mornings that made it hard to move, but promised perfection later in the day.

I wandered out into the woods that surrounded the mountainside and caves that were my home. It was the one time of day that I could have all to myself. It was my time. I didn't have to risk discovery or avoid interruption. It usually never lasted more than fifteen or twenty minutes, but these were precious moments to me.

It was my habit to follow the worn paths that deer and other animals traveled down the slope to a nearby stream. I watched the sun peak over the ridge in the distance. The trees seemed to burn from the yellow and orange that framed them in the mist. The suns rays crawled their way up the sky like a hand clawing at the night. Dew collected on every leaf and stem and turned the landscape into acres of diamonds that seemed to wink back at me.

I don't know how long I stood there in my daze before finally returning to reality and deciding to visit to the stream below. As I looked ahead of me, I saw a large doe with her long dark brown neck stretched down to drink the cool water. I remembered thinking how I might never see anything so beautiful again in my life. An arrow tore violently through her neck, and toppled her into the stream, where she thrashed and bleated wildly to her death.

I stood there, staring in horror, as hunters from my village emerged from between the trees and proceeded to slit her neck, tie her legs, hang her upside down, and cut the flesh from her body.

I remembered thinking, 'I should go down and stop them, but knew it was useless. The doe was dead.' I thought, 'I should be appalled, and that a better person would have been sickened. A weaker person would have thrown up in the grass, but we needed the meat.' I turned around, and walked back to the caves.

It bothered me lately that every time I finally discovered something beautiful, I was forced to watch it destroyed. Why in the hell was it that when I had the tiniest bit of joy, it had to be snuffed out of existence? Why every time?

We're dazzled so easily when we are young, and it took so little to destroy our worlds. In youth we were innocent and naive in our wonders and devastations. A butterfly could draw our attention for endless moments, and a harsh word could crush us. We grow, we age, and we see more magnificent destruction. It's almost as though each lash from the whip of life numbs us against the next. I wait to feel or witness something even more beautiful, hoping my soul will respond. Then I watch its execution with morbid curiosity.

I have watched the happy people and I still didn't know how they were so fortunate. I liked to console myself with the thought that, maybe... they were just faking it. I didn't know anymore. Happy people didn't seem to work harder for it, or deserve it more than someone else. It just happened. Everything seemed to fall into place for them as if they were entitled to it.

I've had lovers that I have buried, lovers that I have left, and lovers that have left me. I have never felt the joy of their company, without the thought of what my time limit would be. More often than not, I'd been prone to prolonging my agony just to avoid the effort of starting over again. I suppose it's easier to take the beating one knows, than to risk the unknown. I think, sometimes, a soul just becomes weary.

I've seen bad people go unpunished; and good people devastated by life. In my 1600 years I've often seen retribution for the evil a person has loosed upon the world, but not every time. My conclusion was this. It didn't make one fucking bit of difference what someone did. Try your best to be happy, and if you're happy being an asshole, go for it.

Bransen entered my quarters. I lay still in bed, and sighed to let him know I was awake. I felt him crawl onto the bed on top the covers. The fabric tightened against me and pulled along my hip as he moved closer. He wrapped his arm around me and squeezed me beneath the blankets. I didn't respond.

It's not his fault. I didn't want to be cruel, but right now, I really didn't want someone being nice to me. I needed to be alone to think. I wanted to be hidden away from the whole world, surrounded only by eyes that couldn't speak about what they saw. I couldn't do that here and I couldn't do that with Bransen. I've spent hundreds of years alone in my own mind, with only an occasional distraction. I felt crowded.

"Hey, you okay?" He gave me a squeeze. I suppose he recognized the silence.

Normally I would have answered with a lie. 'Hell yeah... everything is fucking great!' I didn't have the strength for the deception.

"No. I need your MFM, and please don't come looking for me," I spoke in a hushed tone before turning to look him in the eyes. I could see worry there, but I didn't have it in me to dispel his concern.

"Please?"

Silence filled the room and he finally spoke. "Anything for you."

I pulled him into a deep awkward kiss, feeling my heart double over on itself at the thought of leaving him behind.

"Thank you," was all I was able to say as I climbed out of the bed and dressed. I pulled a satchel from the bottom of the wardrobe, throwing in a few odds and ends to get me by.

"I'll be back before test day," I said, zipping up the satchel. I was trying desperately to pay more attention to what I was doing, than to the pained expression I saw in my peripheral vision.

"That's two weeks away!" Bransen said, hopping out of bed. "What's going on? What's wrong? What did I do?"

A sad laugh escaped my chest. "Nothing. I just have some things I need to sort out. I can take care of myself. I can always fold myself here to safety if something happens. Right now, I just need to be alone."

"It's only two weeks," I said, smiling at him.

It was nice, for a change, to feel that my absence would seem like an eternity to someone. I hoisted the bag over my shoulder and walked to the door.

"I love you," I said with a smile and walked out the door. "By the way, the tracking device you hid in the sole of my shoe is in your top left desk drawer." With that, I folded myself out of the complex and deep into the jungle.

I probably should have left him with his illusions of having an eye on me, but I didn't. It seems we measure worth in how much we'd miss something, if it was gone. I hoped that Bransen would miss me desperately. He does have a hold on my heart, and I don't know if I have the stamina to watch another beautiful thing die.

I wandered through what felt like mountains of brush, following animal-made paths as often as I could find them. I could hear water ahead and hoped for a clearing of some sort where I might rest. As the dull roar of water became louder, I found myself walking onto a plateau of sorts.

There were no trees in the area, but there was so much plant life I had to wade through it like it was rushing river, pulling against me. I finally made it to the water's edge where large boulders stopped at least some of the advancing wildlife. One particular boulder, nearly eight feet long, jutted up from the earth, providing a decent place to rest.

I climbed its lichen slick side before finding a rougher but dry flat spot to sit. Everything was so alive that it practically made my skin crawl. Everywhere you looked there was something crawling, slithering, or flitting through the air. I felt claustrophobic and created a barrier about myself to keep out unwanted visitors. Calming myself, I looked at the landscape. It was beautiful with its flowers, plants, and many multi-colored birds that flew from one giant mound to another.

It was a spectacular panorama, as I gazed at the valley that appeared almost too perfect to be by accident. Some 300 yards ahead of me were gigantic mounds of growth that peeked from the canopy of trees showing large flat stone tops. This place was man made, though long before the Thorens had come to the world and before the human's recorded history.

Thinking back to when we had first arrived, I remember reviewing ancient human civilizations. This had been the site of one of many Mayan pyramids that dotted the landscape in this region. I was awestruck. Advanced human civilization had been all but reclaimed by the Earth, but these monuments still stood. These people had been remarkable indeed to stand strong against the passage of time. It shamed me to ponder the unbelievable advancements the Humans had made in only a thousand years. At their rate of progress, if they didn't destroy themselves, they would be fast approaching Thoren technology. Humans were such a chaotic race though.

I reached out with my mind and felt precision cut stones line a road beneath the many vines and plant life that went directly ahead of me for nearly a mile. I reached further out to the sides, feeling the four massive structures on either side of the road. The alignment of the structures, the road and the massive overgrown pyramid at the end of the road, were in direct alignment with the sun and moon. The place felt alive with memories and I searched deeper, noting much of the ruins had sunk. Still further, I realized that it had not sunk so much as the ruins had been linked together. Below, there were massive caverns and pockets that once housed thousands. Those areas, by some great miracle, were left untouched and undiscovered.

I reveled in how magnificent a people they must have been. They must have been extremely advanced at such an early stage of life on this planet. What also intrigued and perplexed me was that every entrance into the extensive honeycomb of tunnels below, had been covered by a massive carved stone. I was perplexed by thoughts of how they could have placed such intricately cut stone with such precision. Surely I could move these stones with little effort, but how would they have performed the task? I didn't sense any pulley system. I wondered if they possessed the ability of mind to perform such a feat. I don't remember any scientific documentation on it other than a few fleeting texts that appeared after the 1500's.

I strengthened the barrier around me to help ease my way along the mile of road to the massive pyramid ahead of me. The closer I came to the man made jungle-covered mountain, the larger it loomed above me. It was massive, nearly 100 feet in height. I made my way to the base where large stones sat to either side of the roadway. Atop each was a long since weathered hunk of rock that was probably once a statue of some kind. Below the left stone was an access way to the catacombs. It was approximately ten feet wide, ten feet tall and ten feet deep. It had to weigh over eight tons.

Curiosity overwhelmed me and I concentrated on the stone, expanding its molecules until it weighed barely more than a few pounds. I slid it to the side, tearing centuries of vines and undergrowth as it moved. Once the seal was broken, a gust of air burst out of the exposed opening. An exhale of death and decay pushed out from the crypt. Taking the flashlight from my satchel, I turned it on and pointed it into the shadowed parts of the entrance that were not lit by the sun overhead.

The corridor was carved of stone and led downward in narrow but steep stairs. Two men would barely be able to pass each other shoulder to shoulder. Cobwebs lined every possible corner, making it difficult to see any distance. Pushing the cobwebs away with my mind I started my decent into the darkness, led only by the beam of light from my flashlight. The air stunk of dried up, long forgotten things.

Every one hundred steps or so, on opposite sides, an opening led into large natural caverns within the granite. In each cavern I could see hundreds of skeletons amongst the dust and debris of rotted cloth and dirt. This place was a tomb of thousands. Stranger yet was that there were skeletons in every stage of growth. It looked as though both young and old had come here to die at the same time.

Stretching my senses ahead of me, I searched for the end of the stairway. An end existed in another fifty feet, but I couldn't determine what was beyond that point. As I crept my mind along its surface, I could only determine that it was massive and unidentifiable. Whatever it was, though, had come alive with the touch of my mind. I could feel it vibrate back at me with an almost audible hum. Stumbling in my daze, I caught myself with my outstretched hands against the walls of the stairway.

I felt compelled to continue down the hall. I had to keep going until I found the end of this. Moments later I reached the end of my descent and stood facing a large square stone surface chiseled with writing I recognized.

It was Thoren writing. It was an ancient dialect long since dead. The Thorens had been here before when this planet had just sprouted its first civilizations.

Ancient civilizations were an idle preoccupation of mine. I had studied Thoren culture intensely when I was only a few thousand years old. I had never actually given up my study, though in the past few hundred years, I seldom had time to review old thoughts.

I directed the light against the flat carved surface. One phrase was all that was written.

"One People May Not Enter"

I reached out to the carving to brush some dust away from the inscription, to be sure I hadn't mistaken the symbols.

As my fingertips brushed the surface, it pulsed. A thin horizontal ray of white light blazed from it and moved against me from head to toe, freezing me in place. As the light completed its pass, the wall became an archway much like the way Cavrium did on Thoren Sphere Major today. It seemed to merge into the surroundings to form an entrance.

I was able to move again, but the fact that only a second ago I couldn't, put me on edge. I walked through the archway, then turned to see it sealing behind me, as my surroundings seem to burst to life. I was in a ship, a very, very, old Thoren ship. I was giddy with fear. Instantly I turned and sent the command for the arch to open and nothing happened. I sent the command again in the old tongue and an arch formed. The ship was taking its first breath and I decided now might be a good time to move the stone in place at the surface to seal myself in, and slow down anyone who might detect this marvel. I watched the light wink away as I moved the stone back into place and then commanded the arch to close behind me.

I stood in a bay area at least the size of the entire pyramid. The air was clean. In fact, every surface was devoid of even the slightest amount of dust as though the entire area had been vacuum packed for an eternity, waiting to be opened. As the bay seemed to light itself with activity, I noticed two raised panels atop metallic pedestals that looked like some sort of communications area and computer access terminal. I stepped in front of the access panel and noted the symbols, shutting off my flashlight.

Touching the face of the panel, a blue light seemed to center on me and illuminate the computer station and myself. I realized that it was reacting to me. The door had said "One People May Not Enter". I was Thoren, and Human at the same time. Someone had configured this thing to only allow entrance to beings that were a mix of the two. Pulling up records, as best I could, I read through the symbols and found a schematic. It was definitely a ship. Not just any ship, this was the Cystos.

The Cystos was a prototype battleship created over half a billion years ago when the Thorens were at war with other races far across the galaxy. Experimental technology led the ship off course during its first tests of stealth travel, and it was never seen again. It had somehow landed here, galaxies away. The story goes that the technology had been completely abandoned and another path was sought. Centuries of work had been undone in seconds. It had been a devastating blow, and nearly caused the Thorens to lose the war against the Velo.

The stealth technology was still active, according to the panel. It made sense to me now why it had not been discovered already by the Thorens, and explained why I was unable to see beyond its walls. To say that this ship was massive wouldn't even begin to explain the size. A sphere major, when seen in the sky, looked as big as the moon. It was really only about a mile in diameter. This ship could easily have held ten of them.

A hologram appeared before me.

"Greetings," it said in the old dialect. "I am Captain Talp of the Battlecruiser Cystos. It seems you have found our tomb, and are worthy of it. Chronometer readings indicate that cloak has been maintained for 687,000 years. We changed the DNA sequence indicator to allow only Human and Thoren hybrids to enter this ship. We did this for two reasons. One, left to our own devices, we corrupted a civilization, letting them worship us as gods and, as self inflicted punishment, removed them and ourselves from this existence. It was our hope that should ever a Thoren/Human hybrid find it, it would be used with a better purpose than what brought us here."

The hologram continued in the old language. "The second reason is far less pleasant. One possibility is that we Thorens have lost the war and have run so far from our own system that we are near extinction. If that is the case, then a new tactic must be pursued, and we have found this species has great potential for genetic compatibility. Another possibility is that we have won the war, and have completely taken over the known galaxies, spreading further than any one species should ever control."

"Logic dictated that we create a situation where neither, full blooded Human nor Thoren could enter this ship. One People or One Race may not enter. In this way, we ensured that both species would live on so neither could gain an advantage over the other. A natural melding of species would have to occur. Your DNA structure has already been scanned and entered into the system. You and only those like you, or with a natural strain variant of your DNA, will be allowed entrance, unless you specify otherwise. Anyone else attempting to enter the ship will be instantly destroyed without warning, as were my copilot and I once we started this program."

"I hope it is good fortune that has brought you here and not our fears. We have since corrected the cloaking technology that placed us here. The ship is fully functional, and yours to command. Only you, your mate, or your descendants may command or destroy this ship. Control of this ship can be relinquished, but only for a maximum of 100 hours, upon which time, if you, your mate, or a descendant hasn't indicated otherwise, the ship will self destruct."

"Ship schematics and technology are available at any computer interface, and to any whom you grant access. Media scanning has indicated several thousand languages have been written and spoken over the last 687,000 years. Please select your preferred interface language," it said for the last time in the old dialect.

"21st century English," I answered.

"Personality level," the hologram asked.

"Level of what?" I asked.

"Personality level," the hologram repeated.

"What do you mean level, level as pertaining to what?" I asked again.

"Please indicate a level setting between 1 and 5." The hologram said a third time.

"Fuck! Okay, let's go for middle of the road. Personality Level 3," I said as a guess more than an answer.

"Personality level 3 encoded. Program complete," the hologram spoke and then faded.

The entire ship came to life. Everything was lit in a light I wasn't familiar with. It wasn't the bright of the day, and it wasn't the blue of the Thorens, nor was it the artificial light of the complex that never stretched more than a few feet. This light made dark flesh seem darker and pale skin somehow even whiter. The glow seemed to stretch on forever.

"Follow the indicator lights on the side walls to find your quarters. Make it quick, I can't have you sleeping in the halls like some homeless dude," the computer said, with a voice of a 20th age young male voice.

"Move your ass! I know you're tired," the voice snapped.

"Computer, what would have been the result if I had asked for Level 1 on personality?" I asked.

"Then you would have had a royal bitch to contend with."

"And if I had requested level 5?" I asked.

"That would have been the ice cube. No personality at all. Aren't you the lucky one, you chose me" the voice answered.

"How would I reset that?"

"You can't. It was kind of their last joke before leaving this existence. You're stuck with me. Get used to it, and get to bed."

"Damn, I'd hate to see the bitch mode," I mumbled, following the indicator lights leading to my quarters.

"I heard that."

I paused and took a moment to collect myself. I was exhausted and had been down here for quite a while. With the travel, and all that had transpired, it had to be well past midnight. I followed the movement of the light until it terminated at an entrance arch. I sent the command to 'OPEN' and the arch cleared and I walked into the room.

"Damn!" I said, looking around as the arch closed behind me.

"Sweet ain't it. Good Night, Captain"

I had memories of luxury and the feel of such fine cloth against my body, but my skin had never truly touched it other than the clothes I had taken from Kelay. The room wasn't large so much as it was functional, but when you've slept in a cave for 1600 years this seemed extravagant. My last upgrade, from stone floor and feather stuffed fabric, to my quarters in the complex, seemed phenomenal. This, however, made that pale in comparison. There was a large sleeping area that you could easily walk around without tripping, with a very wide and comfortable looking bed. It was large enough to sleep four people.

There was a table set up with two chairs, and a couch directly in front of the entrance. The grey chairs in the living area were thin by design and curved seamlessly from top to base in one solid piece, in the shape of a hook. The couch looked as though it would comfortably seat two and matched the chairs in color, but not quite in design. It was padded heavily so that if you were to sit, the bloated cushions would form to you. Beside each, was a short clear glass table. Across from the entrance, behind the sitting area, were two large windows that now had stone for the view. My mind wandered, imagining stars skimming passed.

The bathroom to the right had a bathtub that would easily fit several people. The interior was a matching black and white cracked marble design. It was overwhelming. I would have to do more exploring tomorrow, but right now, all I wanted to explore was my dreams.

I stripped off my clothing, stumbled over to the enormous bed, and climbed between the covers, and lay my head on the silky pillows. If I hadn't been so overwhelmed by sensation and exhaustion, I think I could have cum from the touch of the silky fabric that seemed to lick my flesh.

I finally awoke from the best rest I could ever remember having. I missed Bransen's embrace as I wiped the sleep from my eyes. Sliding from bed, I went to the bathroom. I drew a huge bath of hot steamy water, and soaked in it until the water was almost to cold to tolerate. I felt refreshed beyond words. I toweled off and went back to the sleeping area, opened the wardrobe, decided on a white opalescent pull over shirt with half sleeves, and an opaque flat black set of tight pants.

"I wonder what time it is," I mumbled to myself as I sat on the bed.

"It is 7:02 am, Captain. The funny looking box with the numbers '7:02' across from you on the counter, is your clock. It's an amazing coincidence, I know," came the smart ass reply.

I really wish I would have picked a personality different level. I suppose it could be worse.

"Computer, do you have a name?" I asked.

"Yes Captain, it is TK3400, but you may call me TK or computer," the voice replied.

"Ah, well TK, I have one as well, and it's Khore. From this point forward, please address me as such," I said, stretching out my arms to evict the last remnants of sleep.

"Whatever..." came the quick reply.

"TK, I'm going to be leaving for a short while, and when I return I will be bringing my Mate and Lover. I expect him to have full access. He will be the only one accompanying me so I don't want a fight about this." I said.

"Yes, Khore..." TK answered with an exasperated sigh.

The computer just sighed at me! It wasn't just a sigh, but it was a sigh with attitude! The previous inhabitants definitely had a twisted sense of humor.

Due to the type of cloaking this ship possessed, I didn't want to chance folding space until I had a better understanding of the technology. This was for more ancient than Kelay or myself and the thought of emerging in a solid mass of rock did not thrill me.

"TK," I said as I exited my quarters. "Show me to the bay in which I first arrived, please."

"That would be Cargo Bay 15," TK answered. Amber lights pulsed through the same narrow strip in the center of the wall I had followed to get here now, but led in the opposite direction.

I had a bounce in my step that even I couldn't deny. I grabbed my bag and made my way back toward the arch. I couldn't wait to see my Bransen again and get him in that great big bed!

I entered the cargo bay and walked past the two terminals that rose from the floor. I commanded the arch to open and fished the flashlight from my bag. Turning it on, I went through the arch and it closed behind me. Darkness surrounded me, and I commanded the arch open and closed again, just to make sure it would reopen.

I made my way about 30 to 40 steps up the stairway before reaching my mind out to my room in the complex. It was empty and I folded space letting the light slide me into my quarters.

"Bransen," I said, bringing the wrist COM to my mouth. "Please come to my quarters!"

"Khore?" Bransen practically yelled back at me.

"Yes, it's me. Come quick!"

I had barely finished the sentence when the door slid open with a clunk and Bransen came running in. He picked me up, spinning, and squeezing me too tightly. We hugged and kissed. I spied people walking past with barely hidden grins as they averted their eyes before the door closed. We clung to each other for long tender moments before he put me back down.

"Wow!" he said, backing away looking at me, "You look great! And those clothes. We don't have that type of cloth here. Where have you been?"

"That's what I want to show you. I think I have found our new home. Not only that, but there is room enough for thousands," I said.

He stood there eyeing me as though I had gone completely insane.

"It's true! Radio the team that you will be leaving the facility for a few hours and I'll show you." I was practically crawling out of my skin with excitement. I pulled at his wrist, and pushed the COM toward his mouth.

"Okay! Okay!" he giggled and activated the COM. "Khore and I will be leaving the complex for approximately 2 hours. An emergency team meeting will be held in Conference room three on level five at 17:00 hours. Attendance is mandatory."

"Grab a flash light, and let's go! You're not going to believe this," I handed him a flashlight from the shelf above my desk.

"Hold me tight," I said as I pulled him in close, grinding against him. I breathed in the smell of him as I nestled my head against his chest. I folded us into the dark stairwell and turned on my flashlight. Bransen loosened one arm, examining the walls and floor where we had emerged.

"Oh... a dark stairwell. No... wait... a smelly dark stairwell?" I heard the questions in his voice.

"Follow me, and be careful, it's steep. It's only about 50 feet further." I said, starting down the ancient stairway.

We climbed down the steps and I sent the command to open the arch. I took Bransen by the hand and pulled him in, instructing the arch close behind us.

"Welcome back, Khore," TK said as I felt Bransen nearly jump out of his skin. I couldn't help but chuckle.

"Kind of skittish, isn't he. Nice ass, though!" TK announced.

"Watch your tone TK, this is the love of my life you're talking about." I warned before planting a kiss on Bransen's neck.

"Who the hell is that?" he asked, glancing around the bay in wonder.

"That's TK, he's the ship's computer. I'll explain the attitude later."

"Attitude? I'm crushed... NOT!" the computer responded.

I pulled Bransen into me, giving him yet another deep kiss. I felt as though I had the last 24 hours to make up for.

"Follow me!" I said, nearly jogging down the hallway. We reached the door to my quarters. I was hoping this would soon become 'our' quarters.

The arch opened and we entered. Bransen just stood staring into the room.

"How did you find this?" Bransen asked, looking completely overwhelmed.

"I was hiking, and I found the ruins that are above us. While reaching out with my mind, I found a stairway beneath a huge square cut stone and decided to see where it led. It led here!"

"Okay, but what is this place?" he said, looking a little suspicious.

"This is the largest, most powerful battle cruiser in the Thoren fleet, or it had been until about 687,000 years ago. Being Khore's Mate and Lover, you also captain and command this ship. Only you or your children and their descendants may ever command this vessel," answered TK.

"Come here," I said, pulling his bewildered face to mine, running my fingers through his hair. Our lips and tongues wrestled with each other.

"Get your groove on!" TK broke the silence and our bliss.

"TK!"

"Yes, oh lustful one?" TK responded.

"You are not to initiate communication or give commentary while we are in this room unless specifically addressed, or unless the ship or its crew is in some form of danger." My voice was stern and probably a little too loud, but the computer seemed to have more attitude than I was willing to put up with.

"Whatever..." The computer responded.

Bransen looked questioningly into my eyes as his furrowed eyebrows creased his forehead. They always did that when he had a question for me, but didn't want to ask it aloud.

"Later. How about we take a peek around our ship?" I asked.

"You haven't yet?" He asked, looking at me, amazed.

"No, I found the stairway and this ship late in the afternoon. I was so tired from pushing through the jungle that I went straight to bed." I paused. "I missed you." I wanted to pull him so close our hearts would touch.

Chapter 9
Revelations

"Khore, what's going on?" Bransen's frustration was obvious as he snapped at me.

"Okay, let's slow this down a little." I sat on the couch and pulled him on top of me. I didn't have the bulk or size of body he did to press him into myself. I cradled him the best I could, as I rested my head in the nape of his neck and wrapped my arms around him.

"I was feeling a bit out of sorts yesterday, not that you could tell. I needed a moment to slow down and a place away from the chaos. I've watched time and the Thorens destroy everyone and everything around me, like some kind of spectator. I know you know what I'm talking about. You've seen more death than most." His heartbeat thrummed in my ear and his sweet musky scent drifted passed my nose.

"I'm from a simple place. I haven't existed in battle for centuries like you have. I never lived on the edge. My most stressful moments were a furtive glance or avoiding a disapproving eye. Then I woke up, and had my entire life ripped from me in a matter of minutes. I've been so careful to make sure my soul wasn't stretched too thin, but as usual, I failed."

"After a few hours sleep, I opened my eyes and the mirror showed me someone I didn't know. I like this new person I've become, but I think it's going to be a little while before I'm fully comfortable with myself." Bransen's emerald green eyes shimmered in the light of our new quarters as he listened to me try and explain myself.

"I think, for once, I'm going to be one of the happy people." A smile stretched my lips and I gave his neck a subtle nibble. To be honest, the prospect terrified me. I didn't have the best track record when it came to happiness.

"I guess I'm just frightened of the unknown. Now get off me you whale... my legs are going numb!" I poked him in the side and tried to shove him off of me.

"Hey!" he twisted in my lap, giving my sides and stomach sharp jabs. As much as I tried I couldn't twist away from his tickling attacks.

"Okay! Okay!!!" I coughed out in hysterics. "You're not a whale. You're not a whale!" I felt as though my heart might explode if he didn't stop soon, and I loved every second of his torture.

"That's better." His supple lips spread in a smug grin as he leaned in and gave me a gentle kiss and his shoulder length blond hair tickled my cheek.

"So, when I awoke this morning, I left the Cystos, folded back to my quarters, called you... and the rest you know." I grunted as he slid off my lap and into the spot beside me on the couch.

Bransen sat there for the next few minutes and his brow furrowed. It was the same expression he always wore when his thoughts led to something I probably didn't want to hear. He was thinking, but I didn't know what about. I was tempted to pry, but I wouldn't break my word by reading his thoughts without permission.

He sucked in a deep breath and let it out. "Okay."

"Okay? That's all you have to say? Just... Ok?" My words seemed to burst past my lips and my voice was louder than I intended.

"Okay... Now I know what's going on. Computer, what is the status of this ship?" Bransen was always matter-of-fact, but I had hoped for a little more reaction.

"All systems are operating within normal parameters, Sweetmeat." TK, the ships' computer replied with a growing attitude. I seriously wished I could take back the personality setting I chose when I boarded the ship. The original occupants had a sense of humor that was going to take some getting used to.

"TK! Please address Bransen by his name and cut the shit." I knew better than to let it get to me, but the flippant reply grated on my nerves.

"Whatever..."

Bransen leaned forward and studied the computer panel on the coffee table. "Computer, please display a schematic of the ship and indicate our position within it."

The black panel displayed a horizontal raindrop shape showing key systems and level separation. It wasn't your average Thoren ship. The basic Thoren design had been and was still, a sphere. While a sphere had served their kind well over the millennia, the shape of a falling raindrop is perfectly aerodynamic in every way. I had never seen anything like it. Not even from the memories I possessed that were transferred to me from my dead father, Kelay.

Redundancies in the ship's major systems boggled my mind. It wasn't built with the two standard back ups that current Thoren ships possessed, but more in a grid, wherein if any one system failed, it would be automatically rerouted to another junction. All major systems were built with a spider web design that had been spun on its axis. This ship however, could literally shed its skin layer by layer and remain completely intact as a smaller version of itself. It would simply absorb the previous layer, to perform repairs and store in reserve whatever was not needed.

All key systems were located in the center like a heart that pumped the ship; Weapons, Communications, Environmental, Tactical, and Propulsion. The 5th dimensional material that powered all this was located at the absolute center.

"Computer, what is the total occupancy of this ship?" Bransen was furrowing his brow again, and as usual, it worried me.

"Approximately one million, Bransen, and please call me TK." The ship replied.

"OK then, how long would it take to destroy every Sphere Major?" Bransen continued.

"If they were not fighting back, approximately three days nine hours and twenty three minutes?" TK answered.

"How long would it take if they were resisting?" There was no doubt in my mind now that I didn't like where this line of questions was leading.

"If they were resisting, this ship would not survive. You would never accomplish your goal. There are too many. 83% of them would be destroyed, but you would not survive the conflict in an enduring battle." TK answered, calmer than I would have liked. One would think that the smart ass would have at least some reaction and sense of self preservation.

"How long would it take for the Thorens to destroy this planet?" I asked, seeing Bransen's head snap to my direction.

"Total Earth devastation by the Thorens would take approximately 37 minutes." TK answered.

"How long would it take the Cystos to destroy the Earth?" I asked, more out of morbid curiosity than anything else.

"24 seconds." TK answered.

My skin seemed to crawl with the answer. A shiver rode across my flesh like some small terror. "TK, how is that possible?" I was stunned.

"Detonation of 5th dimensional matter would destroy this world in approximately 24 seconds, the system in approximately 21 minutes, and the galaxy in about 4 hours and 6 minutes." TK announced.

I gazed over at Bransen who sat beside me, staring back in horror. The line of questioning had given us some answers we weren't prepared for.

"It isn't by coincidence that you are here, Khore. The emergency transmission during the cloaking error took approximately 512,000 years to reach the Thoren home world. The Thorens are here looking for me as much as they are here looking for the cure to their longevity. We knew once we found the anomaly in our genetic code that this would be the destination of the Thoren. It was only a matter of time. The Thorens are here by design. This was never a serendipitous destination. We weren't, however, sure of the circumstances of your arrival, and that is why only those of mixed heritage are allowed entrance." TK started referring to itself as we, and I knew that the answer was programmed into the computer by, Talp and Berlit, the original pilots of the Cystos.

"It is inconceivable that someone had the forethought to do this." I tried to wrap my mind around it. My heart was pounding and I didn't want to believe that Keelon had fooled us all.

"Yeah, crafty little fuckers, weren't they, and that Talp was hung like a horse!" TK added.

"Well thank you for that tidbit of information." I snapped.

"Bransen," I said, more a question than anything. "What are we going to do?"

I was at a total loss for words. There were too many possibilities. For once we had the means to do something, but I wasn't sure what. It was simple enough when one make decisions that only affect them and a select few around them, but how the hell does someone decide what is best for an entire race or two, and the world?! Heh! No pressure there!

Bransen sat for a moment and opened his mouth, and then stopped to think some more. I was glad not to be the only one at a loss for words. What do you do, given the options we now had? I had to admit that the idea of just running away with Bransen, leaving them all to their own future, crossed my mind. I knew I couldn't do it, but I wanted to. That selfish part of me wanted to get what was mine and run. I never imagined that where we went from here would be such a difficult decision.

I rose from the couch and removed my shirt, tugging it slowly over my head, pulling my hair from it as I tossed it to the floor. I could feel the feathery weight tickling my upper chest as I moved, shifting my weight, working the clasp on my pants. I didn't know what I was going to do tomorrow, or even later today, but I did know at that moment I wanted to feel his hard body against mine. I kicked off my shoes, unfastened my pants, and slid them down my legs, giving them a little nudge with my foot as I shook them from my feet.

I turned away from Bransen and walked toward the bed. Looking back as I climbed onto the bed, I saw Bransen, now standing. He already removed his shirt. His bronze muscles tapered to his waist which was still covered by his silken pants. His sex stretched down his leg, and was bursting to get out, as a ravenous passion filled his eyes.

As I rolled onto my side, he ran to the bed and climbed on top of me, thrusting into me with his crotch as his lips pressed feverishly against my own. Gripping at his pants I roughly loosened the bindings and, with his help, was able to work them down and free his seeping cock. He shook the pants the rest of the way off his legs and we ground our hips into each other.

He leaned back, grasped both of my ankles and gave a strong pull, bringing me closer to him. Reaching under my knees, he brought them up and dove between the cheeks of my ass, making a meal of me. His movements were violent but tender in their urgency. He devoured my asshole with loving quick nibbles and the feathery touch of his tongue.

When I thought I was going to go insane from the sensations his tongue was giving me, I grabbed a fistful of his hair in each hand and pulled him up. "Fuck me!" I commanded. His eight inch rod was ready, and I was desperate for the feeling of fullness it would give me. His cock jutted out and throbbed as the precum glistened along its length. He slid into me, slowly but without stopping, until he was buried completely. Laying flat against my chest, we kissed passionately while I clung to his strong body with my arms and legs. We ground against each other as he worked in and out of my ass.

We held on to each other in our rhythm of lust and pleasure, and slowed to an uneven but sensual glide. His hard, slick abdomen wrung so much juice from me it felt as though I had already come. The friction against my cock, trapped blissfully between us, was bringing me to the point of no return. The delicate brush of his hefty balls tapped against my opening, and the assault against my prostate threatened to send me over the edge. Bransen gave me more of a bite than a tender nibble, as he buried his face into my neck. The action sent me soaring. I felt my asshole contract as I shot my load between us. I clenched around his still working cock. As my ass clamped and twitched around him, Bransen came, thrusting into me one last time before emptying his balls as we both grunted and moaned.

We lay like that for several minutes, catching our breath, before Bransen pulled his softening cock from the velvet recess of my ass. It felt so good inside me I hated to part with it. He rolled off onto his back, eyes still closed, with a smirk across his face.

"TK, wake us at 4:00 pm please." I whispered sedately, and rested my head on Bransen's chest as the rise and fall of his chest rocked me to sleep.

"Yes, Khore." Bransen's labored breath and Tk's words were the last thing I heard before drifting off to sleep.

Sirens shattered the silence and Bransen literally flung me from on top of him, throwing me out of the bed and onto the floor. The lights were flashing and the siren's wail was deafening. My heart felt like it was going to explode in my chest while my mind tried to figure out what was going on.

"TK!" Bransen yelled. "What the hell is happening!?"

The sirens and strobe lights stopped, instantly. The computer spoke two words.

"Wakey, Wakey"

"TK! You fucker!!" My sleep didn't just leave me, it was ripped from my mind and was replaced with rage. "You ever do that again and I swear I'll set this ship to self destruct!" I growled while pulling myself up from the floor, rubbing the bump above my left eyebrow where I had hit the bedside table. The bump was shrinking as I stood in a huff, looking over at Bransen who had the biggest shit eating grin on his face. He burst out laughing.

"Oh, ha, ha." I tried not to grin. "Sure, it's funny to you. You didn't get thrown out of bed!"

Bransen pulled me into him. "Sorry babe," he said and kissed me on the forehead.

"TK." I smiled as I leaned against Bransen. "Next time, a simple vocal indication will be sufficient. Maybe even a some gentle music."

"Suit yourself, sleepy head, though my method seems to have been quite effective." TK giggled through the ships speaker.

"We've got to get everyone moved here so TK will have someone else to torment." I ran my fingers through the blond chaos of Bransen's hair and kissed him gently on the lips.

After I stood and stretched, I walked over to the bathroom and began to fill the bath tub. The roar of water echoed against the walls of the room as it gushed out of the faucet. I waited until the water was about three feet deep and shut off the flow of water. Wisps of feathery steam rose from its surface like a mist covered lake on an cool morning.

Testing the water with my foot, I eased my body into the water. I got used to the burning sensation as each inch of flesh submerged. Holding my breath, and with a quick hop, I went from hip to chest into the water, finally settling on the ledge.

"Well stinky, you coming?" I asked as I hung my head back and gazed down my nose at Bransen across the room.

He stood and stretched, flexing muscle from his legs to his powerful chest like a cat after an afternoon nap. His curly golden hair swept across his shoulders and broad chiseled chest. I could see him like this every day and never stop finding a new beautiful line of muscle. He seemed to glide over to the bathtub and climbed the marbled steps to the tubs edge. He sat slowly, letting only his legs submerge to the shins. Grabbing his left leg I gave him a quick tug, and pulled him into the water with a huge splash. He coughed and spluttered as his body rushed to acclimate to the nearly scalding water.

"Wakey, Wakey!" I choked out through my laughter and he pushed a huge wave of water into my face.

"Okay! Okay! Truce!" I chuckled at him and smiled.

I scooted over next to Bransen letting our legs brush against each other as they floated in the water. "So, what do we do now?"

"Well, we need to explore the ship, investigate its abilities, and learn its systems. Then, I suppose we need to decide what to do with our new found home." He looking at me and then leaned over and gave me a chaste kiss.

"What we do with the Cystos after that, is what scares me. The Thorens know this ship is here somewhere, and they are going to want it. They won't be able to detect the cloak, and most likely won't even try so long as we stay quiet and bide our time. I don't want to end up in a battle where everything is destroyed, specifically this planet. I worry that if Keelon becomes desperate enough he'll ask to trade me for his promise not to destroy the Earth." My mind was doing flip-flops again at the endless possibilities. There were too many options to consider and I was having a difficult time trying to focus on any one given thing.

"Let's take this slowly, inform the team of your find, and begin after the meeting. We have more time now than we did before. We should be safe for a while yet. In two weeks you'll be testing everyone, and we can continue from there." Bransen seemed to settle on the idea as he stared at nothing in particular and resolved himself with his proposed course of action.

"I won't allow the destruction of the Thorens." I said gravely. "Many of them are good people and have been friends for thousands of years. Trax may be able to help us."

We both washed and dried ourselves and made our way to the panel that covered the garment storage. Bransen had become quiet, and it worried me. As we dressed in silence I began to worry. He still hadn't spoken a word.

Taking his hand in mine, I looked into his eyes. "You know I would always pick you before anyone and anything else. I just don't think I could survive watching the genocide of an entire race, friends, and memories. There has to be another option."

Bransen sighed. "A lot of people will probably die, but if we do this right, maybe we can save ourselves and the Thorens."

"Thank you for saying that. It's really been weighing on my mind." I couldn't help but love him more with each passing day. We were partners in life and love as well as well as our goals for our people and those we cared about.

"Well then, I suppose we should head back to the complex and update the team. They're going to shit when they see this place." An awkward smile curled my lips. It was the kind that nervousness brings when a body is so exited they don't know how to act.

"So, are you going to fold us there from here?" Bransen seemed to be waiting for me.

"No, I haven't tried to fold from behind the ships cloak. I'm not sure if it would be safe. Honestly, I don't know if I could do it or not, and the idea of emerging in the center of a rock scares the living shit out of me. I folded us by sheer panic when we were almost killed. I didn't know if it would work or if it was even possible. I knew the physics of the process, but in that panicked chaos, instinct took over and it just sort of happened." It was something I had hoped I wouldn't have to explain, but I should have known better.

"So you folded us through space not knowing if we would survive??! You hadn't done it before?" Bransen's voice was strained and he didn't bother to hide his surprise or disapproval.

"We were dead either way, what else could I do!? I've been flying by the seat of my pants as much as anyone! I was just a farm boy before all this started remember? Well, a human and Thoren hybrid, but I didn't know it then! I didn't have Kelay's memories to help me before I was taken. Everything has been happening so fast, I haven't had much time to sort it all out." My words came out to fast and in a jumble as I tried to explain myself.

"You're doing great," Bransen gave my shoulder a reassuring squeeze and then he smiled.

"I'm not a fighter Bransen." I reminded him.

"You became a fighter when you escaped from the Thorens. It was a fighter that killed the Thorens and destroyed the Sphere Major. You didn't hesitate." His voice was even and I knew that he meant the words, but it was still difficult to accept.

"Yeah, I know," I said, not at all comfortable with the memory. "I know if I had hesitated we all would have died, but it could just as easily have all gone to hell. I'm a scientist and pacifist. I was fighting for my lover and our lives. I feel like I'm teetering at the edge of the abyss waiting for someone kick me in the ass," I said, pulling him in tighter.

"I'm scared, Bransen. Of myself and for our future," I whispered to him.

"It's okay," Bransen paused, "we'll get through this. I'd be more worried if you weren't scared.

"TK," I paused.

"Yes Khore?" the computer replied.

"Will the cloaking method of this ship interfere with folding space?" I asked. Why I hadn't thought to ask the computer before embarrassed me.

"Working," TK answered.

"Fourth dimensional travel should have no impact on the cloaking system or fifth dimensional matter in the power drive. Transport by this method is theoretically possible."

"So that means?" I asked

"A little more than maybe, and a bit less than probably. Act like you have a pair of balls you big baby!" TK snapped.

"Thanks TK, you're my eternal crutch and support," I muttered hoping that he noted my sarcasm. The last thing I wanted was for him to actually believe that was true.

"Well then, I suppose there is only one way to find out." I said as I began to envision the cargo bay.

I concentrated, clearing my mind, remembering the exact layout of the cargo bay. Creating the spatial distortion, I moved through the fold and emerged in the cargo bay in a flash of white light. Checking to make sure I still had all of my parts, I breathed a sigh of relief.

"Well, I guess it's safe," I mumbled before folding Bransen and myself to conference room three on level five within the complex. There had been a slight hiccup. For a moment we had been within the granite surrounding the complex, but I was able to make corrections for the shifts the fifth dimensional matter had caused. They were minor, but enough to scare the hell out of me.

"I could have sworn I was in that wall!" Bransen said, eyes wide as he pointed across the room, staring at me.

"For a moment you were," I said with a nervous shake in my voice.

Bransen was a little upset with me, but was calming. "Next time warn me, okay?" He elbowed me in the side, but his grin told me I was out of trouble.

"I'm sorry," I said aiming my best puppy dog eyes at him. "But, now we know! It's a little tricky, but it's doable."

We had arrived about ten minutes early and no one had yet shown up in the conference room. It was odd that even Doc wasn't here. He always arrived early, though I wondered if he had adopted some of Chris's bad habits or, more likely,... was 'preoccupied' with Chris.

"So, meeting aboard the Cystos then?" I looked at Bransen, questioning.

Grinning, he nodded and lifted his wrist COM to his mouth to speak. "All team members are to be in the Level five conference room three NOW," he announced sharply.

Smiling at Bransen I nodded, letting him know that I was preparing. As our team would enter the room, they would walk through the fold at the entrance, bringing them all to the bay on the ship.

"Let's go prepare." I said, and envisioned the bay. I could not see beyond the cloak of the ship, but I could see the bay within my mind as though I were looking at it with my own eyes.

We folded into the bay of Cystos, blinking out and back with a flash.

"TK, we have company coming. You will not harm them," I announced as Doc and Chris popped into view moments later.

"Whatever," came the familiar reply.

"Table seating 12, approximately fifteen feet long, four feet wide with chairs, please," I stated as they morphed from the floor in a black and silver blob before taking complete shape.

"Please have a seat," Bransen spoke, breaking the silence as they all made their way to the elongated table and chairs.

As the rest emerged, we directed them to the table with Bransen and me standing at the front.

When everyone had finally arrived, I released the fold that brought them here. I was getting better at this. It had barely taxed my mind at all. I let the blue light that blazed from my eyes die back down to their natural icy grey blue color.

The ship's bay was nearly half the size of the entire complex. I could see their furtive glances and the confusion cross their faces as they took their seats. Dusty seemed to be absolutely giddy with the construction of the place as he looked beneath the table and across at the walls of the bay.

Bransen and I took the seats at the head of the table. We let everyone have a long look at the area before we continued.

"Khore found this ship yesterday when he left. TK," he announced, "Give them the rundown please."

They all just stared in awe as TK began to explain. A three-dimensional silhouette emerged about four feet above the table. It was a scale hologram of the ship itself about 8 feet long and 5 feet wide.

"687,000 years ago the Cystos was built by the Thorens during their war with the Velo. A mishap with the cloaking device folded us through space to Earth. An emergency message was sent, but the communications array had been damaged during our materialization into this place. The message would not be received for another 512,000 years."

"Due to the massive loss of technology and time, the Thorens completely abandoned the technology and changed their tactics, finally winning the war several hundred years later."

"Talp and his lover Berlit found themselves trapped here for a short while, eighty thousand years or so, before they were able to correct the anomalies in the cloaking system. They had been weary of war, and finding the emerging Mayan civilization here, they molded an empire where they let themselves be worshiped as gods. They had interrupted the natural development of these people. It wasn't long before they got tired of playing god. They had considered going back to the Thoren home world, but had also discovered in their research that they were dying. They couldn't return for fear of what they had done to these people. It was beyond reproach to interfere with a culture so young so, with no home to go home to, and only death waiting in the wings, they took the Mayan people down into the catacombs with them and killed them all."

"Talp and Berlit then programmed this ship, and your fabulous computer, me, to ensure that this would never happen again by only allowing entry to a race that was a mix of both Thoren and Human genes. Anyone else who attempted to enter would be instantly vaporized."

"Any questions so far?" TK asked.

Sweed had started to speak when TK cut in. "I wasn't serious. Sit there and be quiet until I'm done ya big oaf."

I noticed Sweed's face blaze red as I waved to him. hoping he would let it go.

"Anyway, where was I? Oh, well, the last program that Talp and Berlit executed to ensure only a mixed race would enter, also killed them. It was quick and painless, as it was for the Mayans, and I've sat here ever since waiting for someone to find me. Bout fucking time, too!"

"The ship has five basic systems, Environmental, Weapons, Tactical, Communications, and Power. Each system is based in the center sphere of the ship with duplicates on every level spanning outward exponentially. If at any time one system is damaged on any given level it can be routed to another module on either the same or a different level."

"Cavrium 2 is the liquid metal substance used in construction of the current Spheres. Cavrium 3 is the base of the Cystos. While it acts almost identically to Cavrium 2, it possesses a stronger make-up, allowing for high speed atmospheric travel. For those of you who aren't following me, it means I'm harder to damage than a standard Thoren ship. It is also the reason for the darker metallic color of the exterior and the presence of more standard coloration on the interior of the ship."

"Each level extends outward from the center core in rings. The core of the ship consists of 150 levels in size, approximately two miles in diameter. The ship levels then rotate. In rotation you will find one crew quarters level, one recreational level, one hydroponics level, one operations level and one command level."

"The operations, hydroponics and recreational levels are split into three equal sectors. They are signified by color; Red, Yellow, and Green. On operations levels, red signifies Propulsion, Yellow is sensors, and Green is Environmental. On recreational levels, Red is fitness and activity, Yellow is 'alternative' and standard entertainment, and Green is the dining and relaxation area. Food can be dispensed through synthesizers in your quarters as well as from terminals and dining areas in Green sector on recreational levels. The hydroponics Red sector is mountainous forest, Blue is fertile flatland, and Green is Tropical Jungle and oceanic coastline."

"All those that board this ship must wear a PDD or Person Detection Device. It monitors your health and location for inter ship transport."

Finally there was a pause as small metallic beads about the size of a pea appeared before each of us.

"Please place the PDD in the palm of your right hand to activate absorption and ship registration."

I looked at Bransen, wondering why this was the first we had heard of it. I suppose we should have asked for the tour, but it was just as well we didn't have to sit through this twice.

We watched as Bransen picked up the small silver ball and placed it in his palm. It seemed to melt and soak into his skin. Seeing that he was okay we all followed suit.

"Crew encoded. To activate intraship transport you must address me as Computer or TK and then state your desired location. You will then be transported to your specified location. Internal to external transport is not possible and such requests will be ignored."

"Additional information can be accessed from any data access terminal located in your quarters and throughout the ship. While this has been as much fun as analyzing the pattern of hair on the oaf's ass, this concludes your tour. You have bored me."

Chapter 10

I Am

The team stared at us from around the table. It was too much information in too short a time. They were on sensory overload. I wanted to say, "Welcome to my world!" but decided against it, considering their already battered sanity.

Bransen's eyes glanced around the table, taking stock of our team. He stood and introduced the team to the computer, indicating each with his hand as he spoke.

"TK, This is Doc, Chris, Sweed, Raven, Rift, Twist, Neek, and Dusty. I think you're all familiar with the ship's smart ass computer."

"Bite me!" TK interrupted.

Bransen breathed a deep sigh.

"As I was saying… we can't change the computer. It has been programmed this way. You're all going to have to deal with TK in your own way. Please acquaint yourselves with your new quarters and take the evening off. Explore the ship, relax, do whatever you like. Tomorrow is going to be a full day and I will need you fresh."

TK spoke. "Everyone has been assigned separate compartments. If the groping and foot play under the table are any indicator, I will be expecting room assignment updates. If you're going to be bumping uglies and sleeping together, please occupy only one room. There is sufficient space for two people. My power supply may be endless, but you don't need to piss it away by keeping separate quarters." There was a slight pause. "Incidentally, I'm not a smart ass. I'm fucking witty!" The next sound heard was a computer generated raspberry.

I know that the computer didn't have a mouth or lips, but the sound was duplicated expertly. I could almost hear the barrage of spittle. Watching the muscles ripple in the angle of Bransen's jaw, I could see the raspberry had been effective. My laugh shattered the tense silence.

Sweed's cheeks burned as he brought his hands up from beneath the table. The look on his face made me laugh even louder. Sweed's gentleness of spirit is one of many endearing qualities. His blue eyes were focusing on anything but the others seated around the table.

Raven looked guilty, too, but did not divert his eyes. His cheeks were now only slightly less flushed than Sweed's. He peered though black wisps of hair daring anyone to comment. I envy the way he can appear so menacing while shorter than an average man. Images of an innocent black furred puppy came to mind. This puppy however, stared back defiantly after shitting on the floor, bearing sharp teeth behind raised quivering lips.

Twist and Rift were grinning at Sweed's embarrassment. I had been referring to them as the twins in my mind. Except for Twist's slightly more pointed chin and auburn hair, they could have been brothers. Their overall beauty is what might be best described as 'those guys' that provide the erotic images that speed you to climax with night's handy work.

Doc and Chris were smiling at each other with knowing eyes. I noticed Dusty give Neek a slight elbow and quick nod in Sweed's direction.

"Ahhhh, isn't the big guy just adorable," came the smart ass remark from the ships computer.

"That's it!" yelled Raven, slamming his fist into the table. Jumping up he pulled a gun from his side holster, aiming it at the source of the voice.

"Holster your weapon, spaz," TK commanded.

"One more fucking word and I'll shoot your ass!" His black eyes were slits as the cords of his neck strained.

"Wrong answer," spouted TK.

A white flash of light replaced Raven only seconds before another flash returned him. He no longer had his gun. What was most noticeable was a wet brown liquid soaking him from head to toe. It was difficult at first to identify what he had been submerged in. That question was answered as the rancid stench of sewage quickly filled the room. Raven best resembled a freshly submerged cat at bath time. Pissed off!

"TK, transport Raven to his quarters immediately!"

A flash of white light replaced Raven once more as the room exploded into laughter. The stench was awful as I walked over to a very sober looking Sweed.

"He'll be okay." I gave his shoulder a little squeeze. "Do you want to go to him?"

Sweed nodded weakly as he stared at the floor.

"TK, transport Sweed to Raven's quarters," I ordered and Sweed was flashed away.

Upon his departure I stifled a couple of giggles before regaining control of myself and returning to Bransen's side. His laughter had been instant and quickly subdued as he trained the smile from his face. I worried for Sweed. The image of wet cat and paralyzed mouse came to mind.

"You have to do something about this," I sent the thought to Bransen.

"I'm about to," he thought back to me.

"Okay people, let's calm down for a second. In light of recent events, I expect *all* of you, *especially* you, Twist, to never mention what just happened here. Don't talk about it outside of your quarters. No rude comments or statements that even remotely allude to it. If you are afraid you may slip, do not speak to him. If by some strange twist of fate he brings up the incident, listen and then let the topic die," Bransen paused.

"You all know Raven, and what kind of man he is. This is the first public display of affection Raven has shown in over fifty years. It didn't end well, and I'm worried about Sweed. Any harassment," Bransen centered his eyes on Twist, "could do serious damage to their relationship. If you fuck with me on this, your new home will be where Raven has just been."

"One last thing," his voice had softened and a smile crept across his face, "I would strongly recommend against any attempts to shoot the ship."

Sporadic giggles and laughter echoed from the shadowed walls of the bay.

"Alright then, have a good evening. TK, transport all but Khore and me to their quarters, please," Bransen ordered.

The rest of the team was blinked out of the room simultaneously, leaving us alone.

I turned and wrapped my arms around Bransen, squeezing him tightly to me. I felt his strong arms wrap around me pulling me closer.

I tilted my head upward and whispered in his ear, "You're a good man, Bransen."

"Yeah, I know," he chuckled as we separated.

I pressed against him for a swift kiss. His lips were so inviting I was tempted to linger.

"Would you mind if I spent the next few hours alone? I kind of need some time to myself. With all of this I haven't really had the chance, you know?" I was afraid of his reaction and had spewed the words out in a quick jumble.

"I don't see why that should be a problem," he said, looking into my eyes, "but with two conditions. One, you have to be back by 23:00 hours and two, I get a goodbye kiss!" he said as he gripped my ass pulling me into him.

"My pleasure," I answered, leaning into him

Our lips met in a slow but passionate kiss, before reluctantly pulling apart.

"Thank you," I said, running my fingers through his silky golden hair and down his strong square jaw.

"TK, Random level, Hydroponics, Green Sector."

The scenery changed in a flash of light. I was standing on a white sandy beach looking out to an ocean that appeared to have no end. I knew much of it was simulated and illusion, but it looked real enough to me. I sat down in the white sand, resting my elbows on my knees and my chin in the cup of my palms.

The crash of waves brought the smell of the sea to me as I gazed out at the purple and pink hue of sunset. The salty breeze caressed my skin as I sat thinking about nothing at all. This was the perfect place I had only imagined before in my mind. I watched as a seagull plunged into the water in pursuit of its evening meal.

I closed my eyes to better savor the world around me. I wanted this moment. I wanted every smell and sound of this perfect place etched into my mind forever. I sat completely still, opening my eyes on occasion to see a new and spectacular panorama of color.

I didn't so much feel the passage of time as I simply knew it existed. The simulated sun sank into the horizon with an almost audible hiss.

Thoughts were rolling around in the back of my mind like so many distractions. I shifted my weight and struggled back to my feet. I felt the weakness in my legs from their lack of movement.

"TK, mirror, one meter wide by three meters tall."

I watched as an upright mirror grew from the sand, showing me myself.

I marveled at my reflection in the red and purple light of sunset. I pulled my skin-tight shirt over my head and tossed it to the side. I then pulled off my pants and sent them away with a weak kicking motion from my right leg.

I stared at the person in the mirror. It's strange. I can peer into someone else's eyes, but I have never been able to look past my own. I tried, yet again, focusing my attention on the grey flecks within the icy blue of the iris that stared back at me. With all that I am, I still could not focus on the soul behind my eyes. Had it been someone else, I would be able to see but my focus still flickered from eye to eye, catching on remnants of grey. It was distracting.

A feathered movement caught my attention. The wind had bent a curl of my mid length dark brown hair as it spilled down my neck and past my shoulders. The thick white streak seemed to take on the hues of sunset, framing my face as if by design.

My dark, long, thick eyelashes winked at me as I followed their curve to my thin but average nose. It was nestled between the non-descript ridges of my cheek bones and the fleshy pink peaks of my upper lip. My lower lip pouted into the curve of my tapered chin and jaw line which wrapped squarely to below my ears.

I glanced further down to the hollow at the base of my neck. I had missed too many meals, but work in the gardens had kept my neck strong as it merged into my shoulders. My lack of exposure to the sunlight over the last two weeks had faded the bronze color of my skin, making it a muted tan.

The transformation had left me with cut lines of muscle at my shoulders that creased like crows feet at my armpits. Young unblemished skin stretched across my developed chest and abdomen, leaving sharp furrows that baby fat had hidden for the past 1600 years.

The flesh continued to undulate across the bone and muscle of my ribs as it tapered to my waist. My eyes followed the gradual thickening trail of dark fuzz from my naval to my ample cock. The hair branched out only slightly, framing my egg-sized balls that rested against two hearty cut thighs. They were an athlete's legs. The weight played across my thighs and calves as I shifted from one leg to another, watching each flex from hip to toe.

For the very first time in my life, I saw myself as beautiful. It was a difficult perception to accept when I had viewed myself so differently over the millennia. It is a rare thing to see ourselves as others might. We tend to linger on the miniscule flaws that draw our fleeting attention.

Taking one last glance at the purple and grey hued sunset, I turned away from the mirror. I looked out to the ocean as the water rushed against the beach, smelling the salt-soaked moisture as it passed my nose.

"I'll be damned," I thought. "I was here the whole time."

"TK, remove the mirror," I ordered and watched as it melted into the white sand, disappearing completely.

Darkness surrounded me as I dressed and stars emerged by the millions. They were tiny pin pricks of light that seemed to wink at you if you looked hard enough. Turning, I saw a sliver of a moon slashed by shadow as it crept from behind the canopy of the jungle. My eyes had never seen a sky without Thoren ships interrupting the view. It felt like a promise of things to come.

I reached out with my mind to find Bransen. I *had* to show him this! He was in our quarters at a black desk that sat against the far wall, behind the couch and chairs. It was nestled into the right hand corner beneath the windows. Both Bransen and the desk faced the bathroom, showing their silhouette to whoever might walk through the door.

"What you doing?" I sent him the question.

"I'm reviewing Blade schematics. There are hangers and hangers of Blade fighter ships here." I could hear his excitement in my mind.

"Do you have a moment?" I asked.

"Sure, this can wait, what do..."

"TK, transport Bransen to my location," I commanded, after hearing 'sure'.

The white flash of light that brought him momentarily blinded me. Hearing a thud, I realized a better idea would have been to have him standing first.

"I'm sorry, Bransen," I giggled as I sat.

"I thought you might want to see this," I explained as I reached out to the sound of him falling while my sight returned to normal.

I found Bransen's hand and wrapped it around my chest as I scooted between his legs with my back to him. Resting my head against his muscled shoulder, we sat staring out at the blanket of stars. I felt a small shudder escape him.

"Are you okay?" Maybe this had been a bad idea.

Bransen cleared his throat. He was trying to disguise the emotion that was causing the ache in his chest. "Tough guy to the end," I thought to myself. I felt his chest expand, taking in a deep breath before exhaling slowly.

"I never thought I'd see it." Bransen's rich deep voice cracked.

Clearing his throat I felt Bransen's strong arms pull me tighter. "Thank you, Khore."

Bransen hadn't ever seen the sky without Thoren ships. I had memories of it, but had never really 'seen' it either. We sat dazzled as the breeze rolled over our bodies. The view was hypnotic as stars combined with the low roar of waves rushing against the sand.

I don't know how long we stared at this perfect world before a hollow pang from my stomach pulled me back to reality. I hadn't eaten yet today. This had been my diet for too long. Life always seemed to need so much work that eating became a low priority for me. I usually snuck in quick meals with food in one hand and work in the other. I couldn't put it off any longer.

"Bransen," I whispered in his ear. "I need to eat. I'm going to head back to our quarters, okay?"

My tenor voice roused him from his daze as I pulled my head from his shoulder. "I'll be there in a bit," he answered.

I couldn't blame him for wanting more time with this perfection. I let loose his hand and kissed him lightly on the cheek.

"Close your eyes," I told him.

"Huh?! Oh, okay"

"TK, quarters." As quickly as I spoke the words, I was transported to our new home.

The dim lighting gave the white walls a grey pallor. I stood and walked over to the food dispenser and requested broiled cod with lemon on a bed of wild rice, a small plain bowl of shredded lettuce, and green tea.

Kelay had loved this dish and I hoped I wouldn't be disappointed. A red flash lit the framed edges of the panel before it opened. The sweet smell of butter and the sea mingled in the air.

I balanced my tray precariously as I stepped slowly to the couch. I gave the fish a moment to cool as I broke a chunk off with my fork. I pushed the lemon-buttery fish into my mouth and savored it. I ceremoniously devoured my meal. It was the kind of quick meal we have when we love what we put in our mouths so much we barely take the time to taste it. The crispness of lettuce and grainy texture of fish raced across my tongue. Five minutes later I washed down the last of my meal with the earthy green tea.

I sat the tray on the knee high table in front of me and leaned back, draping my arms along the length of the couch. As I glanced down I could see the slight pooch of my well fed belly. I tilted my head back and closed my eyes, resting my mind. I drifted in that place between waking and dreams.

A burst of color from the backs of my eyelids brought me back as they popped open to see Bransen had returned. He was sitting on the floor facing me on the opposite side of the small table.

"I love you," he said, pausing before he stood.

"I love you, too, Bransen," I answered.

"Could you send Chris and Doc back to the complex conference room?" he asked me. "They've been away from the infirmary for too long and we need a Team member in the complex."

"Of course." I worked myself upright. "Standard communications protocol, TK?" I asked.

"No! Aboard the Cystos, you must press your ass cheeks firmly together and fart out your message in Morse code." TK paused, "DUUUUUUUuuuuuuuuuuuhhhhhh! Yes, standard communications protocol, Khore.

"Whatever," I snapped back as I sat upright.

"Doc," I paused to establish the com link.

"Are you ready for transport?" I asked.

An unsure voice answered me. It was Doc. "Uhhhh hello? Yeah, I think so," he replied.

I unfurled my mind through the levels, crawling out like smoke along the floor. Finding Doc and Chris, I folded them to the conference room within the complex.

"We need to get everyone aboard the ship as soon as possible," I thought to Doc with my eyes still radiating the blue glow from my recent work.

"Please announce that testing will be tomorrow. I will search their minds to see who they are. We cannot take the chance that a Thoren spy might board this ship."

A late night announcement from Doc erupted from the speakers throughout the complex. "There has been a schedule change. Khore will be testing you tomorrow. Please get as much rest as possible. You'll need it."

Chapter 11

The Trials

"Schedule change," I smiled at Bransen while my eyes returned to their more natural icy blue color. "I had Doc make the announcement that trials will begin in the morning."

Bransen walked over to the couch and I scooted over for him to have a seat. "I thought you were going to wait two more weeks?" he questioned as he sat down beside me.

"I don't think we can put it off any longer. Everyone should continue with their training, but I don't want to risk an unknown spy coming aboard the ship." I felt the heat from Bransen's body warming my side.

A crease appeared in his forehead as his eyebrows tried to pinch together. It was the look that twisted his face when his mind was working too hard on something.

"You're going to be scanning their minds then?" There was too much worry in his eyes.

"Yes," I said as I gave a short nod.

Bransen's eyes seemed to darken. I could see the tension stretch out across his body as he shifted his weight. "I don't like this, Khore. Not one fucking bit!" His voice sounded short and angry as the images played across his mind behind his eyes.

"Twist and Rift will accompany you for protection," he said resolutely.

"Actually, I was hoping you could all come with me." I stood and started pulling off my shirt as I walked toward the bed. "TK, please wake me at 3am. GENTLY!" I tugged the laces at the waist of my pants and let them fall to the floor.

"3am?!? What is going on Khore?" He asked as he stood and walked toward the bed.

"I don't know," I said and crawled into bed as he stood there staring at me.

"I'm sorry Bransen, I know I should have talked to your first, but we are out of time. When I folded Doc and Chris back to the complex I felt something. It was like a darkness slithering up my spine." The memory made me shiver. "Something is coming and we have to get them out of there now and we can't afford to bring in any spies. Please trust me on this."

"I do trust you," he said, taking off his shirt exposing his muscled chest and abs. He unfastened his pants at the hip and slid the fabric down his legs. Pulling back the covers, he climbed into bed and leaned into me giving my shoulder a subtle nudge. "So what's the plan?"

We worked out the details before Bransen spoke.

"COM. Ship-wide. Attention all team members. You will transport to Cargo Bay 15 at 0400 hours. I repeat, all team members are to be geared up and ready in Cargo Bay 15 at 0400 hours."

"TK, please wake everyone at 0300 hours, GENTLY," Bransen said as he situated the covers around himself.

"TK, lights," I commanded as we leaned in for a kiss. I turned on my side and pulled Bransen's arm around me. It was going to be a busy morning.

It seemed I had barely closed my eyes when a loud voice shattered my dreams. "Get your asses up! Wake up!"

White light flooded the room as pain shot through my eyes. Bransen made a little grunt as his arm gave me a gentle squeeze.

"Are you bitches getting up?" TK's voice blasted at us again.

"YES TK! We're getting up!" I snapped back. Throwing off my covers I begrudgingly slid out of Bransen's embrace and stood on shaky, tired legs. My body hadn't quite come to life yet and was resisting me.

Bransen sat up, crawled out of the bed, and trudged to the food dispenser.

"TK, Coffee," was all he said, leaning against the wall.

A red flash peaked through the edge of the panel before it opened. The smell of coffee lured my body over to Bransen. Grabbing the mug from the tray, I brought it to my lips to give it a casual breath of air hoping to cool the surface. I needed the caffeine but blew again, deciding the pain from the molten liquid wasn't quite worth the result.

I took a quick sip, letting the bitter liquid fire bite against my tongue. It had been my morning ritual since arriving at the complex. After enough pain, numbness would set in and I would be able to swallow my coffee in proper doses that would rouse my mind.

As the caffeine took hold of my nervous system my eyes began to appreciate the view. We stood naked, nursing our mugs side by side.

"TK, 2 more coffees, please." Bransen commanded as I kissed his cheek.

"Morning," I slurred with my sleep tinged voice. "TK, replace the bath with a four person shower."

We watched as the black and white marbled rippled and morphed into a silver color and reform, creating the new floor and walls. The liquid metal surged into its new shape and solidified to a black and white marble décor.

"I need to shower. Care to join me?" My eyes lingered on the pale grey flecks in his eyes before roaming down his muscled body. 'If only we had more time,' I thought. I felt a slight pulse in my balls and brought my eyes back to Bransen's smiling face.

Pulling Bransen by the hand we entered the shower that, only moments ago, had been our Jacuzzi-style bathtub. The hot jets of water blasted off the previous days sweat and twenty minutes later we were out of the shower, dried, and dressed. Showers always seemed so much faster. Albeit soothing, a shower just doesn't provide the same comfort as lounging in a nice hot bath.

I sped myself around the room, picking up our coffee tray and placing it in the food dispenser return slot. Nervous energy pushed me through the room, picking up our clothes and tidying up before I was left with nothing else to do. I stood, picking at my fingernails, staring at the floor and trying not to think about the work ahead.

"Why don't you come over here and take a break before we go?" Bransen patted the cushion beside him on the couch.

We had fifteen minutes before it would be 0400 hours and I couldn't think of any place I'd rather be as I sat beside him and leaned against his muscled warmth. I could still smell the slight cologne of soap on his flesh as I nuzzled into his neck. His arm slid down from the lip of the couch and squeezed my shoulder, causing me to jump. My head snapped up into his jaw causing his teeth to click.

"Ow!" Bransen piped, rubbing his jaw. "Jumpy?" Bransen's asked though now his tongue sounded too big for his mouth.

"I'm sorry. I'm nervous." Leaning over, I kissed where my head had jacked his jaw.

"Good, you're supposed to be. Relax," he said, noting the worry in my eyes. "It'll be okay."

His words comforted me because he believed them. I don't know where someone finds that confidence, but I needed to find some of my own, and soon. This nervousness was not going to be productive. I glanced over to the clock next to the bed. We had five more minutes.

"Well, let's do this," I said, pushing myself up from the couch.

Bransen stood beside me and gave the command. "TK, transport us to Cargo Bay 15"

The white flash of light deposited us in the cargo bay before the rest of the team arrived. They were all dressed, awake and waiting.

I let the silence of the room surround me as I pulled in the energy around and through me. My eyes blazed icy blue as an indigo and white fire erupted along my skin. With a pulse of energy and concentration I transported Doc and Chris from their bed in the complex to their bed aboard ship.

"COM, Doc and Chris. Go to med level 5 and remain on stand by. We may have casualties," I noticed all eyes were now on me. This had gotten their attention as much as the strange fire that rode across my body.

Bransen gave me a nod, "They know what to do."

I folded Twist and Rift to the bowels of the complex to complete their work.

Bransen explained. "Khore will be folding people, ten at a time, to this bay. He is going to scan their minds, checking for possible spies. Once cleared, TK will transport them to individual quarters aboard ship where they will remain confined. TK will be orienting them to the ship and encoding them with PDD's as we work."

"What the hell is going on, Bransen?" Neek shifted his weight, sounding a bit too agitated. "We don't get any weapons?"

"TK, knife. Eight inches long with a five inch handle." The knife emerged from the floor like a piece of buoyant wood might find its way to the surface in a deep lake.

Instantly I took hold of it with my mind, sending it in a speeding blur, stopping an inch from Neek's left eye. I let it twist and turn, causing the light to play along the shiny blade poised to strike into his brain

"You'd give spies something to use against you?" I asked, before letting it fall to the floor. "TK, take the knife." It sank into the floor like a rock in quicksand.

"I see your point," Neek answered.

My voice sounded hollow as blue energy pulsed around me. "No guns, no weapons. Use the air around you and your minds. Use your abilities now to create a barrier around yourselves. Envision it like a force field nothing can penetrate. This 'should' cushion the blow of an attack."

Bransen added, "We are going to form an arch formation. Khore and I will be in the center. Sweed and Raven, I want you on our right. Dusty and Neek on our left. Khore is going to bring them in about ten meters ahead of us in a row of ten. Most of the complex's personnel should be asleep, except for a few guards, so this will be to our advantage," Bransen paused, "Take your positions."

I watched as they gathered around us in a half moon formation.

"TK, increase the cloak to maximum strength. I want all available power diverted to the cloak at the first sign of trouble. Oh, and don't be incinerating anyone.

"Yes, Khore," TK replied.   I was thankful for the lack of harassment.

"Let's begin," I said as ten sleeping bodies appeared on the floor ahead of us. I searched their dreaming minds as they roused from their sleep. I drifted along their memories like the waves of a storm, catching glimpses of their lives.

"Clear," I spoke, and TK transported them to their new quarters.

We continued this for the next two hours, without incident. Many were apparently fond of sleeping nude. While the curve of flesh and furrow of muscle was a nice distraction, I couldn't let it keep me from the task at hand. I whisked them along their way to their new beds to minimize their embarrassment. It seemed to be going smoothly, and I felt the tension drop a few notches before I pulled in one of the final groups of ten. It was a mix of three standing security personnel and seven sleeping men.

I began searching their minds like I had the last two hundred, but was blocked. It was too late. The surprise showed in their expression as their eyes erupted with light like my own.

Instantly, three buffets of blue energy traveled from them toward us, throwing Sweed and Raven to the ground with a sickening crunch. I folded the remaining seven waking bodies to the infirmary. "Hold them!" I thought to Doc.

Another series of energy waves exploded from them, sending Bransen, Neek and Dusty flying backwards. The scream I heard from Bransen tore at my heart. He was hurt.

My anger flared with light. I was the only one who remained standing. They had hurt Bransen but I could feel him alive behind me against the cold floor.

I screamed as the rage took hold, sending out a blast, throwing them backwards. The light flared around my flesh as I advanced. They crawled away with broken bodies while sending buffets of energy in my direction.

I focused on the guard to the right sending his body into an internal blaze of fire, burning like a dried leaf floating into the air. The wall of red and orange crept across his skin as inhuman shrieks of anguish pierced the chaos.

I reached out my arm to focus the energy, lifting the remaining two into the air. Their eyes widened as I dived into their minds like a thousand spears.

"You will tell me," I yelled as I raped their thoughts without remorse. Like scraping ice from a window, I shaved the memories from them as they screamed in torment. I tore what they knew from their minds as trails of blood trickled from their eyes and nose. Their screams reverberated against the walls of the bay as I clutched their brains and spinal cords and crushed them. Finally, I let them fall to the floor like so much dead meat.

We were out of time. The Thorens were arriving at the complex and I folded the last forty-two of it's occupants to the bay. I let my mind sweep out amongst the crowd violently tearing through their most intimate and private thoughts.

There was a fourth spy and I folded him before me, letting him hover above the floor. I knew from the memories I had stolen, that he was the last. His eyes burst like cracked eggs as I tore through his mind. He was the one that was supposed to kill Bransen. Cold crept across my skin as I ripped his mind to shreds. He writhed, making frighteningly strangled sounds. I twisted him like a wash cloth and tore his body in half, sending it in opposite directions, splattering to the floor.

I swept across the onlooker's minds a little too harshly, watching the sea of horror gaze back at me.

"Clear," I said in a hollow voice and TK transported them to their new living units.

I folded the four piles of gore to the entrance of the complex for the Thorens to find. An explosion erupted in the bowels of the complex. They could have the useless pile of twisted metal and dead computer system. Twist and Rift had done their job well.

"TK, Transport all team members to Med Level 5."

"Yes Khore," the computer replied and they were whisked away instantaneously.

I remained standing in place.

"TK!" I snapped, "I said all!"

"I, I cannot transport you in your current state." TK stammered.

I let the energy roll off of me in layers trying to calm myself and the blue fire that danced across my skin faded to nothing. I took a deep breath and relaxed. Every muscle in my body ached as though stretched too tight, only now being able to expand to its regular state.

"TK. Med level 5 please," I asked. A white flash of light changed the scenery as I appeared in the medical facility. Doc and Chris were busy working to see that everyone was ok.

"How are they, Doc?" I asked.

Everyone stopped and stared back at me. They all looked to be fine, from what I could see. Bransen, Twist, Rift, Raven, Sweed, Dusty, Neek. They were all healthy and accounted for.

"What's wrong?!" I asked.

Bransen brought over a damp wash cloth and dabbed at my face, removing bits of dried blood and gore.

"What was that, Khore?" Bransen continued to wash away bits and chunks of the last spy that managed to land on my neck. "What did you do to them? What the hell was that!?!"

"I killed them." I didn't understand what he was asking me.

He continued to move the rub the cloth against my flesh clearing away the larger pieces of gore. He hand trembled against my skin as he worked down to a large gash on my arm. I hissed at the pain as the two met. He jerked back, watching the wound close with a blue glow, then busied himself with what was still stuck of me of the last traitor.

"A bullet to the head kills someone. I can't even describe what I saw you do. What the hell was that?" Bransen asked again, he was scared. Scared of me, and I couldn't quite understand what he found so terrible about what I had done.

"Oh," I paused. "I raped their minds and destroyed their bodies. The last one was supposed to kill you. That won't happen now."

The tone of my voice was even and sure. It was almost like I was hearing someone else speak the words. There was no regret and no remorse. I had done what needed to be done.

"But... you were so brutal." A shudder passed through Bransen's body.

"What would you have had me do, Bransen? The Thorens were knocking on the front door of the complex and we were out of time. I couldn't take the chance that they might hurt us again. I couldn't let them transmit our location to the Thorens. What was I supposed to do? Kill them slowly?" I was quickly losing my composure, feeling the anger boil up inside me. Why was he asking me this?

As I explained I sensed Doc moving up behind me. He had a syringe in his hands.

"Don't do it Doc. No drugs," I said coldly as I mentally ripped the syringe from his hand, sending it into the wall across the room in an explosion of glass. I backed away from them and felt a slight outrage quickly building in my chest. 'How could they not trust me?'

"What the hell is wrong with you people?!" I yelled. I could feel the blaze returning to my eyes.

"Back off everyone. Calm down!" Bransen commanded. "I'm worried about you Khore."

"Well don't be. I'm fine," I yelled, pulling back the glow.

"Hell hath no fury like a parent protecting their child," TK's voice interrupted.

The sharp intake of breath made it sound as though the entire room had just inhaled. They stared at me in stunned silence.

"You're pregnant?" Bransen asked, wide eyed.

"Yes... and so are you Bransen." TK answered for me.

Doc feinted.

"Well for shit sake! We're pregnant and he passes out," I sighed and wanted to cry but for once was grateful that I couldn't feel anything.

"Why didn't you tell me!?" Bransen demanded.

"Would you have agreed to my plan if you had known?" I asked.

"No..." Bransen answered, looking defeated. "I suppose I wouldn't have."

"Well then, now you know," I answered.

Chapter 12

And Baby Made Four

I watched the color drain from Bransen's face.

"Uh, maybe you should sit down." I grasped Bransen's hand and led him to a nearby bed.

"We're pregnant. We're pregnant? Doc? Where's Doc?" Bransen eyes were searching the room for Doc.

"Okay everyone, you're clear to go." Chris was shooing them out of the room as he knelt on the floor, trying to revive Doc.

"We're both pregnant?" Bransen was rambling.

"It's okay," I said, trying to calm Bransen.

I hadn't been any more prepared than he was when I heard the news. Even a couple of days ago, when TK blurted it out to me, I didn't exactly 'feature' the idea. After TK scanned the embryo and confirmed it was Bransen's, I relaxed somewhat. That was until the thoughts of midnight feedings and diaper changes started to flood my mind. What the hell did I know about raising a child; and now two?

"Come back to me," I said as I leaned in and kissed him gently on the cheek.

Bransen's eyes focused on my smiling face. "So we're both pregnant..." he said as a goofy grin curved his lips.

"Yep. We're going to be fathers. How about we go back to our quarters and I get cleaned up? I could use some breakfast, too. I'm starving," I said, pulling him to his feet.

"Time to feed the boys!" Bransen announced, smiling as wide as I had ever seen him.

"Chris, send up the Doc in about an hour, 'eh? He is okay isn't he?" I asked.

"Yeah, he's okay. We didn't exactly get a lot of sleep before we were transported over here last night," he said with a sly grin.

"TK. Please..."

"Double check the load capacity on the power lift?? Widen the doorways?" TK interrupted. "Daddy Khore... has such a sweet ring to it."

I clenched my jaw. "Go piss up a rope, TK. Transport us to our quarters. NOW!"

A long whistle echoed through the room. "If you're this bitchy after a couple days of pregnancy, I just can't WAIT until next month!"

"NOW, TK!" I yelled.

A white flash of light enveloped us and we were back in our living area.

The truth was, I was edgy. Had we not left the complex when we did, many would have died. I was quickly becoming a burden and savior to these people, and I didn't like it. With all the wonders of this place, a piece of me still missed the caverns and forest of home. I felt guilty for building a new family so quickly after having lost my previous one. There were still days when I opened my eyes in the morning wondering if I had the strength to push on. I reminded myself of the cardinal rule that had gotten me this far. "It is what it is. Accept it. Life goes on." My feelings of betrayal didn't diminish though. It's not supposed to be easy to leave the past behind is it?

"I'm going to clean up real quick," I said, selecting a fresh set of clothes from the dresser against the wall. "TK, subdued lighting."

I relished dimmed lighting. It reminded me of the dawn when I was back at the caverns. It had been my private time. The walls of the shower shut me away from everyone and everything as I let the warm water beat against my sore muscles. I stretched out my arms against the wall, letting my head hang between them. My mind wandered as streams of water found new paths down my body and into the drain.

I stood, oblivious, in the spray of water when it struck. There was a slight push of darkness. I shifted my weight to my left leg, watching the rivers change path and work their way down my thighs and calves. I shook off the cold dark feeling and went back to my sweet oblivion surrounded by the hiss of water.

I stood there in my own world when a scene flashed across my mind. It was darkness, complete darkness, but something with sharp, cut, jagged edges shown through it. I could see faint lines travel along the shape of it as it shifted. It was alive!

"BRANSEN!!!" I yelled. The cold of the image left me huddled in the corner of the shower for warmth. I was freezing and terrified! I could feel the involuntary spasms of my muscles shiver in some feable attempt to warm my body. My quiet place of paradise had somehow become a torment.

The next thing I knew Bransen was carrying me to our bed and tucking the covers around me.

"COM Doc: I need you here, NOW," he yelled. His words were urgent, but he seemed so distant. It was as though someone were screaming in the next room.

I was so cold. I curled into a ball, eyeing the shadows of the room. They were in the shadows. I could still feel their touch.

"They're coming!" I yelled as my muscles twisted from the burning cold.

"The baby is fine," I heard Doc say.

"Thank the gods," Bransen's voice replied.

I opened my eyes to find myself wrapped in too many blankets on our bed. Bransen's fingers were working their way across my scalp, combing my hair with his fingertips. The idea of being tied down made me stretch out to see how much I could move.

"He's coming to," Doc said.

Coming to? I was waking up. What the hell?

"Sorry Doc, that hour went by quicker than I expected," I said, trying to make my words clear behind the blanket of sleep.

They were silent for too long. Something was definitely wrong.

"What? Did I over sleep?" What the hell was wrong with these people?

"Khore, that was 18 hours ago. We almost lost you. I still don't quite know how you're alive right now." Doc's face wore the lines of exhaustion.

Bransen stared down at me. He remained silent and it worried me.

"What happened??? I was in the shower," I began, when the image flashed through my mind.

"They're coming!" I yelled as I tried to crawl away from them, banging my head against the wall. I was terrified and didn't know why. The feeling was instant and so so cold. It gripped me like a vice as my breath sped and heart felt as though it might burst through my chest. Then, as quickly as it came, it was gone. It seemed more like a half forgotten nightmare.

"Damn it's hot in here!" I said, noticing the trickles of sweat and shine of Doc and Bransen's face.

"What are you trying to do? Cook me?" I asked.

"TK, what is the temperature in here?" I asked.

"125 degrees Fahrenheit, ice queen," came the reply.

"What the hell! TK, adjust environmental to 68 degrees Fahrenheit, please. What is wrong with you people?" I stared back at them.

"It wasn't a dream, was it?" I said, already knowing the answer.

Bransen shook his head. "No."

The water in the shower, as well as the liquid metal around it, was frozen in mid stream. The black and white marbled wall of the shower was frosted to a grey color, creeping out in random patterns. I scanned it with my mind. The sub atomic particles hadn't just slowed, they had stopped. They were frozen in place, creating the hardest and yet the most fragile substance. I sped the particles heating them with my mind until they became pools of black silver sludge. Increasing their speed even more, they turned into the liquid metal that composed the most base element of the ship.

"Who is coming, Khore?" Bransen asked.

I grasped at the fleeting image, but I didn't really want to remember.

"They call themselves the Kotan. That is all I know." I shivered at the memory.

I draped my fingertips along Bransen's cheeks, letting them slide to his shoulder. I saw him grimace as he jerked back like I had burned him.

"Doc?" I asked, looking in his direction.

"Show him, Bransen," Doc answered.

Bransen gently lifted the left side of his shirt, showing me dead white flesh where normally bronze skin stretched across his abdomen. The grayish white impression was outlined in a deep red. I sat up as Bransen continued raising his shirt, displaying more impressions against the right side of his chest. The tissue damage must have been massive for it not to have been repaired yet.

I looked into his eyes. "Bransen?" I was too ashamed to ask.

"It happened when he carried you to bed," Doc answered my unspoken question.

My heart ached. The last thing I ever wanted to do was hurt him, and there was the proof of it across his body. Tears filled my eyes at the very thought of it. I drew in energy and placed my palm over his heart.

"I'm so sorry," I said as I took hold of the energy within his body.

My palm erupted in fiery blue light as cell by cell I concentrated on the damage. Each cracked frozen membrane was repaired and brought to life. Like a fall wind across a field of wheat, the color surged back to bronze across his abdomen. I warmed the remaining damaged muscles and nerves as they sparked back to life. Bransen moaned and threw his head back as if in ecstasy, but I knew that the painful sensation would not bring about any passion or the exquisite release our normal sex play included. Removing my hand from his chest I pulled him into me and I tightly wrapped my arms around him.

"I'm sorry, Bransen," I whispered in his ear.

"You don't have anything to apologize for. I love you," Bransen whispered back.

I pulled back. "I love you, too."

I yawned loudly and settled back into the bed. I wasn't sure how long I would be able to stay as I began to feel the cold pull again.

I spoke quickly, feeling another pulse of cold rush through me. "Bransen, I don't think I have long before they pull me back so please listen. Try to keep my little problem a secret, if possible. I don't know how long I will be frozen, but for the god's sake don't bury me. Push everyone to learn the ship's systems as fast as they can."

"I will." His voice shook as his eyes filled with tears.

"Don't worry about me, Bransen. Bransen Junior and I will be just fine," I smiled, patting my belly.

"Give me a kiss to come back to?" I said, pushing myself up.

Bransen leaned into me as our lips met. His warm sweet lips gripped and pulled at mine. Kissing him was like touching my soul to his. It felt like I was complete in a way I hadn't been before. I loved him. In the past, each time I had allowed myself to love, it had been special. Each person I let into my heart was been special. I loved them in different ways. They were very different people.

Bransen is the other half of my soul. I don't remember it happening, but it was true. He is the other half of who I am now, and who I will become in the future. I knew now that I could never survive the exquisite anguish that would mirror this love if I ever lost him.

We separated as I lowered myself back into the bulk of covers. I didn't want to leave yet, but I could feel them rising through my mind. The cold was beginning to grip me and caused my breath to sputter.

"Bransen," my voice shuddered.

"Yes, Khore?" he answered.

My mouth moved but I was having a hard time pushing air out of my lungs. I took in a deep breath. "The enemy of your enemy is not always your friend."

The cold stole me into a frozen darkness. I seemed to be swimming around in the void. I was no place at all. The lack of feeling overwhelmed me. There was nothing.

"Who are you?" I sent the thought outward. There was no answer. I concentrated and sent it with more intensity. "Who are you?"

The darkness swirled around me and through me as though I had no substance at all. I don't suppose I did. My body lay frozen in the ship while my consciousness had been pulled here alone. Maybe they could not understand me.

I formed my thoughts and amplified them, screaming into the void. "WHO ARE YOU!?"

"SILENCE!" A wave of destruction pulsed through me the likes of which I had never felt before. Thousands of voices erupted in my mind in unison.

It had somehow weakened me. I didn't know what would be left of me if I endured too much more of that torment. I rested and gathered strength. I couldn't feel the passage of time and it worried me. How long had I been here? I thought for a bit. Maybe it wasn't the words that were the problem. I had understood their demand of silence. Perhaps it was the question.

"What are you?" I sent.

"We are Kotan," the chorus of thoughts replied.

"Who are the Kotan," I thought.

The chorus replied "We are one of many."

It seemed this was a collective conscience. So many minds merged for a common purpose. Individuality must be inconceivable to these things.

"Who leads you?" I thought to it.

"You," replied the chorus.

What the hell? I wasn't leading these things. I didn't command it to steal me away from Bransen. If I was the leader then they should follow my commands.

"Stop!" I sent the thought but there was no answer.

"Show me the Kotan," I thought to it.

My thoughts burst with vivid clarity. In my mind I saw a mass of black crystals. They weren't so much black as they had no color. The glimmer of distant stars framed its edges, but there was no reflection. Each snowflake like figure seemed to absorb the light around it. It was a collection of crystals pointing outward in all directions from a central mass completely devoid of color. The edges were only perceptible against the backdrop of stars. It was beautiful as it rolled like a tumbleweed through space.

"What do you want?" I thought to it. Again there was no answer. It was beginning to piss me off! Again, maybe it was the question.

"What do you seek?" I asked.

"FOOD," the chorus replied.

I was afraid to ask.

"Show me food," I sent.

Again my mind exploded with a new image. It was a planet in the neighboring solar system. I watched as the swarm of Kotan dropped from the sky and plunged into the planet below. There were too many to count.

The Kotan dotted the surface of the planet like a ferocious hive of stinging bees. Ripples of white energy worked along the peaks of the crystal talons to its core. They were only about a 100 feet in width and height. There were so many, it reminded me of locust in a field. In a matter of hours, the once lush planet had become a simple rock in space, floating around the neighboring star. They didn't simply devour the energy from the soil. They absorbed it all.

"Kotan, what is leader?" I asked.

"LEADER IS FOOD," the chorus answered.

I was the bright petals of the flower that drew the bee. Intergalactic bugs had somehow caught my scent and were working their way toward Earth. Great, Just fucking great!

Chapter 13

Home Away From Home

"TK" I asked.

"Yes sweet Bransen?"

Damn, I wish Khore could fix that fucking computer! I wiped the tears from my eyes. "COM. Shipwide."

"All personnel will report to Cargo Bay 15 at 1600 hours. EVERYONE is to attend."

I had almost forgotten Doc was still standing there. "Doc, I need you to find out what is going on with Khore, and stop whatever is happening to him. Learn the function of every piece of equipment in the med bay if you haven't. Sleep until 1530 hours if you must, but make it happen. You may go."

Doc's bloodshot tired blue eyes blinked at me as though my head were spinning in place. It had not been the best day for him either.

"I need to transport Khore to the med facility." He was using his concerned voice, and its deep timber did not sooth me.

I nodded to the Doc before looking away from him to where Khore lay. The covers I had piled on him before were a chaos of frozen fabric.

"This is to stay between us, Doc. TK, transport Doc and Khore to Med level 5." Seconds later they were gone.

My eyes burned and it felt like my stomach was eating away at itself. I had gone too long without sleep, but couldn't comprehend lying in our bed without him. The room felt so empty. The deafening silence reminded me of places I had buried the dead.

"TK, extend the couch 2 meters in length. I will also need a pillow and blanket."

The couch reverted to liquid metal and extended its silvery fluid before solidifying with a folded blanket and pillow on its grey cushions.

"TK, wake me at 1400 hours," I said as I made a bed of the couch, pulling the blanket over me. I gave the pillow a few punches, venting anger more than fixing its shape for sleep. I lay there, pissed off and worrying. The more indestructible Khore seemed, the more I gave him my heart. It had been so easily and completely given when I thought nothing could touch him.

"Bransen, time to wake up," TK announced. "Wake up, you're going to be late for your own assembly."

TK was being a bit more gentle than the last time and it surprised me. I lay there and grunted my response.

"Get your ASS UP!" TK's voice boomed.

I swung my legs to the floor, preparing to cuss that damn computer but decided against it. I just didn't need any more aggravation right now, and instead trudged over to the food dispenser.

"Two coffees. Black." The blink of red peaked from the edges before I realized I had requested one for Khore. My heart ached as I looked back at the bed, wishing I would see his blue wolf's eyes staring back at me.

I leaned against the wall as I sipped my coffee, waiting for my mind to clear. Once I Finished my coffee, I showered and dressed and found myself standing in the middle of our quarters alone. It was nearly time for the assembly to begin. Running a comb through my still damp blond hair, I pulled at the knots. I didn't want to be around anyone, but there was work to do.

"TK. Cargo Bay 15."

I had to admit, this was much more convenient that taking the lift in the complex. I arrived in the bay and it appeared nearly everyone was there. I watched as intermittent flashes brought in the last few stragglers.

"TK, what is the time?"

"1558 hours, Bransen"

"TK, how many are still not here, excluding Khore?" I growled out the question.

"Twenty-three are still not in attendance," came the reply.

"COM. Shipwide. Those who are not in Cargo Bay 15 in one minute will be escorted from the ship PERMANENTLY." I barked out the announcement. I was angry and everyone around me was going to bear the brunt of it. Several flashes brought the last few as some were still putting on clothes.

"Is everyone here, TK?" I asked.

"All required personnel are in attendance," TK announced.

"Listen up! You will ALL attend mandatory meetings, prepared and on time. Those of you who do not will be removed from this ship. If you fear you may forget, ask TK to give you a reminder. If you do not attend a mandatory meeting without a valid excuse you will be transported to my office and I will personally kick your ass off this ship."

Twist, Rift, Raven and the other team members had worked their way through the crowd and stood on either side of me during the announcement. I looked to Doc, and his expression told me Khore's condition had not changed.

"Starting now you will all associate yourself with Team One members. You all had your duties at the complex; it will not be any different here. Those of you who wish to work preparing meals may still do so. Those of you who wish to pursue a different interest may do so," I paused.

"TK, place all Team One members in pairs in the following pattern; perpendicular to myself, and eighty feet apart, thirty feet ahead of me. Dusty and Neek, Engineering. Raven and Sweed, Tactical. Rift and Twist, Weapons. Doc and Chris, Medical. Khore and myself will be Operations. Those of you who choose Service please stay where you are. You have five minutes to choose. TK, announce when 5 minutes have passed," TK transported them as I listed the names and designations.

"Yes, master," announced across the COM.

Several nervous laughs escaped the crowd as people diverted their eyes and moved through the bay. Most hadn't changed their duties but I did notice a few had ventured out for something new. My mind was glad. I wanted everyone to enjoy their work, but right now I wasn't happy and my heart wanted everyone else to feel as miserable as I did. I was being a hard core solid gold asshole and I didn't know if I could stop.

"Five minutes have passed, Bransen."

I looked at the three individuals who had moved to my side for the Operations group. Jake had been the first to approach. He was taller than most people, standing at 6'3" and was awkward looking. His nose was large and hooked and his hazel eyes seemed set too far apart. His jaw line rounded down his pasty white face to an almost undetectable chin. His head was topped with muddy brown hair that seemed to never have been introduced to a comb. It looked like the permanent home to some large rodent I hoped never to meet. His body was thin and lanky, making him appear even taller than he was. He had a warm heart and a sharp mind and I was glad he stood there.

Next to him stood Morland, more commonly known as 'Mouse.' He was even shorter than Khore, standing at 5'2". His small willowy frame reminded me of someone who had eaten only the least bit of food for the last century. He looked almost fragile. That he was able to walk up to me after my tirade impressed me. Mouse had earned his name from his shyness and from hardly ever speaking above a whisper. It had happened many times that Mouse would be in a room and, later, seem to have completely disappeared. He had large dark eyes, a small pointed nose, and pert thin lips. His pale skin seemed to make his dark brown shoulder length hair look almost black. He was so nondescript that I had a hard time remembering when he had joined us, but I was certain it wasn't more than a year ago.

Next to Mouse stood Kent. He was young, barely 180 years old, and eager to impress. He had joined us about six months ago after having been rescued during one of our better planned raids. He had been one of the Thorens' toys and, to hear him tell it, extremely popular. I later heard that this had not been because of his average endowments but, instead, due to his over achieving tongue. Kent had flawless olive skin and an almost too-perfect body. His 5'11 frame was packed with muscle, similar to my own. It was hard and defined, but not bulky. His dishwater blond hair feathered forward to his face and down to his neck. His deep green eyes were framed by long eyelashes that led to a strong straight nose. His plump lips were quick to smile and fit perfectly in his square jaw that ended at the dimple in his chin. He was handsome and he knew it. I was forever curbing the urge to push my fist into his face. He was a kind and jovial young man, but something about him aggravated me. He brought out that dark side of me that wanted to destroy an oddity of perfection that had no place in my world.

"You all have some balls coming over here," I growled.

"Yes, captain!" Kent and Mouse said in unison.

I squeezed my eyelids into slits. "Call me that again and I'll see to it what little manhood you possess is removed." I growled again.

Mouse looked like he could have crawled through the floor to escape while Kent looked like he may have just shit his pants. I could see the smirk on Jake's face out of the corner of my eye. It had been a running joke for the long timers. Tell the new meat that I insisted on being called captain and then watch me shred them when they did. It was an informal initiation into the family.

"Relax you two," I softened my voice, "and please call me Bransen." I smiled to let them know there were no hard feelings. Normally I would have laughed, but right now I just didn't have it in me.

The groups were almost evenly distributed. I was relieved that at least this part of my day had not been complicated.

"Team Leaders, I want you to assign separate systems to individuals or small groups. Those individuals will need to learn their assigned system and every facet of its operation and then transfer that knowledge to you. You will then transfer that information back to the rest of the members of your group."

I took a breath, letting what I was telling them sink in. I decided not to tell them about the Kotan just yet. I didn't know exactly what they were or if they were a threat. I let some of the harshness of my voice leak away and continued. "Look people, we need to know these systems backwards and forwards in case we are discovered by the Thorens. TK can't do all of the work, though I'm sure he'd tell you otherwise."

"You cut me, Bransen. You cut me deep!" TK interrupted, following with a quick raspberry.

I hate that computer. If I could find its electronic tongue and lips I'd nail them to the floor! I took another deep breath and continued.

"We will begin now and continue until 20:00 hours. Starting tomorrow we will study these systems from 08:00 hours until 20:00 hours every day. You have seven days to complete this task.

"Team Leaders will report to my office at 21:00 hours tomorrow and each day thereafter with a status report."

"TK, transport all but my group to their designated areas." The entire room emptied with a flash.

"Jake, you're in charge tonight. Assign yourself, Kent and Mouse each a separate system and we'll discuss your findings in the morning."

Jake nodded to me. "TK, transport Mouse, Kent and Jake to the operations room.

There was finally silence in the bay and I found myself hating it.

"TK, transport me to Khore."

I arrived in the room with Khore frozen exactly as he had been in our bed but now on the medical platform. Several silver thermal blankets had been placed over him but had failed in their purpose. The top most layers had already become dusted with frost. I noticed an extra bed had been placed in the room that wouldn't normally have been here. Doc must have instructed TK to add it and I'd have to make a point of thanking him later.

"TK, what can you tell me about Khore's condition?" I asked, while sitting on the bed across from him.

"He has stopped," TK replied. "Khore is in a form of stasis I have not encountered before. He has paused on a molecular level. Any further attempts to warm him will likely result in cell damage. Brain activity is at an elevated but steady rate."

"Come back to me, Khore," I whispered as the arch to the room formed.

"I thought I might find you here," Doc said in a quiet voice as he made his way past me to more closely inspect Khore. One of Doc's many new interns walked past the arch, stopped, with a look of horror on his face as the portal closed.

"Any status changes, TK?" Doc asked.

"No," was the simple reply.

"Continue running scans and notify me if there is any change." Doc sighed before settling in beside me on the bed.

"I thought I asked you to keep this quiet!" I felt my anger flaring.

"Since when was there ever a secret in the complex? Did you think it would be any different here?" Doc shifted his weight, aiming those all-knowing slate blue eyes at me.

"You could have transported in here," I said, beginning to wonder if it hadn't been deliberate.

"Yes. That would have been one option. What do you think would have drawn more attention? Me teleporting to a room not eight feet away, or walking through the door?" He continued to stare at me with his tired eyes. His logic was pissing me off.

"You can't do this to yourself again, Bransen. It wasn't your fault then, and it's not your fault now," he said in a hushed even tone. "Let it go."

I felt my skin flush at the memory and bristled against it. This was a low blow even for the Doc. He had no right!

"This isn't the same, Doc, and you fucking know it. He is so much stronger!" I was quickly losing control. I could feel my face flush and felt the temptation to rip his head off. I know he meant the best. He knew me better than anyone, but at the moment I wanted him to get the hell away from me.

"Oh?" he said standing. "I would have thought someone as old as you would have known better by now."

I stared at him as he walked through the newly formed arch and left me alone with my thoughts.

Damn him! Doc had been there when I watched the coma eat away at my son's body before time finally took him from me. He had been there the day I buried him. Doc let me cry on his shoulder after the news of Kelay's passing. He had become one of the few permanent fixtures in my unstable world and now I almost hated him for it.

A yawn broke my thoughts as I looked across the room again at Khore as he lay frozen. I breathed a deep sigh and lay back onto the bed. Pulling the covers around me, I situated myself so that if I woke I would see his face. It wasn't long before sleep pulled me to its familiar horrors.

The scene played across my mind like it did on so many nights. Torel had died giving birth to our son Vaden. Images of our son growing older stuttered like slides in my mind until the day of his first mission.

It had been a normal day, like any other. It was mid-summer, the season where the moon and sun shared the sky. The moon had been witness to the sunset hours ago and now shown alone in the night. The humidity seemed to capture the smell of the soil and plant life in the air as we made our way through the thick vegetation of the jungle that surrounded us. Our scouts had discovered a small group of Thorens and their human slaves performing some type of scientific study as they took samples of various plants and wildlife.

Our plan had been a simple one. Move in, liberate the humans, and kill the Thorens. My son Vaden had become impatient and was discovered before we were ready to spring our trap. A Thoren hit him with a wave of mental energy that caught his side, sending him to the ground. It turned from a simple extraction to a cluster fuck of mass chaos.

When the smoke cleared I found Vaden barely alive, lying on the ground in too much of his own blood. The energy blast hadn't done as much damage as the sharp rock that his head had struck when he fell. I never heard his voice after that day. He lingered for too long in the complex's medical facility before he finally passed.

I woke up with hot tears streaming down my face. The memory was fresh but fleeting in my mind. I glanced over at Khore, seeing him unchanged. How many times had I repeated this scene with Vaden? The memories were opening an old wound.

I sat up and looked more closely at Khore. He lay like a statue of cold. It isn't natural for a parent out live their child. It seemed like some kind of sick blasphemy that it could happened. I would not outlive Khore or our unborn children. They were going to live even if I couldn't. I would not be witness to this horror again.

"TK, time," I whispered as though I might wake Khore.

"It is 0400 hours, Bransen."

I pulled the covers from me and sat up in the bed, swinging my feet to the floor. I waited for sleep to leave me before standing.

"Come back to me, Khore," I whispered to his cold unmoving form. I hoped for movement but there was none.

I took a moment to memorize his face before exiting the room as an arch formed. The light was harsh and nearly blinded me as I made my way into the main medical bay. The arch closed behind me as my eyes adjusted to the bright white light. There were several sets of eyes staring at me. They quickly looked away, trying to appear busy with their work. Doc had apparently set his new interns into shifts. Smart man, that Doc. There were 20 to 25 people studying at different consoles in groups of four and five.

I decided I would take a more scenic route back to my quarters. I hadn't truly seen much of the ship other than the bay, hydroponics, and this med level. I exited through another archway into a long, curved hallway.

Looking in both directions, I could see the brightly lit hallway appeared to cut off about 100 meters in either direction. Looking over my shoulder, behind where the arch had been, was a large "M5A" in black print high on the blue and white split wall. The floor was white and seemed to swallow my steps like sand, but left no footprint.

I turned to my right and started down the hall. Except for the almost unperceivable hum of the ship, the brush of fabric was the only sound I heard. The walls were a weak shade of blue from the floor to shoulder height before being split by an eight inch black line. Above that, the white wall extended for another five feet. Black print, the same as I noticed before, indicated the level and function of each area and the presence of an entry arch.

I didn't remember the long drawn-out explanation TK had given about the layout of the ship. I remembered that sections of each level had been split like a pie cut into thirds but not much beyond on that. It had been too much information. It wasn't set up much differently than our old complex.

The print indicators helped paint my mental picture as the walls shifted from blue to red. I didn't remember TK explaining the medical level of the ship though everything from that day had seemed so much a blur.

"TK, what does the Red color of this area indicate?" I asked, noting the R5A indicator of an access arch.

"This is research level five, Bransen. The alcove to your left is a data access terminal and food dispensary station. The A indicates upper levels, above the ship's equator," TK informed me.

Paying closer attention to the inset arch and data panels on my left, I noticed that there were several food dispenser panels much like the one in our room. The inset arch was maybe only a foot deep, but eight feet high, rounded, and at least 20 feet wide. It was wide enough to stand eight men side by side.

I was still having problems grasping the layout of the ship, and it was nice, for a change, to have something else to occupy my mind.

"TK, what is on the level above us?" I asked.

"The levels are split above and below the equator of the ship. Levels above the equator, are labeled A, those below are labeled B. The level directly above this one contains living quarters, storage and ship bays," TK explained.

"TK? Weren't crew quarters on a separate level from ship bays before?" I was feeling a bit confused. I had studied the ship bays personally through the data access panel in our room. The idea of piloting one of smaller ships had made my flesh crawl with excitement.

"Yes, Bransen," he replied.

"But they're not now?" I asked

"No," TK answered.

I continued to walk down the quiet hallway. I was now in the research area of the med level. The silence was eerie. There was no sound other than the movement of fabric against itself as I made my way through the ship. It sent a chill up my spine. No silence of this sort had ever been a good thing. I felt my dark mood returning quickly. What the hell was happening. This wasn't what I remembered at all from our overwhelming orientation. How could the ship not be as it was before?

"Khore restructured the ship two days ago for better functionality," came the booming response. I hadn't spoken the question, but the answer had come just the same. TK's words sliced the silence around me so abruptly it made me jump.

"TK, can you read my thoughts?"

"Yes, Bransen," came the familiar voice. This time the answer entered my mind but not my ears.

"Why didn't you say something before?" I asked aloud.

"Two reasons. One, you didn't ask. Two, Khore told me not to," came TK's reply.

I felt a tinge of jealousy and anger. Why didn't he tell me?

"Because a direct downlink of all ship information would kill you." TK's voice invaded my mind. "You are not Thoren. You are not quite human any longer either. He instructed me to allow you to learn the systems of this ship naturally. You humans waste much space," TK answered.

"WHAT!? What do you mean we waste space?" I projected.

"Your minds. You use so little of your brain, and it leaks. Khore says you are not ready."

"BULLSHIT! TK, I want all ship information! I want it now!" I insisted.

"No," answered Khore, in my thoughts.

I fell to my knees. Hot wet tears streamed down my cheeks. I was elated to hear his voice if only in my mind.

"Khore?" I asked.

"Yes, Bransen. I'm here," came Khore's reply.

"Are you OK?"

"No, and you cannot help me. The Kotan are little more than bugs. They have but one purpose, to feed and multiply and my mind is trapped in their web. Have the team absorb what knowledge they can and pass it to those in their group. It hurts, Bransen. I love you. Please do as I ask." The sound of Khore's voice broke into pieces across my mind and he was gone.

Chapter 14

Descent

I was so happy to hear Khore's voice, but it hadn't exactly been good news. They had him, or at least the part of him that I thought mattered. I wiped my eyes as I rose from the floor. I started walking, again, through the hallway.

"TK, Khore said that I was not allowed to absorb all ship information?" I asked aloud.

"Yes, Bransen, that is what Khore instructed, and what you just heard. It's for your own safety. It would never have been allowed even if he had not stated it. I'm not allowed to harm you or do anything that might, as a result of my actions, cause you harm," TK answered.

"Sounds like a lot of double talk to me," I huffed.

"Sucks to be you!" TK quipped.

"Maybe, maybe not," I answered.

"TK, Khore said that the Kotan are coming. Have you any records of such a race?" I asked.

"No, Bransen."

"Have you detected anything moving in this direction?"

"Yes, Bransen. There are approximately 32,295,185 objects coming in this general direction at this moment. Meteorites, debris, asteroids, and a very large concentration of objects on the edge of this solar system."

"TK, the large concentration of objects, what are they?"

"Unknown."

"Are they heading in our direction?"

"The objects are moving from the remains of the previous planet and are now moving toward the fifth astral body in this solar system," TK answered.

"Did it NOT occur to you that these might be the Kotan?" I snapped, quickly losing my temper. "And what do you mean 'remains' of the previous planet?"

"Weeellllll excuuuussssse me! I have no reference point to say what might or might not be the Kotan, though these objects do seem to be moving with some form of intelligence. They have just altered their course since entering this solar system. From this recent course change there is an 83% probability they will continue from planet to planet until they have arrived at this one," TK snapped at me.

"You said that they were now heading for the fifth planet? What happened going to the planets between that and the other planets?"

"Their current orbits place them at a greater distance than the fifth planet," answered TK

"TK, I want you to give me all command and operations information. Download it to my leaky brain." I commanded.

"I'm sorry Bransen, Khore's orders were clear about downloading ship information to your mind," TK answered.

"Khore said you were not allowed to give me all ship information. He did not say you couldn't give me parts of it," I smirked at the thought.

There was a moment of silence. "Agreed," TK finally replied.

Images flashed through my mind as I saw the intricacies of ship systems and how they interacted. It was so much information I found myself squeezing my eyes shut in a weak attempt to avert sensory overload. I was lost in numbers and images, feeling them pile over my mind, threatening to spill out like from a bowl of water. When I thought there couldn't possibly be any more information, it continued to push and push. The saying "Pounding ten pounds of shit in a five pound bag" came to mind as my world spun.

"Complete," was the last word I heard before feeling the cool floor slam against my body.

"Welcome back, Captain Dumbass," came TK's voice.

I opened my eyes. I was happy the lighting was lower than the brightness of the hallway I had just been in. I had passed out and been transported here. I felt the information surge through my mind. I now knew every bypass and energy flow as different systems went on and off line during almost instantaneous repair. It was deafening and made me dizzy. I groaned.

"TK, is there anything we can do to cut down on the background noise in his mind?" Doc asked from 1.3 meters from my position. *OUCH. Too much information. Weight 183 pounds, height 5'9, Hair Blond, age approximately 420 years. He lied to me!*

Every miniscule piece of data concerning the Doc was racing through my mind. Facts were filling my head faster than I could comprehend them. It was a jumble of noise and it was driving me insane. It was like listening to music so loud all you heard was static! Then suddenly it all stopped.

"Bransen? Can you hear me?" I heard Doc's voice as he walked around from behind where I lay, coming into view.

"What happened?" I asked.

The look on Doc's face was not encouraging. He looked worried, and he looked pissed. It was the look my father had when he found me in the forest as a child. He had taken a nap and I had gone wondering and had gotten lost. I don't remember seeing anyone so happy and angry at the same time. I also remember getting the beating of my life shortly after returning home. Well, 'Welcome Back!'. I only hoped this time it would end less painfully.

"What were you thinking, Bransen? You nearly killed the rest of the team, and destroyed the ship," He was in a huff though the creases in his forehead had started to smooth. He was happy I was awake.

I remembered now. I had instructed the ship to download ship information to team members according to their area of responsibility. I also remember accidentally powering up weapons and nearly disabling the cloak before TK's systems shut down the process. I had leaked. Random thoughts became commands direct to the ship's computer. Millions of details and systems flooding in and out of my mind had been too much.

"I'm sorry, Doc. Khore talked to me. I heard him. Did you know the ship was telepathic? They're hurting him, Doc. The Kotan are coming! They're eating whole worlds!" I had a hundred things to say and my lips were barely able to keep up. I felt like I was crawling out of my skin.

"Shhhhh, listen for a moment," Doc hushed me. "TK, explain to him what has happened."

"You cheated," TK answered.

"The details, TK, damn!" Doc shouted.

A long sigh sounded through the room. "You asked for operations and command system information to be absorbed. I performed your request. After you had operations information, you circumvented security protocol, pulling in the rest of the ships systems, justifying that they were needed for operations. Basically you raped me. I feel so violated! (sniff, sniff)"

"Cut the drama, TK," Doc grumbled. "Basically you have been in contact with the Thoren science systems since you passed out. Or at least TK has been. They've been insisting on face to face communication for the last three days and we aren't going to be able to stall them any longer. TK, only acknowledge verbal commands from Bransen and cut off all but basic communications between his mind and your systems."

"Agreed," was TK's response.

The low roar of my mind calmed. There were a hundred different thoughts buzzing around like flies but they were more manageable than I had expected. My training with Khore had helped more than I had realized.

"How is the Team, Doc?" I asked, sitting up in bed.

"They are doing well. You're contact with Kelay at the time of Khore's conception, and then again when Khore mingled with Dusty, is the only thing that saved you, but we can discuss that later," Doc said, eyeing me as I hopped off the bed.

Seeing me sway, Doc was quick to grab my arm. I was dizzy for a moment but it passed.

"It's okay, Doc. I got it now," I reassured him.

"TK, Command Level 1," I thought, seeing the flash transport me to the command deck.

"COM, Shipwide. All team members transport to Command Level 1 immediately," I announced.

I was standing on the command deck that floated in the center of the massive command station. Almost instantly I watched as Dusty and Neek were transported to the propulsion and power regulation station on my lower left. Sweed and Raven appeared in a flash at the tactical station to my lower right. Twist and Rift appeared to my upper left on the weapons platform. Doc and Chris appeared on my upper right at the communications station.

Every station had been built for two, and I missed my other half as I sat down in front of my console. "Please be seated," I commanded. Each sat at their station, pulling the access terminal before them into place.

"TK, open ship operations to my mind, limiting it to only essential system; Propulsion, Tactical, Weapons, Communications, and Environmental."

The information flooded my mind but was subdued. Concentrating, I could single out smaller pieces of the noise. It was disorienting, but was becoming easier to handle.

"Let's get airborn, gentlemen," I announced.

The command deck was phenomenal. A 360 degree virtual display surrounded us as we hovered at the core. On all sides I could see rock and the land outside of us. Altering the view, I could see past the stone that encased us into the atmosphere and beyond. It was more than a panoramic view. It was three dimensional in every detail, as if in the center of a transparent sphere, looking out.

"Activate the displacement cloak," I commanded.

I could see the stone and earth on the surface of the ship as we hollowed out our space within it. It looked like a bubble floating in water that was actually rock around us.

"Dusty, Neek, get us out of this rock and don't take your time. They may not be able to see the ship, but they will definitely notice a huge hole appearing out of no where. Take a route behind the moon and match its orbit."

The ship rose as stone and earth seemed to crumble off the ship. We lifted into the night, before traveling at unknown speeds through the atmosphere and into space, past the Sphere Major. The point of our raindrop-shaped ship led the way as we came about behind the moon.

Neek answered, "We are in position." His muddy brown eyes looked out in wonder. You could hear the awe in his voice.

"Pretty fucking sweet, ain't it!" TK blurted.

I noticed Dusty give Neek's thigh a little squeeze as they smiled at one another. Raven's deep black eyes just stared. His white skin and dark features seemed to contrast against the black field of stars. Sweed didn't seem to be taking it as well as some of the others. His color had changed to a sickly green.

"You okay over there, Sweed?"

He was breathing quickly but finally answered. "I'm afraid of heights," he said very quietly as he white-knuckled the base of his seat.

"Let go of your seat, Sweed," I commanded.

He sat in place, arms flexing to get a better hold, shaking his head back and forth.

"TK, transport Sweed one meter to the right of his current position," I commanded.

A white flash took him from his chair as he floated in place, flailing his arms and legs. He was hollering as though he had been splashed with icy water. We all watched as he finally calmed down and just floated in place, regaining his composure. I couldn't help but laugh.

"You cannot fall here, Sweed. You'll be okay. Put him back, TK," I ordered, still chuckling.

"Yes, Bransen," and with a flash Sweed was back in his chair, looking relieved. I still had to chuckle as I noticed his left hand reaching out to Raven's for comfort. What surprised me more was that Raven actually gave it to him. Maybe Raven was coming around after all. Who'd have thought being dunked in a shit tank would have such a positive affect on someone.

Rift and Twist sat staring at the view. The starlight played along Rift's auburn hair as he leaned into his companion. Twist jumped from the sudden contact but you could see him warm into the gentle pressure.

Doc gaped as a giggle escaped Chris. Chris' green eyes glimmered with excitement while it looked like Doc was preparing for his first coronary.

"It's so small!" the Doc gasped referring to Earth.

"That's not what you were yelling last night!" TK snapped.

"Bite me!" Doc shot back.

"Yep, that was one of the phrases! Save it for your office though, hot stuff, I don't want that mess on my console," TK's replied.

The rest of us were in hysterics. Sometimes, I was thankful for TK's attitude. It definitely helped to ease the tension of the moment. The noise dwindled down to sporadic giggles as we regained our composure.

"Chris, I want you to triangulate Keelon's position as soon as we get a reply. I want to know EXACTLY where he is. Patch the coordinates to my terminal." I said, glancing at Chris.

"Move us in front of the moon. I want a clear shot, Neek. Twist, I want him targeted as soon as the coordinates are known. Rift, be prepared to cover our ass. Dusty, make sure that cloak comes back online as soon as possible if we fire. I don't want to stick around and be anyone's target," I ordered.

"Communication will be telepathic if we establish communications with Keelon."

"Chris, begin a transmission on all frequencies, voice only," I commanded.

"Keelon, Leader of the Thoren people, The Kotan are coming to devour this planet and everything in their path. I would fight against these creatures, but I do not have the time to battle two enemies. I would like to reach some sort of agreement. I await your reply," *End Transmission*

We sat in silence for several long minutes before receiving an answer.

A three dimensional image formed ahead of us. It was transparent but not completely devoid of shape and color. "I would see the faces of those who stole the Cystos before continuing further." The image was of an older man of 60th age. I could not comprehend the passage of time that this thing before us had been witness to, but I also doubted this was Keelon. A vain megalomaniac, so bent on living forever, would never let himself age like this.

I stood at my station.

Chris: Open the signal video and audio.

"I am Bransen, Captain of the Battlecruiser Cystos. Let's dispense with the games, shall we? I am well aware you are not Keelon," I replied.

The image shifted. Before us now sat a much younger looking man of maybe 21st age. He had long black curly hair that cascaded down his sides and hung to his knees. His icy blue eyes glowed with power. His nose was thin, leading to even thinner lips which curved into his pointed spear-like jaw. His skin was almost a blue white in color that stretched across his strong lithe body. He wore a white opalescent garment that gaped at the chest and billowed across his ivory muscle. It was gathered at the waist then continued to his feet. He possessed a demon like beauty.

"Indeed," Keelon's low timbered voice cut through the silence. "I had hoped to see specimen 143977."

"If you are referring to Khore, he has other duties to attend to." I hoped the pain I felt didn't betray me.

Chris! Where are those coordinates!

I'm sorry, Bransen, they're bouncing the signal all over hell.

FIND HIM!

"So then, are you prepared to return our property?" Keelon grinned.

"You're more than welcome to come aboard any time you like, Keelon," I smiled back.

"Try it, Keely boy, and I'll BBQ your wrinkled ass!" TK all but yelled.

TK! NOT NOW!

The image of Keelon doubled over with laughter.

WHERE ARE THOSE COORDINATES, CHRIS!?

"Talp and Feril were always the tricksters," Keelon said, calming himself. "I assume then that no Human or Thoren of pure blood may set foot on the ship then. No matter."

I've almost got them.

"We're wasting time, Keelon," I stated.

"Time is all we have now, Bransen," Keelon answered. "Our scientists have gleaned enough genetic material to advance us another hundred thousand years. We will find another planet and let the Kotan have their way with this world."

The transmission is originating from the third Sphere Major above the continent known as Australia. The coordinates are being fed to your terminals now.

"Partial to Kangaroos and Kuala Bears, Keelon?" I asked.

Keelon's eyes widened in surprise.

Give it all you've got, TK.

"Your time is up, Keelon," I said with a smile. *End Transmission*

FIRE!

The ship de-cloaked as silver and blue light rippled along its surface from base to tip. The point erupted, sending a thick beam of destructive energy to the Sphere Major, causing it to explode in a halo of blue fire. Several beams of light from multiple Sphere Major rocked the ship before we were able to maneuver behind the moon. The redundancy of systems repaired the damage and we were cloaked in seconds.

"Move us to the destroyed sphere's location now! Level off above its previous coordinates. Give us a wide berth," I commanded.

In seconds we sped from behind the moon to a position some six miles above the destroyed Sphere Major, dodging random beams of light. What better place to hide I thought.

We watched as the Spheres suddenly attacked each other. It was complete chaos as they battled. We positioned ourselves eighty miles from the planet. We watched, wide eyed, as the battle continued for hours, as hundreds of Spheres destroyed each other.

The battle of Sphere against Sphere finally ended as they spread themselves out, now much thinner across the planet.

An image appeared before us. "This is acting Captain Trax of the science guild. We mean you no harm. I would speak with Khore, immediately, please."

Before us stood the image of a man of maybe 30th age. He was thin and tired looking. His dirty unkempt blond hair barely capped his head, being cut short at the ears and neck. His eyes were large and friendly, framed in long dark lashes. He had an average nose and kind mouth with supple, almost abnormally large, lips. His body was thin and frail, but poised. Every movement was subtle and controlled as if choreographed.

Chapter 15

Loss

"Open a signal, Chris."

"Khore is detained at the moment. I am Captain Bransen. Anything you would say to him, you may say to me now." Each time I heard Khore's name cross someone's lips it ate at my heart. I worried about him and our unborn child. Still we were in deep shit, now more than ever.

"Ahhh, I see," Trax answered gravely, giving a small nod. "He was the one caught in the telepathic web then, I presume. Our sensors allow us to see the net of it. It seems to center on your ship. Obviously, we did not share this information."

The team turned, with questions on their faces, waiting for an explanation. I hadn't told them and apparently the gossip had, for once, not traveled at its usual near-blinding speed throughout the ship.

"Yes, that seems to be the situation. We are unsure how to free him. Khore and my unborn child lie frozen in our Med bay. That isn't our biggest problem, however. The Kotan are coming to devour this world and, I imagine, us along with it unless we run. That part of Khore that is Kelay mentioned that you might be helpful in putting an end to this conflict between the Thorens and Humans. I hoped it wouldn't have taken this much death. It has left us with too few to fight."

Trax considered my words before answering. "For many millennia we have been subject to Keelon's insanity. We owe you our gratitude for this new freedom. We also have a great debt to pay for the atrocities to your race." Fatigue and sympathy played across his face.

"Keelon greatly exaggerated our advancements toward our own longevity. You still provide our best chance at regaining our immortality. I speak for the Thoren people when I say we will abide by your decision, even if it means the extinction of both our races," Trax paused to take a short breath and shift his weight. It was strange to see the simplest movement be a thing of grace.

"If we could share the data you have compiled regarding the Kotan with our own long range scans, we may yet find a solution. Would this be acceptable?" Trax asked.

I searched the eyes of our team. Each reflected the stubborn determination and loyalty I loved in them. After a unanimous nod of agreement, I gave my answer.

"We have approximately two days before the Kotan arrive. We will share our data and continue scans until the last moment. I cannot condemn two races for the sake of this planet or my love. If we do not find a viable solution in that time, then I will remain here with the Cystos. If that happens, you and the occupants of this ship are to flee.

"TK, establish a scientific data link with the remaining Thoren fleet. Coordinate data and possible options." Trax's words seemed genuine, but I wouldn't let my guard down completely. There was too much history to give them access to all data.

"Understood." Trax gave a nod and the image before us dissipated like a warm breath on a cold winter day.

"We won't leave you, Bransen," Doc insisted.

"You will do as you're told!" I said, too harshly.

"TK, Take me to Khore," I thought the command.

My surroundings flashed and changed to the scenery of the room where Khore lay. My hopes were destroyed, along with the many Sphere Major that fell in their personal struggle over command of their people.

I sat on the bed that TK had created for me across from Khore. The same doubts that threatened my sanity when my own son had lain in such a bed haunted me. His body dead to the world and me with fleeting hope beyond hope he would come back to me. He didn't, though. First it had been my lover, and then my son. A parent isn't supposed to watch their child pass before them. It's against the natural order of things. I had been living against the order of things for so very long. Over 1700 years had passed with me as a pivot point, watching life wither and decay and then renew itself.

I suppose I had clung to the fantasy that one day Kelay and I would be whisked away to live out eternity in each others arms. I did love him, but I know now that I loved the possibility of a forever that, for once, would not end. Suddenly eternity seemed like a possible blessing instead of a curse. Now Kelay was gone too. The part of him that remains is Khore. Khore's smile captured my love as much as his strength. There is an empathy and anguish in him that rivals my own in understanding. And now, yet again, I had been misled by fate, cruel bitch that it is. I've seen the bitterness fate has spawned over time. Until now, I don't think I had ever felt it cut so deep.

Anger boiled through me as did the hollow ache within my chest. I took a deep breath, remembering Khore's words: "It is what it is. Accept it and move on." The soldier in me was beginning to rage against Khore's words. I may have to accept the situation, but I didn't have to let it roll over me. I am going to fight! With renewed purpose I felt the rush of adrenalin quickly leaving my body. It was late, and in truth I was mentally exhausted. Hell, it had been a busy day.

I stared at Khore, trying to engrave every line and curve of his face onto my mind. I lay back on the bed finally, closed my eyes and tried to calm myself. The whiplash of events in the last few weeks had taken its toll. I was tired, and let sleep take me.

I dreamed.

I felt the sun warming my skin as I lay nude in a field of grass and wild flowers most would consider weeds. I was barely able to peer over the endless field of thigh high grasses. The smell of something earthy and sweet was in the air and hinted at long forgotten memories. Insects dotted the horizon in chaotic patterns over the foxtail, thistle and pink clover. The hills in the distance seemed to sway like the waves of the ocean, stretching their green and gold colors to the sky. There was a rushing hiss as the breeze tussled the leaves of a nearby copse of trees. They were large ancient oaks that seemed to be waving back at me as their leaves flickered green and grey. It was a perfect place and I knew it wasn't real.

I caught another taste of the sweet scent as the wind washed over my skin. It was honeysuckle. I couldn't remember the last time I had smelled its sweetness. I had forgotten such things existed. I don't suppose there was a place for this in my world. The faster life seemed to move, the more simple pleasures necessity disposed of. I would be lying if I said that there wasn't enough time. It's strange how duty, commitments, and responsibilities seem to push aside the things that truly matter. It only takes a second to stop and look at the beauty around us.

This was a good dream. The horrors of most nights didn't invade my thoughts and I let regret leave me. I was going to keep this moment even if for only a little while. The blue sky was dusted with small bits of white that let me know how far away they truly were. I felt something to my side and turned to see Khore standing with the sun behind him, highlighting the edges of his dark brown hair. He was nude, also, and the contrast of light crawled across the curve of his chest, hips and thighs, almost hiding his expression. He was smiling and he was beautiful.

"Khore?"

"Yes, Bransen, I'm here." He answered as he knelt beside me in the den of bent grasses my body had made. It felt so real.

"I know I'm dreaming."

"Yes and no," Khore answered as he lay down beside me, placing his head on my chest.

I could feel the weight of him against me and the tickle of wind-blown hair across my skin. I could smell the faint musk that was Khore. It reminded me how he slept wrapped in my arms. Sometimes at night when I breathed deeply I would catch a hint of it from his hair or neck. I held him close, watching his head rise and fall with my breath. It was more than comfortable. It was perfect and safe.

"I want you to think of this place and remember me," Khore whispered.

"Always," I answered.

An eternity seemed to pass too quickly as Khore stretched against my body. I tilted my head to meet his gentle lips in a fleeting kiss before parting.

"The Kotan are crystalline creatures and too many to blast from the sky. Weapons might not have any affect at all on them, and may even feed them. You might be able to shatter them with sound. There is some small hope in that." Khore was tracing his fingertips through my hair and along my temple.

"I love you, Khore," I spoke too quickly. I didn't want it left unsaid.

"I love you, Bransen. Raise our son well."

My eyes shot open as I sprang up in bed. My heart felt as if someone had crushed it.

"TK, status on Khore!" I yelled. I felt like I was losing my breath as my heart threatened to explode within my chest.

"Status unchanged." TK replied.

It had sounded too much like goodbye. I was half afraid to look at him but I had to. He was still dusted with a shimmer of frost, seeming more statue than person. He had said to take care of our son. Not our 'sons' and the realization crept up my spine like ice.

I hopped off the bed, trying to escape the suffocating cold. It crept across my flesh, leaving goose bumps in its wake. I was angry and terrified. The fury was taking hold.

I began pacing the eight foot path between our beds.

"There is NO WAY IN HELL you're going to lay there and tell me that this space bug has beaten you!" I yelled, feeling tears form at the corners of my eyes. Even this small weakness fueled my frustration as I wiped them away violently.

"Fuck tears, fuck the Kotan, and FUCK YOU KHORE if you let them take you and our child from me!" I screamed, regretting the words as fast as they left my lips. My whole body trembled out of control.

I glimpsed a blue flash in the mirror as I paced in my rage before finally pausing to see that it was me. Khore's eyes shown back at me, but they were my own. It was a cruel memory that brought a guttural cry from my throat.

The arch opened to the room as Doc rushed in.

"What is.." was all Doc was able to say before my mental blast sent him flying into the far wall with a crash.

"DON'T TOUCH ME!" I screamed.

"DOC!" Chris yelled, racing past me. Blood trickled from Doc's brow as Chris huddled against him.

"Doc," I stopped as he flinched away from me.

I felt my anger melting away. I had never so much as raised a fist to him and now he cowered.

"I.. I'm sorry." This would be another of too many regrets.

"TK, Command Level 1." I projected the command.

A white flash moved me to the center of the command station. I slumped in my chair, catching my breath. I attempted to gather the shattered remnants of my sanity. This was serving no purpose and I had other responsibilities. The safety of my team and the people on this ship diverted my attention. I welcomed the distraction.

"Incoming transmission from Trax," TK announced.

"Go ahead," I answered, straightening my sleep-pressed clothing.

"Captain."

"Please call me Bransen," I interrupted.

"Excuse me, Bransen," Trax paused. "We just monitored an energy spike from your location. Is everything alright?"

His voice was filled with genuine concern and it caused the guilt to press heavily on my heart.

"Yes. Everything is fine. We dropped our cloak hours ago. I didn't know such things were of consequence," I lied.

"I see," Trax answered.

I suppose my lies were better served elsewhere. The emotional pain was raw and open and I'm sure read like a book in my expression. I don't think I had ever felt so out of control in my life.

"I want you to investigate the possibility of using a high frequency resonance burst to shatter the Kotan life forms. Khore…..," I choked on his name. "Khore believes that this may be the means to defeating them."

"Interesting, we will look into this. Without something more substantial to test with, we will not know the appropriate frequency or even if this is a viable possibility. Don't give up hope just yet, Bransen. We still have time." The image faded.

"COM: Shipwide. I want all personnel to run drills on emergency escape procedures until further notice." I announced.

I thought my next command. "TK, transport me to the oceanside where Khore and I spent our first day aboard ship, please."

A bright flash brought me to the beach as I felt my feet sink into the hot sand. I sat down and rested my head against my knees, wrapping my arms around my legs. I closed my eyes and let the roar of the ocean breaking against the sand lull me away from my worries. The distant call of gulls and other birds pierced the roar as they fought over the latest catch.

I sat there for hours, doing nothing but concentrating on the roar of the ocean. I felt so helpless and time was running out. I felt someone beside me, though I didn't know for sure who had tracked me down. Whoever it was, was not welcome, but I didn't have it in me to care anymore.

"Hey there, guy," came the quiet voice. It was Rift. Rift didn't speak unless it was important and I think that fact worried me more than anything.

"Hey," I mumbled back, not bothering to look up.

I heard his body hit the sand with a dull thump as he sat beside me.

"Rough day I hear." He said quietly.

"Yeah," I sighed. "How's Doc?" I didn't really want to hear the answer. It shamed me to think what I had done.

"He's fine. Worried about you though," Rift answered.

"It's killing him, Rift," My breath caught in my throat as I fought against my sorrow. "They're killing Khore and my unborn son."

We sat in silence for some time, feeling the spray of water as the mists gathered against our skin. The cold damp made me shiver.

"I'm jealous," Rift said quietly.

I hadn't expected to hear this as I lifted my head from the cradle of my knees.

"You're jealous? You've had so much time with Twist, how could you possibly be jealous?" I asked.

"It takes a special love to cause that much pain, Bransen. Don't misunderstand. I love Twist very much, but I have never been so wounded as the pain I see in your eyes. It's a double-edged knife, Bransen. You cannot have the good without the bad. Without the depths of sorrow, how could you compare the joy? One is nothing without the other. I envy you that joy," Rift paused.

"When I was a very young child, I remember going through the fields to pick flowers for my pouch father. I had spent hours selecting just the right ones to make the most beautiful bouquet for him. I made sure the flowers were just so, and that every petal was in place. The colors were divided and all was perfect. I brought them home to him and he placed them in a container of water so that they might last longer."

Rift continued after a deep breath. "The next day, as I climbed from my bed, I walked into the room that held the container of the beautiful flowers for my father. It had been late fall then. They had all died. They had wilted, sagged, and turned brown from the cold harsh night. I remember crying and crying. They were gone and I had worked so hard to make something special for my father. I felt so cheated."

"He came rushing into the room that brisk morning to see why I was wailing away and laughed at my tears as he hugged me tightly. As he brushed away my tears, he told me a secret. We took the flowers and buried them outside our door. The next summer we had a living bouquet just outside," Rift smiled as he spoke.

"We all build our own gardens, Bransen," he finished, pressing against my shoulder, then getting up from the sand.

"Trim back the dead so new growth might flourish," he smiled and a flash of light stole him away.

"What the hell do you trim back when the roots have rotted?" I yelled to no one in particular.

"You plant the leaf," TK answered.

Well, I suppose I could grapple with my fate like an ant under the looking glass, or I could emerge like the butterfly before having its wings ripped off. You have to love the possibilities. In the past I had always expected little and got less. Goddamnit, this time I wanted it all.

"COM: Trax. Status on the resonance burst for the Kotan," I asked.

"It has merit, Bransen. We can't say for sure what, if any, affect it will have on Khore. He could be released, or destroyed along with them, IF it happens to work. There are too many variables," Trax answered. "Kotan ETA is in eight hours. They laid waste to the last planet. Even if we succeed, the debris in our orbit will likely rip this planet to ribbons. You've got work to do."

"Trax, if it comes to that, I want you to take your people and go. Take as many as you can. You said you'd follow my decision. I expect you to keep your word," I replied.

"Sometimes the good guys win, Bransen," Trax said with a smile.

"Not in my world. Not for the last 1700 years," I snapped, watching him blanch at my reply.

It was now nearly 2200 hours. In eight hours they would swarm our world. I was prepared for my oblivion. They would be here at 0600 hours.

"TK, Take me to Khore's Room," I commanded.

The flash of light moved me, morphing the background into my new surroundings. TK might be a smartass, but he was also efficient.

"Thank you, TK," I answered. It seemed odd thanking a computer, but he had become a member of the team as much as anyone.

"You're welcome, Bransen," TK answered me almost immediately.

I pressed my lips against his biting cold skin before I left. This wasn't our final goodbye.

"COM: Shipwide. All personnel will board escape pods at 0500 hours.

All those not in compliance will be executed," I ended the transmission.

"TK, transport me to Command Level 1," I commanded.

One by one the team members emerged within the command area, taking their posts. I noticed the dark red of Doc's stitches and glanced away in my embarrassment. I had lost control.

"I'm sorry, Doc," I said in front of the team.

"It was never a problem, Bransen. How are you doing?" Doc asked.

I suppose the sadness in my eyes answered his question because he didn't pursue the silence

"I'm okay, Doc," I answered, finally seeing a smile cross his face.

This was my family. It was my job to protect them and I would, whether they liked it or not.

We sat looking at the view screen for the next few hours before the first remnants of our doom encroached upon the world. Like a plague of locust they filled the sky and darkened our world.

The Sphere Major stationed with the Cystos had positioned us to emit the high frequency burst.

I watched as the sharp black talons of these things plunged into Sphere Major, the Cystos and the Earth. They were a blanket of destruction that literally blocked out the sun as dawn came and passed without recognition.

We initiated the high frequency harmonic pulse. It seemed effective but it didn't destroy them all. It had actually taken only a small fraction of the swarm that tore across us and this world. We increased the intensity of the pulse, destroying some of the larger crystals before they began to converge on the Earth below.

They had reacted instinctively. They merged, creating a greater crystal, growing in strength and size exponentially. We simply didn't have the power to destroy them and now they were bleeding the energy from the atmosphere itself.

We began the use of conventional weapons against the darkness of the crystal only to watch it grow as if we had force fed it. We simply couldn't harm it. We had lost. Our time was done.

"TK, take me to Khore." I commanded.

The familiar flash pulled me to his room and I stared as him. Too many days were spent without him and now there would be no more. Explosions and power outages rocked the ship as our doom approached.

It hadn't been so much the attack they used, but the cold that had frozen our liquid metal exteriors. We were like fragile glass at a shooting contest and all we could do was sit there.

In my final moments I decided on the company of Khore. How could I choose anything else? I remembered the field of green and gold. It hadn't been a difficult decision. There was no one else I'd rather be with. He held my heart. What do you do when that happens?

The power drain was collapsing the ship, layer by layer, threatening to hit the core and the 5th dimensional material that powered it. I didn't honestly care much any more. Yes, this would probably fix our problem, but, it would, unfortunately, kill us too. So, it wasn't a good thing.

I sat staring at Khore as the world around us crumbled. I noticed the frost begin to melt against his nose. He was losing the frost.

"TK, status on Khore!" I yelled hopefully.

"I'm sorry Bransen, Khore is gone." came my reply.

The words echoed through my mind like a thousand explosions. Then I settled. I lay my head against the cool flesh of his chest. A calm overcame me. I didn't fear it anymore. We were moving on, and I didn't worry so much. There was unfinished business, there were regrets, but this did promise me Khore. It was all I ever wanted to start with.

I suppose I learned to cherish the simple things after all.

Chapter 16

Emergence

I don't how long I swam in my frozen prison. They had left me alone after devouring the previous planet. It seemed the promise of the next planet, my planet, had their complete attention.

In my attempts to divert the swarm of Kotan, I had been punished several times. Each attempt only weakened me more and I was getting no where. I did learn some things as I delved into their consciousness, however. They were like a colony of intergalactic bees but with no queen. They shared the safety of their number and a single-minded purpose. FEED.

Their sense for finding food was much like a shark's but on a much grander scale. While a shark might smell a drop of blood in twenty five gallons of water, the Kotan could discern energy over a distance of light years. Much like a shark, they would sense the energy and follow the strongest source that met their taste. They would pick out a particular strong source of that energy and store it within themselves. Unfortunately, that had been me.

Otherwise, I suppose, they would move between energy sources with the off chance of never finding a specific destination if they sensed another yet more powerful source while in transit. Nature had a way of working things out and it did not surprise me that it had done its work for these creatures as well.

I decided on another tactic. I had said my goodbyes to Bransen, but I was not giving up. It was only my struggles that caused my pain. Time passed and I found myself regaining my strength more quickly than I had expected.

I sensed them begin to feed again and knew it was Earth they had landed on. I had to escape now or it was going to be too late. I focused my mind and, thinking of my sons and Bransen, let forth a burst of energy that could have flattened a mountain. A concussion reverted back into me that all but destroyed my mind and spat me out.

There was nothing but a void of darkness surrounding me. It was no longer cold as I lingered, trying to collect my obliterated thoughts. I didn't know where I was, but I knew I was no longer linked to my Kotan captor. I feared there was nothing left of my body to return to or, more possibly, not enough of my ravaged mind. Had I died? Worse, what has happened to our unborn children and Bransen?

I was suddenly pulled as if by slingshot into myself. I was back in my body and it was still frozen, but quickly thawing. I felt the heat growing within me. I don't know how, but my son had fanned the flames of life within me. It had been gentle at first but was quickly turning into a raging inferno.

My eyes opened as the white blue fire swept across my body.

"I take it that we aren't winning," My voice was a bit hoarse but the sound of it seemed to give Bransen a heart attack.

"I KNEW they couldn't beat you, Khore!" Bransen yelled as he hugged me, nearly ripping me from the bed.

"Actually, they killed me. Bransen Jr., on the other hand, seems to want to keep me around," I said, smiling back at him. It felt so good to have him in my arms. I wanted to melt into him and stay like this forever.

At that moment a twinkling of blue light emerged from my pouch. I had only seen this once before, and that was when Kelay had passed on. The thought filled me with horror at what might happen next. Kelay had burst into a thousand stars. I couldn't bare the thought of living only long enough to watch the passing of my child and the world around me.

The small blue light danced about as Bransen and I separated. It zipped around the room like a firefly. It passed through my forehead and I was instantly revived. It started swirling around Bransen. It looked like it was playing with him. It darted around him like some pesky insect that wouldn't be shooed away. It had been racing around his abdomen, passing through him several times, before a second twinkling blue light burst from Bransen. Now there were two and there was no doubt in my mind these were our children.

I had seen many amazing things in my time, but nothing like this.

The lights flared against each other, growing in size and intensity. They had centered on me, spinning. A thought came to me. "LEAD" I knew what I had to do.

"Three minutes until containment failure of fifth dimensional material. We are soooo fucked," announced TK.

"Welcome back, Khore. You have front row seats for the big boom. Nice timing, bitch," TK snapped.

I gave Bransen a quick but tight hug and hopped off the bed. I folded myself high into the sky only moments before our children flashed next to me. The blue lights began to spin around me in a blur, now looking like a single ring of bright blue light. We had to pull the Kotan from the planet. They didn't have my mind as their fix any longer and we had to give them a better target.

I focused and calmed my mind. The blue light of the souls of our children were building a sphere of power around us. For my children, my Bransen, and our world I pulled within myself and erupted pure power, feeding this sphere. I funneled power from the earth and sun and even the Kotan themselves, building the sphere. The sphere continued to grow as the Kotan had swarmed to its surface in a feeding frenzy.

My body couldn't be seen more than what appeared to be a star blazing white hot in the sky. We built the sphere, pushing them back, as they fed from the energy that drew each of them to the growing surface. The speed at which they absorbed the power and multiplied was amazing.

It was now or never. I sent the thought to my sons' light. "NOW".

The blazing white lights of them merged with me and I pulled in the sphere upon us. The Kotan were quickly approaching. Almost reaching us, we released the energy like a supernova. A blast of blinding white light erupted outward. As the intense burst exploded it seemed to completely shatter the Kotan like a mosquito slapped as it gorges on your blood. The Kotan broke like glass as the white hot nova continued outward against and through the entire planet before dissipating somewhere too far away to see. The Kotan could feed quickly, but not fast enough. We had filled them beyond their limit and had destroyed them.

Tired and knowing the world was now safe, I folded myself and our children back aboard ship, to the bed in the medical bay. They lingered a little, like drunken pilots, before meandering their way back inside us. I can only imagine they were as weakened as I by the intensity of it all. I let my eyes close and drifted into my dreams.

I woke in my own bed with Bransen's protective arm draped across me. I pulled his arm in tighter. I didn't want to leave this safe place. It comforted me. Everything had been happening so fast.

"Good morning," I heard Bransen say, giving me a tight squeeze.

"Morning," my voice struggled out. "It feels so good to be back in our own bed and in your arms again."

"I suppose we should get back to our world," I said, smiling to myself. Nothing loomed in the future, and by now the Thorens and Humans aboard the remaining spheres would know what we had done.

"Not to alarm you," Bransen interrupted

"Oh for fuck sake now what," I interrupted.

"Nothing major, it's just, well, you don't look exactly like you used too. I think it's quite attractive," he answered with a kiss.

"Huh?!" I sat up too quickly, nearly dislocating Bransen's arm. I hopped out of bed and ran to the bathroom to look in the mirror. "What

NOW?! I have two heads?" I wondered.

Finally in the bathroom, part of me didn't want to look. I glanced up at my reflection to see my same old face but now all my hair was the purest white. SON OF A BITCH! The streak had given me a little dignity, but this; I didn't know if I liked this at all. It was so drastic! The more I looked in the mirror, the more it grew on me. It was the least of battle scars and I finally accepted it. This one I think I could wear with pride. It wasn't all bad, and if nothing else, it did make my eyes stand out even more than they had before. That vain part of me that remained was thankful the color hadn't aged my appearance. I suppose I should be beyond that but, well, I wasn't.

"I guess I could dye it," I said aloud.

"No way! It looks like snow! You better not!" Bransen yelled across the room, now sitting up in the bed.

"It'll definitely make me stand out," I laughed, now looking more at the reflection of Bransen in the mirror than myself.

I was happy and we had been so very lucky. For once, after my world had been torn to shreds, there was something left. This time it was the things I cherished most. These last weeks had been so surreal.

"Oh I can't WAIT until those heathen boys of yours are in their teens!" TK interrupted.

"What's the matter, TK, afraid you can't keep up?" I asked.

"Oh, I see many trips to the sewage tank for those two if they bring me even half the trouble you two have," TK replied.

The thought brought Bransen and me to hysterics, laughing so hard my face hurt. Thank the gods the first 100 years or so would pass in a blur.

I turned and made my way toward Bransen. "Well, Bransen, I suppose we should see what the hell is going on with our new world."

"We didn't lose many. Almost all of the remaining spheres that survived the assassination and coup of Keelon still live. Another few moments and we would have been done for," Bransen answered.

"Another three minutes and you would have all been dust," TK blurted.

"Well then, I guess this 'Bitch' had good timing after all, TK," I answered.

The next sound I heard was a raspberry but, for a change, it had come from Bransen.

I nearly fell to the floor with laughter.

"How RUDE!!" came TK's reply, which made me laugh even harder.

I have to admit, any soul that could survive the roller coaster of fate and laugh at the end had done his work well.

"We have some work to do, and some details to sort out," I said, beaming at my joy as he smiled back at me.

"You two make me want to puke," TK's announced.

"Shall we?" I asked, looking into Bransen's eyes.

He smiled at me and we showered and dressed. It was time to begin again and form our new world. The possibilities were endless.

TK had been directing the recovery of the liquid metal that had fallen to earth during the assault. The remaining spheres were nearly whole again.

The redundant systems of the Cystos had saved the members of our ship. The Sphere Major had similar systems in place that had protected most of those aboard during our conflict. Computer links determined there were 2,392,174 of us remaining, counting Thorens and Humans.

"Are you ready?" I asked, looking at Bransen. His golden hair slipped over the black shimmering fabric of his half sleeve skin tight shirt that tapered expertly to his waist. TK had created our outfits especially for us and had done well. The pants billowed only slightly, making Bransen's thigh look even more powerful than they were. We were in matching clothing. The white of my hair nearly looked out of place against the black, but ultimately accented the ridges and lines of the fabric.

"All Team members report to Command Level 1," Bransen announced.

It was nearly noon the following day after our battle with the Kotan. We all appeared in the command station, including Bransen and me in the center of it. The team just stared at me and I didn't understand for a moment until I remembered my now pure white hair. It made me grin.

"Begin the transmission," Bransen commanded, nodding to Chris.

Chris remained staring and jumped when he heard Bransen clear his throat.

"You're on, Khore," Bransen said to me with a small smile.

"Good afternoon. We are battered and bruised in the wake of all that has happened. Still, through all of this, we have survived. The energy wave that my children and I thrust out has renewed the planet as much as it has you. Your ships' computers will verify you are no longer Human or Thoren, but a mix of both. You will all live forever if you choose."

"There is no longer a 'Ruler' over us as a people. Keelon botched that, and while I'm sure there are good candidates, I won't be a party to it. I would suggest we govern ourselves by majority and with a single law. 'Do No Harm'. We also need to determine a path for our people. We are all free to do as we please so long as it does not break this law. You may leave this world if you please, but not until I know from every individual that they choose to go. Anyone attempting to leave without following this process will be destroyed. I will NOT allow the subjugation of any individual for the convenience of another."

"There will be no more slaves and body guards. We are all equal in our standing, from this point forward. You may choose a life of service in either area, but you will no longer be required. You will all, however, be required to board this ship and will have the opportunity, at that time, to choose a different life. You may stay, or even choose a different sphere on which to reside. There will be no reprimand for your decision. No one will punish you if you choose to stay or leave. This is how it will be. It is the only way to ensure that you are not being coerced or forced into doing something you do not wish." I took a deep breath and paused.

"In light of the past few thousand years, I cannot trust you to break a millennia of habit by my word. We will perform this sorting of all people every year as a celebration of our new freedom."

"Tomorrow, at 1600 hours, your presence is required aboard this ship for a celebration and feast. You will then make your decision. Everyone is to attend, there will be no exceptions. Do not force me to collect you."

"Enjoy your new-found freedom. One last warning, however. Be careful in your love. You are more fertile now than ever before. The affects should diminish after a few months. I guess my sons want someone to play with. Take this time to think about your future."

"Does anyone have a problem following these orders?" I asked.

I knew there were still some who existed that wanted to keep their human sex toys and slaves. They had become used to their self importance and it was going to destroy their ill gotten world. Not my problem.

"TK, you will monitor all the remaining spheres. If any of them attempt to leave, warm them to stay. If they continue their attempt, destroy them before they leave this atmosphere. Continue a sensor scan of all the spheres and notify me if even one individual is harmed or dies."

"End Transmission," I nodded to Chris.

"Damn, Whitie!" Twist yelled. "It's great to see you!"

They all laughed between well wishes and smiles.

"Khore, we have a runner. Sphere 27." TK shouted.

The fire leapt across my body almost instantly. I focused my mind on the ship. I had become more in tune with the people my wave had touched. I was somehow linked to their minds on some subconscious level. The fire flared and I folded all of the people from the sphere to cargo bays 14 and 15. "FIRE"

"Do not let them leave the cargo bays, TK." I thought the command.

The power rippled across the ships surface, sending out the powerful beam of light, destroying the ship a split second later.

"Open a signal, Chris!" I was seething with anger. DAMNIT!

"You are no match for this ship. I will NOT allow any of you to take away any Humans without their opportunity to choose to leave you. I'd rather they all be dead than in your service. Consider it an act of mercy. Is this CLEAR?!" I was yelling the message.

I stood staring at the screen in front of me, waiting for any reply. The fire was riding across my body and my eyes were a blazing blue.

"I will take your silence as agreement. End transmission," I commanded.

"We'll catch up later guys. I have some people to chat with," I said letting the power roll around me.

"Who?" Bransen asked.

"The people I folded into the cargo bay before we blew up that ship," I answered, smiling. "We've had enough death already, don't you think?"

He pulled me tight and we kissed. The fire started working down his skin and the feelings were intensifying. I pulled back with a smile, glancing at his crotch knowing what I'd find.

"Later," I thought to Bransen.

"I always knew Bransen had a thing for old guys. Nice moves there, Grampa!" Twist chided.

Now I know he didn't just call me a grandpa. I smiled wide, staring straight at Twist as the rest of the team seemed to lean back. I folded him to the sewage tank and back again. He was shiny with fluids and debris that made me shudder to think about. He was wide eyed and arching his arms and legs as if trying to get away from himself.

"If I happen to hear any of you call me Grampa ever again, I'll make that your new home," I said with a wide grin. I folded Twist to his quarters.

"OOOOoooo BITCH! I think I like you!" came TK's voice. The rest of the room burst into nervous laughter.

"Well, TK, I learned if from the best," I chuckled.

"Wait a minute, did you just call me a bitch?" TK asked.

"Never," I answered as we laughed even louder.

"OK you guys, you have the rest of the afternoon and night off, by Bransen's orders. Careful though, you're quite fertile," I said with a grin, turning my still blazing eyes at Bransen.

"You and I however, don't have to worry about getting pregnant." I leered at Bransen. "I can do this on my own, but I wouldn't mind some company. I've missed you."

"Works for me," Bransen smiled back at me.

"Okay then, let's get to it. Have fun folks." I paused. "TK, Transport Bransen and me to outside of cargo bay 14."

In moments we were standing in the hallway before the access arch of the bay. I leaned in and gave Bransen a quick kiss.

"Let's get this done quickly," I smiled at him.

"Agreed," Bransen answered.

"Okay, reach out with your mind. Touch across their thoughts. Be gentle. There are twelve conspirators among them. They stand out like a beacon with their fear," I instructed.

Bransen closed his eyes and his own fire lit his flesh. The third wave had moved him to a new level of power. The relief I felt from this was immense. He would most surely now be able to defend against four to five Thorens. Well, he could after some training.

"I see them," Bransen said in wonder.

"Okay, now open your eyes and maintain the power. Let it flow through you," I continued.

Bransen opened his eyes and the power flared a moment when he realized it was his own. He brought it back under control with little effort.

"You could have warned me, you know," he said with a little edge to his voice.

"Yes, but if this little surprise could completely break your concentration, I couldn't let you go in there. Now I'm sure you're safe," I told him.

"The Thorens that are responsible for this are expecting us to transport in. I will fold us in and isolate the twelve. I'll need you to help me hold them there as we enter. Maintain the barrier around yourself like a shield, but help me to keep them in place against the wall. Just don't squash them. Build a barrier around them that will not let them move. Do not push against them or you'll crush them by accident," I instructed.

"Got it," Bransen answered.

"TK, after we enter, transport and confine the remaining people that are not against the wall to individual rooms," I commanded.

"Yes, Khore," came the reply.

"Ready when you are," Bransen announced.

I opened the arch and we walked through as I seized the individuals that had tried to leave the planet. I sent them flying through the air into the far wall. They were resisting but Bransen's focus was helping. TK transported the remaining people into separate rooms.

We walked the mile length of the bay until we stood before them. I plunged my mind into theirs like a dagger. I folded seven of them instantly to a position not far from the moon. No, they were not going to survive. Five of them remained. I had sensed a change in them. They were willing to adapt to a new world, maybe.

"You did not have to run. You could have left of your own free will after tomorrow," I announced.

A rather frail Thoren in the center of the five spoke. His voice quivered with the strain of his resistance and his fear. "Where did the others go?" he asked.

"They are dead," I answered. "This did not have to be, but I could see in their minds that they would subjugate another race even if they left this planet with no humans. They made their decision. Now you have a decision to make. Think it over carefully."

I could see the light of their eyes waning. They had chosen life. I didn't know for sure about the longevity of the decision, but I would watch them. Moments passed.

"TK, transport and confine them to individual rooms," I commanded.

Bransen and I stood in the empty bay like two blue candles.

"One bay down, one to go," I gave Bransen a light elbow. "TK, Transport us outside the entrance of cargo bay 15."

I stretched my mind into the next room. What I found I didn't like. There were a few more this time, thirty one of them. I folded eighteen of them to space before we entered. Thirteen remained. We entered as before, placing them on the far wall with little difficulty. The remaining people were instantly teleported away. We delved into the minds of those struggling against the wall. I could feel Bransen's mind brushing against mine as we searched their thoughts. He nodded to me and I nodded back in agreement.

"The others are dead, but we sense a change in attitude from you. If you are patient with us, you may leave of your own volition after the celebration tomorrow."

"TK, assign them rooms and confine them," I ordered only seconds before they were whisked away in flashes of white.

"So, where were we?" I asked leaning into Bransen, feeling the fire feed between us.

Chapter 17

Earth Reborn

We had our world before us. I was nervous and unsure how to proceed. We had every opportunity for our future, and I was worried I might make a mistake. Luckily, there had been no other attempts to escape throughout the night. For a change, I slept well. I had a thousand things running through my mind. What do you do when you create a new world? I only knew for certain that I needed to create a world our children could live in.

Bransen walked through the door of the bathroom looking at me as I sat up in bed, pondering our future. His long blond hair was still damp from his shower.

"Worried?" he thought to me.

"Yes," I answered aloud.

"There are 38 Sphere Major remaining. Among them, I know there are those that would see us fail. The Thoren are not used to being without their pleasures and subordinates," I said.

"We've restored their immortality. They have no more use for me or this place," I continued. "I'm not sure where this will end."

Bransen carried two cups of coffee as he made his way across the room. He sat on the bed and handed me the dark liquid that would bring me to my senses.

I took a quick sip of the hot coffee. "I have no desire to rule these people, Bransen," I said aloud.

"I don't want some monarchy of hate to exist, ever again. We are better than that. I can hear their thoughts. Every person aboard every Sphere is in my mind. It's deafening," I continued.

I wanted him to hold me. I wanted Bransen to push the thoughts away. It was too much. It was never Kelay's plan to make this new world. I had come into being for a single purpose. Unite the Thoren and Human people. Now we were so few. We had failed on so many levels.

I had a banquet to plan. The sorting would commence and we would begin a new life. I worried about those who might separate from us. I could feel their thoughts against my mind like needles in a pin cushion.

Blue white fire erupted against my skin. I hadn't caused it. It was my unborn son. He sensed my despair and had reacted by instinct.

"Khore?" Bransen asked with concern.

"They know, Bransen. Our children know. We cannot fix this... but maybe they can," I answered.

"Fix what?" Bransen asked.

"My mistakes... Kelay's mistakes. A multitude of bad choices will be their legacy." I paused. "There are so very many," I said, fighting to forget past horrors.

"I don't understand," Bransen said.

Bransen looked at me, confused. I couldn't give him the bulk of our misguided pursuit at longevity. Kelay's memories were mine. The Thoren failures were my own. How do you explain a millennia of bad decisions and atrocity? I didn't want this world to suffer for our errors, but I knew they would. It wasn't my fault, but Kelay's memories made it my problem.

"Never mind," I said with a smile. "I'm just being silly." The blue white fire dwindled against my skin until it was gone.

There wasn't time for this right now and we had much to do. For once, I didn't know where to start. Up to this point, everything had come so fast, there wasn't really time to think. I could only react. It was unsettling.

"What has you so distracted?" Bransen asked.

"Well, to be honest, this is the first time I've actually been able to take a breath you know? Everything came so fast. Now that we have a moment, I'm lost," I chuckled.

Bransen smiled at me and gave an understanding nod.

"TK, release the people we took aboard ship last night. Let them have the run of the ship, but do not allow them entry to Ops or similar systems. I don't want them thinking they are captives aboard this ship. Let them know they are free to move about as they wake. If any are already awake, tell them now," I commanded.

"Whatever," came TK's reply. "Incidentally, there have been 118 conceptions, not including your own, in the past twelve hours. Damn breeders."

Bransen and I stared at each other.

"I guess the boys will have lots of company," Bransen said with a smirk.

"I guess so," I answered. "Didn't I warn them? Didn't I say that they were more fertile and to be careful?   What the hell are we going to do with 120 squalling babies aboard ship!" I felt a panic rising in me.

"Sounds like a lot of shitty diapers and sleepless nights to me!" TK interrupted. "Sucks to be you!"

"No, TK, but it is going to suck to be you. We only have to listen to two babies cry. You will hear them all!" Bransen commented.

"SHIT!" TK replied.

"TK, the Spheres are designed to restructure themselves. Is the Cystos compatible with the Sphere Major?" I asked. Bransen's brow was furrowed again with confusion. Those cute lines wrinkled his forehead whenever he was worried or at a loss.

"Yes, Khore," came TK's reply.

"Well at least there is that," I said again grinning at Bransen.

"We can join the Spheres and the Cystos to make a floating city. They will open up and our children will see a real sky instead of the ones in the habitats." I marveled at the thought.

"So long as the others choose to stay," Bransen added.

"Yes, I suppose that is a possibility, too. I can hope though," I took another sip of my coffee.

"I suppose I should ask. Do you want to stay?" I searched his eyes.

"What?! Well, I never really thought about it," he paused, "Do you?" Bransen returned my question.

"I have Kelay's memories, so I've already traveled the stars. I'd like to raise our children here, but I'll stand by your decision," I answered.

Bransen sat and sipped his coffee for a moment before answering.

"After our children are grown, I think I might like to have a look around, but not for another five or six hundred years, I think," he grinned.

We finished our coffee. Bransen dressed while I showered. After my shower, I dressed and went to the food dispenser and requested two more coffees. I took them to the love seat. Bransen joined me as we sat in silence. I was feeling a bit better now. My shower and the coffee were quickly pushing the sleep from my mind.

"How do you think it will go, later?" I asked.

"Huh?" Bransen snapped back from his daze. "Oh, I really don't know. We certainly can't allow any weapons aboard." He paused. "We need to make sure that every individual, including those on this ship, have the opportunity to choose their own path."

Bransen was picking at his fingernails. It was something he did when he was nervous. That small movement comforted me. It told me he was unsure about our future as well.

"We will continue on whether or not they choose to stay. I'm sure, at the very worst, a few thousand will remain here. In time we would become hundreds of thousands, and then millions. Space is a big place. There's plenty of room for our grandchildren," I answered. The thought made me smile.

"We should probably prepare for this afternoon," Bransen replied.

"Well, which do you want, city planning, or government?" I asked.

"I think with that last display of power, they are going to fear you more than me. I bet that white hair of yours will turn some heads too," he chuckled.

"I'm not interesting in having them fear me Bransen. I only want them to give everyone a chance." I pondered a moment and heaved a sigh.

"You are probably right, though. They will be more compliant after yesterday's display," I continued.

"Okay, you work with TK on city planning and the Sphere merger. I'll deal with the sorting of people and a system of representation. You want the desk or the couch?" I asked.

Bransen leered at me with a smirk. "I want the bed," he answered seductively, setting his coffee cup on the table before us.

I sat my cup next to his. We never did make it to the bed, but the couch is a little worse for wear. I'd have TK fix that later. With a parting kiss, he went to the desk in the corner of the room, and we began our work. We paused for lunch, discussed our progress, and exchanged ideas. A lot depended on the choices made later this afternoon.

I found myself glancing back at the clock every few minutes as 14:00 hours approached. This last hour had been completely useless. I hadn't accomplished a thing. My work was finished almost two hours ago. I had stalled as long as I could to pass the time.

"TK, prepare Bransen and me," I paused, looking over to Bransen. "Black?" I asked.

Bransen answered with a nod.

"Prepare matching clothing for Bransen and me. Make them black dura-silk with an opalescent shine. I want it comfortable and functional. I want a single blue ring one centimeter thick on the upper right sleeve. Make the shirts cross from left to right, tapering at the waist. Make matching clothing for all Alpha Team members. Give them two blue rings one centimeter apart. Instruct them to wear this to the sorting at 16:00 hours."

I thought for a moment and continued.

"Please advise all personnel that levels 50 through 100 will be restructured at 15:00 hours. All persons on those levels at that time, will be transported to their quarters."

"At 15:01 hours, restructure for the sorting." I finished.

We had an hour to shower away the odor of sex from our bodies and dress. That would leave us an hour for the restructuring and adding the final touches to our work.

"TK, bathtub, room for four, please," Bransen ordered with a smile as he turned his eyes toward me.

The shower area morphed back into the black and white marbled tub that had been there when we first arrived. Water flowed into the vast tub as the steam curled across its surface.

Bransen crossed the room and leaned over the back of the couch.

"Let's get ready," he whispered to me. "TK, lights dim."

I nodded as he led me to the over-sized tub. We removed our clothes and stepped into the steaming water. I leaned against the wall of the bathtub, resting my mind. It was so peaceful. The warmth of the steaming water seemed to wash away the tension.

"TK, music, classical, Beethoven, Moonlight Sonata." Bransen ordered.

"A Human wrote this thousands of years ago." Bransen said softly.

I sat up with a quick slosh of water. I listened as the sounds swayed through the room. Kelay's memories told me what music was, but I had never heard it before. In my 1600 years I had never heard music. Oh sure we had songs, but not this. It was beautiful. The sounds were so sad and resolute. How could a Human ever have created this? There were so many sounds at once, but they seemed like they belonged together in a way I can't explain. There was a complex math to it, but I couldn't imagine an equation that would create this. The music seemed to have a soul. It brought tears to my eyes. I had never heard anything so beautiful. I had memories of many forms of music and art, but never anything like this. I laid my head against Bransen's shoulder and relished the sounds as they moved through the room.

"It's amazing." I felt warm tears traveling down my cheek. "Thank you. I've never heard music before."

"What?!" he said with surprise. I could see the flush rise in his cheeks as he remembered my past.

"Surely Kelay had heard music before." He tried to recover from his embarrassment.

"Yes, but it's not the same. I know a lemon is sour. An unripe apple is sour as well. I have eaten apples in the past. I hadn't had lemon until just a few days ago. Kelay's memories told me it was sour. I could even recognize the smell and color, but I found that they are two very different things. It is like the night I brought you to the beach during sunset. Do you understand?" I asked.

He grinned at me. "I do."

We lay against each other, listening to the sonata. What a fabulous people we were. Pride and awe filled me. I also felt a sharp twinge of bitterness. I wondered what we might have become, had the Thoren's not interrupted our world. The Thoren had also given me Bransen, so I let go of my new found resentment.

Bransen asked for names that only Kelay's memories recognized. He requested Vivaldi, Handel, Chopin and more. We listened as music drifted through the air. I hated for it to end, but I knew we were close to the time of restructuring.

We climbed out of the bath tub, rubbed ourselves dry, and pulled on our newly made clothes. The black of the new cloth made my hair seem even whiter.

"Restructuring will be complete in fifteen minutes." TK announced.

"Fifteen minutes?" Bransen asked.

"Hey! If you think you can do it faster, blondie, let me know." TK snapped.

I giggled, seeing Bransen's jaw clench. It was like listening to two children bicker over a toy. I pulled Bransen into my arms. I gazed into his eyes and we kissed. I nestled my head in the curve of his neck, still pulling him against me.

"Our future begins now," I whispered. I relished the feeling of comfort and safety his arms provided me.

"Reconstruction complete, you impatient f..." TK's announcement faded into a mumble.

I felt Bransen tense a bit. We separated. I played with his hair, guiding a few wild curls into place before a smile crept across his face.

"TK, when I fold the occupants of the surrounding Spheres into the ship, do not incinerate them. They are not fully Human or Thoren any longer." I commanded.

"Awwww MAN!" TK wined.

"You are such a child sometimes, TK." I chuckled.

"BITE ME!" TK snapped.

"We better get going," Bransen interrupted.

I gave a quick nod. "TK, transport us to the center of the amphitheatre."

A flash of white brought us to the center of a massive space. I gazed at the rows and rows that circled us. Fifty levels of seating rose from the base and extended outward along the curve of the ship. It most resembled the coliseum of ancient Rome. I had found the diagram in TK's systems and had expanded on the layout. There were thirty eight sections, one for each Sphere Major. The only discernable separation was a waist high partition that split each section. The small wall ran vertically from the lowest to highest row of seating on each side. In the center of each section, another eight foot wall split each Sphere area into upper and lower seating. The wall was level with where Bransen and I stood now. There was a floating platform, large enough for the captain and their second in command to sit.

Above us, when the assembly began, would be a massive hologram that would display the current speaker. Once activated, the hologram would be nearly three hundred feet tall. It would display in four directions for the benefit of those in the upper rows that were nearly a half mile away.

Below us was a platform with seating for about three hundred for the members of the original base.

"Woah," Bransen said, staring.

"Yeah, fifteen minutes, remember?" TK grumbled.

"TK, from this point forward, all communication from you will be to Bransen or myself and only in thought. I do NOT want to hear a single audible comment from you during this assembly, effective immediately," I commanded.

"Care to call the troops?" I asked, giving Bransen a nudge with my elbow.

I saw his chest rise and fall with a deep breath. "TK, COM, Shipwide. All Alpha Team Members please prepare to be transported. You have ten minutes," Bransen announced.

Exactly 10 minutes later, we watched as they appeared on the platform behind us. I know it was silly to feel safer for their presence, but I did. None of them could block a Thoren attack, except, maybe, Bransen. Still it was nice to have them here.

TK, begin transmission. "Thoren commanders, you have all been designated a number. You will approach the Cystos, in order, and be transported aboard. Those who do not comply will be destroyed." I sent.

I pulled the fire from myself and mingled it with the thoughts of work yet to be done. The blue white fire rode across my body. Finally the first Sphere moved to dock with us. I didn't have to concentrate on them anymore. They were lodged in my mind like small beacons. I folded them into the amphitheatre, separating them by Thoren and Human majority. We repeated this until all 37 ships had docked and boarded. Finally, I pulled our guests from the Sphere we destroyed and placed them in the 38th section.

It had been almost no effort at all to move these two million people. It was a bit frightening, considering my limits only weeks ago. We were all in attendance. I stretched my mind to search each Sphere. Everyone was aboard.

"Let's not waste time," I announced. "I know who you are and who would wish me harm. Do it now so that we can continue," I announced as the hologram above me erupted in light and sound.

Silence filled too much space. A current of whispers traveled through the room like a breeze. I let the fire ride along my skin.

"Well, we can wait if you wish," I announced.

"TK, present the feast," I thought.

A flat surface grew along the rows of Human and Thoren majority.

Baked meats and dishes of every style imaginable appeared. We ate. An hour passed as we gorged ourselves. So far no one had died, but we had only just begun.

"If everyone is finished, we'll continue," I announced, rising from my chair.

The food merged into the dark shiny liquid metal. I watched the gaping distance as everyone prepared themselves. Before everyone, now, stood an interactive console of choice.

"Before you is a console that offers you a choice. This is the sorting. It will be done every year from this point forward," I paused.

"Those of you that may fear reprimand for your decision are welcome here. Now is your time. We will guard your choice. That goes for Thoren- and Human-born alike. Now is your chance," I announced. "No one can touch you."

Thousands of Humans left the room almost instantaneously. Surprisingly, many Thoren were transported away as well.

"Ok, then. Captains, you are still the commanders of your Spheres. You are free to stay and flourish with us, or leave," I continued.

"This is ridiculous!!! How can we even consider this? The Humans are a lesser species, bent on their own destruction! We did you a favor!" Laton announced as his platform moved into view.

I knew General Laton. He was strong and powerful. He was also a narrow minded ass.

"You will have more options than the Humans ever had. You have a choice. You may retain your Sphere if you wish to leave. That has never been in question. Leave now, but you will not leave with a single Human that wishes to stay," I announced.

A wave of blue energy burst out from General Laton in my direction. It was a weak blast, even by Thoren standards. He was trying to gage my strength. I formed a barrier around us. The blast rippled toward us and dissipated as it hit the barrier.

"You are nothing, Khore, but a freak. You may have some technology we do not, but you are not more than we are," Laton laughed.

"You are a fool. I would rather not kill you," I replied.

The hall had become deathly quiet. "Please, you can go. You may have your Sphere. It doesn't have to be this way," I continued.

"No, I think you will release the Cystos to my command," Laton said with a devious smile.

"Laton, you are mistaken," I announced as I folded his body before me. He hung in the air like a limp rag. He pushed as much as his mind was able, but there was no way he could break my control.

"Please, Laton, don't do this," I begged.

"You don't have the power. This is a trick. I will not be part of this travesty and you will not take away our Human slaves," he yelled.

"I'm sorry, Laton," I answered.

I filled the center of him with a fire no one could survive. Laton's scream stretched across the expanse of the amphitheatre before I finished him. I pushed the fires and lit him from the inside. It would be quick. His body became engulfed in a flare of blue fire. Then, only ashes remained. The gray flakes fell through the air, drifting like autumn leaves.

"I will not give in on this issue! I already see many Humans that remain loyal to your service. If that is their choice, then I have no objections. Those that remain may continue as they please. There will be only one rule in our society. 'Do No Harm'. We will retain some Spheres in their current form. Others, including the Cystos, will become part of a grand floating city." I paused.

"There will be four factions. They will be Military, Science, Art, and Education. Each will have equal representation. No one group will ever have majority rule, and there will be no dictator," I announced.

Captain Liam moved his platform. He rose above the remainder of the crowd and was projected in the hologram above me. "What will happen to those Captains who have given up their ship for the city?" he asked.

"You can either govern over the portion of the city made by your Sphere as a representative, or move to a remaining Sphere. The choice is yours. You could sit and paint for the next five thousand years. It is entirely up to you," I answered.

Liam nodded. "And if all Thorens choose to leave? What if we all choose to leave with our Sphere and only the Cystos remains?" he asked.

"I would hope, being there are so few of you, that you would condense yourselves and leave us at least half of your Spheres. Considering you made slaves of an entire world, I would think it a very small price to pay. If you chose not to do this, even after I've restored your immortality, then you would leave with all of your Spheres. We will not stop you. It has never been that you cannot leave. You are free to go. You will not, however, leave with even a single Human aboard your ship who wishes to stay," I answered.

Liam nodded again and returned to his original position.

"We will perform this sorting every year. Please understand. This is not a choice on what you will do for the rest of eternity. You only have to decide whether or not you wish to stay. Even that decision is not forever. If, at some time in the future, you wish to venture out into space, no one will stop you." I stopped and watched sporadic white flashes of light remove people from the crowd. "Once you have committed your ship to the city, it will not be returned. Should you change your mind in the future, arrangements will be made to see that you may go as you wish," I continued.

"Those that do leave today will not be allowed to return for five thousand years. If you return before then, we will not acknowledge your communications. You will be destroyed without hesitation. If you leave today, you will vacate this solar system at top speed. Once this is done, you may do as you please," I announced.

"Are there any more questions?" I asked.

Silence filled the make-shift auditorium like something thick and tangible. The white teleporting flashes of light slowed and finally stopped as the minutes passed. Eleven of the original 37 captains remained. There were 327,096 Human and Thoren remaining, scattered among the 38 original sections.

"Your time is up. Very well then. I will ask this one final time. If you wish to stay, please indicate so now," I announced.

There were no additional flashes of light.

"Captains, I will return you to your ships momentarily. I will be transporting the remainder of Thoren and Human people throughout your ships equally. You can decide on their disbursement after you have left this solar system. Is this acceptable?" I asked.

I listened as they answered 'yes' almost in unison.

"You're really going to let us leave?" Captain Tapal asked, skeptically.

"Of course! We've had enough death. What purpose would be served in keeping you here against your will? I have no desire to be a replacement to Keelon. I would like to see you when five thousand years have passed though. It could be a reunion of our kind. Until then, I think we need time to flourish and become what our future allows," I answered.

"If you are ready," I announced with a smile.

The blue light of my eyes flared. I concentrated and moved them to their original Spheres. I split the remaining Human and Thoren among the soon to be departing ships.

"TK, transmit the following message," I thought.

"I wish the best for you, yours, and your future. I hope you find what you are looking for"

Eleven Sphere Major powered up and left our world within a silver blur. TK would monitor their progress and ensure their departure from our solar system.

Chapter 18

A New World

We had done it. There had only been one death. We were free. The elation in my heart threatened to bring tears. I drew in the energy around me and let the fire erupt along my skin. I floated upward, away from our platform and high into the amphitheatre.

I folded everyone from where TK had transported them to safety. back into the massive coliseum. TK removed the separation wall that had split the Thoren and Human born.

The light flared from my body like a blinding blue star.

"We are now one people. There will no longer be Thoren and Human born," I sent to them in thought. "We will now and forever be known as the Huren. We are a new species, and there will be no separation."

We watched as the ceiling of the massive coliseum melted away to reveal the sunset. Bransen had initiated the Sphere merger upon the departure of the last Sphere Major.

Twenty eight Sphere Major remained after the departure. Sixteen merged with the Cystos, creating a landscape of silver. As far as the eye could see, our city formed around us in every direction. The silver landscape crept out from us at the center like a four pointed snowflake. It was spectacular. Twelve Sphere Major remained and circled the city. Each had its purpose and designation. Three were for the military, three for arts, three for education, and three for science.

The city, too, had been split into the same groupings. They jutted outward like talons scraping against the horizon. In the center was a huge silver spire that pierced the clouds.

"Select your destiny," I thought to them. Flashes of white light took them from the coliseum to their new purpose.

I felt the energy burst from the top of the spire to the corners of our new city, creating a massive shield. It would protect us from our enemies.

I settled myself, drifting downward to my place beside Bransen. We were the only ones remaining in the massive coliseum. The sun had set and now stars lit the sky. I couldn't help but marvel at the view.

If only I had anticipated the avarice of man.

About the Author

Shannon Rae

Since I began writing in June of 2005, it has become a passion. My obsession with reading changed to writing and I have learned so much thanks to so many. The only problem of course, is knowing I have so much yet to learn. I grew up in a small town surrounded by cornfields. Alpha, IL, population... a whopping 726 to date. Since then I have lived in Kentucky, Indiana, Florida, Mississippi, and have finally landed in Alabama. Don't let the name fool you, I'm of Irish descent, and a red blooded guy like any other.... who just happens to be gay. While Alpha may be lovely town, you might now understand my penchant for escape. I hope the best for you all. Thank you for reading. Blessed Be!